Dear Little Black Dress Reader,

Thanks for picking up this Little Black Dress book, one of the great new titles from our series of fun, page-turning romance novels. Lucky you – you're about to have a fantastic romantic read that we know you won't be able to put down!

Why don't you make your Little Black Dress experience even better by logging on to

**www.littleblackdressbooks.com**

where you can:

- Enter our **monthly competitions** to win **gorgeous** prizes
- Get **hot-off-the-press** news about our latest titles
- Read **exclusive** preview chapters both from your **favourite** authors and from brilliant new writing talent
- Buy **up-and-coming** books online
- Sign up for an essential slice of romance via our **fortnightly email** r

We love nothing more than t
addictive romance, and so w
into the Little Black Dress cl

With love from,

The

Five interesting things about Kate Lace:

1. When I left school I joined the army instead of going to university – there were 500 men to every woman when I joined up – yesss.

2. While I was there I discovered that there were more sports than hockey and lacrosse and learnt to glide, rock climb, pot hole, sail and ski. I also discovered that I wasn't much good at any of them but I had a lot of fun.

3. I met my husband in the army. We've been married for donkey's years. (I was a child bride.)

4. Since I got married I have moved house 17 times. We now live in our own house and have done for quite a while so we know what is growing in the garden. Also, our children can remember what their address is.

5. I captained the Romantic Novelists' Association team on University Challenge the Professionals in 2005. We got to the grand finals so I got to meet Jeremy Paxman three times.

*By Kate Lace*

The Chalet Girl
The Movie Girl
The Trophy Girl

# The Trophy Girl

Kate Lace

First published in 2008
by LITTLE BLACK DRESS
An imprint of HEADLINE PUBLISHING GROUP

A LITTLE BLACK DRESS paperback

2



ISBN 978 0 7553 3835 1

Typeset in Transit511BT by Avon DataSet Ltd,
Bidford-on-Avon, Warwickshire

Printed and bound in Great Britain by
Clays Ltd, St Ives plc

Headline's policy is to use papers that are natural, renewable and
recyclable products and made from wood grown in sustainable forests.
The logging and manufacturing processes are expected to conform to the
environmental regulations of the country of origin.

HEADLINE PUBLISHING GROUP
An Hachette Livre UK Company
338 Euston Road
London NW1 3BH

www.littleblackdressbooks.com
www.headline.co.uk
www.hachettelivre.co.uk

To my husband of thirty years – Ian: for letting me faff around in front of a keyboard all day and for not insisting I do a proper job.

# Acknowledgements

I owe a big 'thank you' to lots of people: all my friends in the RNA who are simply the best support group for a writer, the lovely people who buy my books and the amazing team at LBD who want me to produce them in the first place. In particular I need to thank Heidi Stewart for answering my inane questions about horses and eventing so patiently, Cat Cobain for putting me in touch with her and my editor, Claire Baldwin, for having faith in this book.

I scanned the small ads at the front of *The Lady*. I needed a new position and I needed it fast. My lovely employers, an American couple with three children, had been told they were moving back to the States at the start of the next month. The move was as big a shock to them as it was to me, but while they were looking at a return to the land of apple pie and Uncle Sam, I was looking at unemployment benefit – unless I could find another nannying position pronto.

Pen in hand, I worked my way through the list crossing out the non-starters and no-hopers as I went. 'Couple wanted . . .' nope. 'Part time . . .' no chance. I need full-time wages. 'North Scotland . . .' Where? I'll freeze! 'Full-time nanny required for large establishment in Oxfordshire . . .' Much more hopeful. I read the rest of the ad and circled it. 'Fun and energetic.' I ticked that box. 'Live in.' Was there any other way to be a proper nanny? 'Sole charge of child.' One child? How easy was that? 'Fluent English, non-smoker, clean driving licence essential, yadda, yadda, yadda . . .' All the standard things the middle classes want from their nannies. Just as well, I thought, they don't generally add 'confident and outgoing'. I wouldn't cut the mustard on that one, but as they never do, I'm all right. I underlined the phone number.

In theory the next bit should have been a doddle: dial the number, say you've read the ad and ask if you can have an interview. Not hard, you might think. Except that it is for me. Nervously I rubbed my hands together and noticed they were damp with sweat. I swallowed and stared at the phone, as if by doing that I could persuade it to make the call on my behalf. I gazed at the receiver for about five minutes before I had raised enough courage to pick it up. Then I put it down again while I found a notebook and paper and wrote out all the likely questions I might get asked. That took a few more minutes. Then I thought I needed a cup of tea beside me in case my throat got dry while I was talking. It was a good half-hour before I finally began to dial with a finger that was shaking with nerves.

After I'd finished the call I felt quite saggy with relief. It had all been straightforward, although why I imagined it might have been anything else I didn't examine, except that I always assumed any new event or hurdle I came across in my life was going to be an ordeal. This time – as anyone would have expected – all that happened was that a woman answered, took my details, asked for my CV and said she would be in touch in due course.

A couple of days later a thick cream envelope arrived in the post for me. As with the telephone call, nerves meant I sat and stared at it for a few minutes, wondering what it contained. Eventually I realised the best way to find out was to open it. The words 'I am pleased' leapt off the page at me. They never said 'I am pleased' if they were giving you the brush-off. My eyes raced down the rest of the page: '. . . invite you for an interview . . . Please bring . . . The successful applicant . . .' All the usual stuff.

I put the letter down on the breakfast table and all my insecurities began piling in again. I'd clocked the address where the interview was to take place – Chelsea. A place in Oxfordshire and a house in a posh bit of London. So my possible future employer was seriously rich. Which meant my chances of being successful had just gone down the pan. I mean, I've got all the right qualifications but mine haven't come from one of those swanky nanny schools which cost a fortune to go to and make you wear a uniform. Which, in my experience, is the sort of nanny the really rich want – the sort of nanny who talks like them, the sort of nanny who knows how to ski, has a double-barrelled name and sees pictures of her relations in *Hello!*.

However, I'd got the interview and I had to give it a shot. Maybe no one else had applied; or, if anyone had, just maybe they hadn't gone to the right nanny schools either. To have any chance at all I had to try. Time was running out for me, and as soon as it did, so would my money and my options.

A few days later I was pacing the streets of Chelsea, killing time till my interview was due. Knowing London traffic and the endless possibilities for delays on its public transport I'd allowed over half an hour extra to reach my destination. As I loafed about the neighbouring streets, the chill February breeze wheedling its way under my scarf and jacket, I wondered about the other interviewees, my chances of landing the job, who my future employers might be in the unlikely event of my success and what I would do next in the more likely event of failure. Going back to Pinner to live with my mum and her boyfriend really wasn't an option and, with rents in London being what they were, affording a place on my own on the dole was about as unlikely as getting the job.

If I'd been nervous at the prospect of making the initial telephone call, it was nothing compared to my blind panic as the hour of my interview approached. I felt sick and sweaty. I'd worried about what I should wear, about finding the house, about my qualifications and my experience, but most of all I'd worried about making the wrong impression. I can't help it, it's how I am. It's probably why I like working with kids.

Generally kids don't judge, and one thing I always worry about is what other people think about me. And generally I assume the kind of people I have to work for aren't rating me very highly. My background – only child of a single mother, father unknown, raised in suburbia, educated at the local comp, never travelled, never done anything the least bit glamorous – is worlds away from theirs. My mum always insisted that I spoke properly and said it would help me get ahead, which it has done. My accent has never been an issue with my employers.

Two minutes before my allotted time I pressed the doorbell with a trembling finger.

As I waited for the door to be opened I noticed that unlike many of the other huge, red-brick houses around this one just had a single bell. It hadn't been broken up into flats. House prices in London meant that 'seriously rich' was probably an understatement. I felt even more shit-scared. I wondered who it might be: some Russian oligarch, a footballer, a rock star? The door opened. I was going to find out soon.

'Yes?' said a woman in a suit.

'I'm here for the job interview,' I said. My heart was pounding and I tried to smile but I was so seized up with nerves that it probably made me look like a halfwit. I wondered who this woman was. Mrs Russian-Oligarch? Staff? Whoever she was, she didn't smile back.

'And your name?'

'Lucy Carter.'

'Follow me please, Miss Carter.'

I stepped into the vast black and white tiled hall. A beautiful staircase swept down into it. In the middle was an oval table with a big flower arrangement on it. I felt as if I was walking into a film set. The place was unreal. Yet again I wondered who owned it, not that it really mattered. If I got the job it was the kid I was going to be responsible for. But it's only human nature to be curious, isn't it?

Nerves made me check my appearance in the big mirror in the hall as I scuttled past. I looked scared, I thought. My eyes looked like those of some small creature about to get pounced on by another, bigger, fiercer animal. However, my short hair was tidy despite the wind outside and my thin face had a nice rosy glow – probably also courtesy of the wind.

I was shown into a book-lined room with a large desk in the middle of the floor. While I waited, I had the chance to take it all in. On the one wall that didn't have floor-to-ceiling bookcases was a fireplace below an oil painting of a stunning young woman posing against a tree in wonderful, landscaped grounds. I knew I'd seen her face before but for a second or two I couldn't pluck her name out of my memory. Then I spotted the horses in the background of the picture. Pennies started not just dropping but cascading. That was it! Of course. She was the world-famous, beautiful, tragic Countess of Arden.

My God, she was a woman who had had everything – and more. The only child of a multi-millionaire, she had become a hugely celebrated three-day eventer before she married the Earl of Arden, and the phrase 'golden couple' didn't even come close to describing how the media and the public loved them. A year after producing a son and heir she'd won gold for Britain at the Olympics and to cap it all the public had voted her 'Sports Personality of the Year'.

And then she'd been killed.

The Countess of Arden, mother of a little boy, young, beautiful, talented, National Sporting Treasure, was dead at the age of thirty. Tragic or what?

I wasn't entirely sure about the details of the accident except that the Countess had been kicked by one of her event horses. Just when her life had reached a peak of perfection it was over.

It was one of those times – like when Princess Diana died – when everyone could remember where they were when they heard the news. I had been in the children's nursery, giving them their supper and chatting to them about their day, when I'd heard a cry from their mother's bedroom. Thinking she'd hurt herself I whizzed into the next room and she was shaking her head and saying 'oh my, oh my' over and over. She'd just heard a news flash announcing Becca's death.

The subsequent public outpouring had been much the same as the one over Diana. And just as there were then, there had been a few unhinged people suggesting that her death might have been not an accident but planned by some mad rival. There was a brief police inquiry into the circumstances of her death but they concluded it was just a desperately sad bit of bad luck: the horse had lashed out and she'd been in the way. However, the inquiry had caused enough of a delay between her death and the funeral for the national psyche to rev itself up to a day of mass hysteria complete with piles of flowers stacked up outside their place in Oxfordshire – Arden Hall – and huge crowds around the little church in the village where her funeral was held.

There had been some obvious differences between the deaths of princess and countess. For a start, the Countess was still happily married. Secondly, no one (apart from a few barking members of the horsy set clinging to the idea of a mad rival) was seriously suggesting there had been any sort of conspiracy about her death, and thirdly, the hullabaloo had died down as soon as the funeral was over.

That had been about a year ago, and I wondered who had been looking after the kid since then. The Earl had never been out of the papers during his brief marriage, but now he had disappeared out of the public's consciousness so maybe he'd taken over.

Staring at the Countess's picture I realised that I didn't know much about the Earl. I'd never even heard of him till he started courting Becca Hetherington. It was Becca that the press was really interested in: a top-class eventer and the beautiful only daughter of a fabulously rich industrialist. When her name became linked romantically with his some of his past had emerged, but all I could really remember was that he'd been in the army and had been decorated for some fantastically heroic act just before his own father had died and he'd inherited the title and the vast family estate. However, what with that and his wife's sporting achievements the papers had had a field day and the couple never seemed to be out of them – a bit like Posh and Becks. And of course, because of his title and her name the papers had dubbed them Posh and Becca.

I felt a wave of sympathy for the poor man. Before her death he'd been half of a perfect partnership, both of them young, beautiful and talented – they'd had everything. No wonder he wasn't seen around much any more. He must be heartbroken.

I heard the door behind me open and I turned. A pleasant-faced woman who looked more like a farmer's wife than someone involved with the glamorous Ardens entered the room.

'Hello,' she said, holding out her hand. 'Miss Carter? I'm Annie.'

'Hello, Annie,' I said, taking her hand. I noticed it was rough and careworn, which reinforced the 'farmer's wife' image. 'Lucy, please.' I hoped I sounded confident and self-assured and not shit-scared, which was the reality.

Annie had obviously spotted me staring at the picture. 'I imagine you've already guessed who your employer will be should you get the position.'

I nodded.

'I'm a friend of the Earl's and currently standing in as Teddy's nanny. The last girl had family problems – her mother was taken ill very suddenly and there was no one else to look after her – so it's all been a bit unsettling for little Teddy as she had to dash off with almost no warning. The Earl has asked me to do the interviews. He's not very experienced in the nuts and bolts of childcare so he's asked me to find someone suitable.' She gestured to two armchairs near the desk.

I sat down, wondering what the relationship between the Earl and this very ordinary middle-aged woman was. She'd said 'a friend' but she certainly didn't look as if she belonged to the sort of set that Becca and Edward had always been seen with. Not that I really cared. Besides, being interviewed by Annie was going to be a lot less scary than being interviewed by the Earl. I counted my blessings.

'Coffee?' she offered.

'Yes, please.'

She moved across to the desk and pressed a button on the intercom. 'Mrs Porter?' A voice crackled in reply. 'May we have coffee for two in the study, please?' Another crackle. Obviously Annie was fluent in crackle because I didn't have a clue what Mrs Porter had said – for all I knew she might have told Annie to naff off – but Annie thanked her and released the intercom button. Then she came and sat beside me, and ran her eye over my life history which she'd picked up off the desk.

'So,' she said, after a moment. 'Why do you want to leave your present job?'

'I'm afraid my job is leaving me.' I explained about my current family returning to the States. 'The news came out of the blue so it's been a bit of a nightmare. However, Mrs van de Berg has said that under the circumstances she wouldn't mind the children flying out to their granny's in Washington a little early if it would help me secure my next job. They're due to go before the move anyway to make it easier for their parents to pack up the house. She says a week or so earlier won't make that much difference to her or her mother but might mean everything to me. She understands I should have had a proper period of notice and wants to do all she can to make it up to me.'

'That's kind.'

'She's a kind woman.'

The coffee arrived, served on a silver tray with milk and cream and home-made biscuits, brought in by the suited lady – Mrs Porter? I thought I could get used to this sort of life. Being waited on hand and foot had its attractions.

'So how will you keep Teddy busy every day?'

'Well, obviously I wouldn't want to change his routine

too much at first. He's . . .' I racked my brains. 'He's about three, isn't he?'

Annie nodded. 'Four in the autumn.'

'I expect you do this already, but I would want to take him out for about an hour each day to play or to walk but mainly to have a good run about and get some fresh air. And we'd play all sorts of games which will help with learning later: measuring, counting or weighing things.'

'How do you feel about television?'

'I think a little now and again is great for children. I hate the thought of its being used as an alternative babysitter, but a few minutes a day doesn't do any harm. In fact I think it can be quite stimulating.'

'And what about bedtime?'

'Routine is essential to small children. They don't like things chopping and changing. They like a structured day. Unless the Earl has strong views otherwise I would expect Teddy to be in bed and asleep by about seven.'

'And what are your views on food?'

'I cook everything from scratch – well, except things like fish fingers, obviously. I believe that children should eat what is put in front of them, within reason, and if there's something they really don't like I try to avoid it. Not that I would serve up artichokes or curry to someone of Teddy's age, of course, but I wouldn't encourage faddiness.'

Annie quizzed me about any number of things from my views on discipline (firm but fair) to the number of points on my driving licence (none).

Then she said, 'Just one more thing, Lucy. How do you think you'll take to living in the heart of the country?'

For some reason I opened up about the dream I'd had ever since I'd read *Swallows and Amazons* as a child; that one day I'd be allowed to go away with a few friends and we'd sail and camp and cook over an open fire and the sun would shine and we'd have fun. But seeing as how I'd never lived more than twelve miles from the centre of London the closest I'd ever got to the great outdoors was Hyde Park. Still, you could dream about it – or I had when I was little. Being a grown-up with a living to earn meant that it was never going to happen now. And, sadly, that sort of unsupervised freedom wasn't a realistic dream for today's kids either.

I smiled wryly, tailing off.

Annie laughed. 'But the Earl did exactly that when he was a nipper. Not that he'd let Teddy do it. Times have changed, unfortunately.' She gave me a long stare, then said, 'Should you be offered the post, there's nothing in your private life which might mean your leaving sooner rather than later? It's just that little Teddy has had a lot of disruption in his life and stability is what he needs.'

Of course it was. His mother had been killed, for heaven's sake, and his last nanny had had to up sticks and go. That was enough disruption for anyone.

'There's nothing. Honest. No boyfriend, no family commitments. I was in both my last jobs for almost two years and I wouldn't plan to be with Teddy for anything less – longer, preferably.'

I left feeling hopeful. I'd done my best, but was my best good enough?

The way I'd felt when I'd walked up to the house in Chelsea was nothing compared to my apprehension when I got off the train at Oxford. Talk about a this-is-the-first-day-of-the-rest-of-your-life moment. I was about to work for someone who until a year or so ago had been one of the most recognisable men in the country, in a big stately home in the middle of Oxfordshire, nowhere near a shop or a bus route or a play park. Supposing I loathed it? Supposing Teddy loathed me? Supposing everyone loathed me? Presumably Annie and the Earl – surely she'd consulted him? – thought I'd be all right, but mistakes happened. The wrong people got the wrong jobs all the time. Maybe I was one of those. Oh, God, the more I thought about it the more neurotic I got.

It was only the fact that my ticket was a single, and I didn't have enough cash on me to buy another one for the next train back to London, that stopped me from fleeing there and then.

I had had to read the letter offering me the job about three times before I finally believed it was true. I bounced around the house like a mad thing for at least an hour afterwards and texted everyone I knew with the good news. I even phoned my mum, but put the receiver down when her vile bloke answered. There was no way I was speaking to him. However, even a close encounter with the hideous Dave couldn't damp my elation. Working for the Earl of Arden had to be about the most desirable nannying job in the world – with the possible exception of looking after Brooklyn, Romeo and Cruz.

Once I'd calmed down a tad I remembered that there was a number in the letter to ring to confirm that I still wanted the job and to tell them about my travel arrangements. I was still so thrilled with my success that I forgot to feel nervous.

The woman I spoke to said to look out for the shooting brake when I got to the station. I'd had to find a dictionary to check out what one of those was as I hadn't wanted to display my complete ignorance of things relating to the country and/or big houses. According to Collins it was a dated term for an estate car. Dated? I should coco. I checked it out with the elderly shop owner where I bought my morning paper and the kids spent their pocket money. She said it was about as modern as calling a coach a charabanc. (I had to look that up too.)

I found the shooting brake – an antique Volvo estate – in the station car park, and approached it nervously, dragging my suitcase behind me. My heart was thumping and my mouth was dry. As I got close a young man with a floppy blond fringe leapt out. He gave me a broad smile and introduced himself as Hugh, the estate manager.

'Welcome,' he said as he clasped my hand. 'Annie has

told me all about you. I think you're going to be perfect for young Teddy. He's really looking forward to meeting you.'

My nerves subsided for a moment. 'Thank you,' I murmured. 'I can't wait to meet him either. It's so sad about his mother.'

Hugh nodded. 'Yes, dreadful. It was a terrible shock to everyone. Here, let me give you a hand,' he added as I struggled to lift my case into the vehicle. He swung it into the back of the car with a bit of grunting, and shoved my backpack in beside it. Then, in a display of old-fashioned manners that I found rather charming, he opened the passenger door for me. When was the last time that had happened to me?

'Good journey?' he asked as he strapped himself in and started the engine.

'Fine.' I was bursting with questions about Teddy and how he was coping without his mother and a million other things, but decided that it would be better if I waited until the information was volunteered. But Hugh must have read my mind.

'So, what do you want to know about the job?'

'How's Teddy?'

'To be honest, he's more upset about his last nanny going than he was about the death of his mother.' Hugh glanced across at me to see if I was shocked. 'Becca was away a lot,' he explained. 'Her eventing took up most of her time and Teddy rarely saw her. When she was around she was up to her ears training her horses. And she liked the London house more than Arden Hall. She stayed up there a lot.' I think he must have clocked my surprised expression. 'I don't think he really understood anything about the accident. He was only two when it happened.'

'I see.' Although I didn't. I suppose life was different for the rich and famous. I didn't understand why Becca hadn't spent all her spare time with her child. I didn't understand how her horses could mean more to her than Teddy. I didn't understand anyone who only wanted to be a part-time mother. My mum hadn't been brilliant but she'd always been around for me. Well, until she'd taken up with Dave.

I changed the subject. 'What's my room like?'

'Nice – you get your own flat. It's a set of rooms that interconnect with Teddy's nursery, in the private family wing. I'm afraid you and he have to share a bathroom. It's a tricky job getting extra bathrooms into a building that age. His last nanny didn't seem to mind. And I hope you don't have a problem with stairs, because there are a lot of them in the Hall. Oh, and you have a car. The keys should be in your flat.'

A car was good, although it was a pretty standard part of the package for most nannies nowadays. It was the only way to get kids to all their after-school activities on time. Hugh kept his eyes firmly on the road as he talked to me, avoiding cyclists and rubber-necking tourists with care.

'I've only seen pictures of the house. Is it as big as it looks?'

'Huge. Completely impractical, of course, and costs a fortune to run, although that's not such a problem these days. Becca's money made an enormous difference to the place. Until then, the Earl had seriously been considering handing the whole place over to the National Trust. It was the only option left, just about.'

We stopped at traffic lights and he gave me a warm smile. I decided I liked him a lot.

'That would have been a shame.'

'The idea was breaking his heart. Anyway, it isn't an issue now. Of course Teddy will have to pay inheritance tax but he won't have to worry about the Hall the way his father had to.'

'No.' It seemed to be dreadfully bad taste to comment that at least something good had come out of the Countess's death, so I kept quiet.

Hugh eased the car through Oxford's busy streets. I looked about me with interest. There were a lot of young, swotty-looking people on bikes, and some very pretty hanging baskets of winter pansies which made the bustling city look rather countrified – which I suppose it was, really. There were loads of ancient stone buildings with olde-worlde mullioned windows and quite a lot of forbidding buildings with large gates – the colleges presumably. All very different from London, I thought.

The only thing I knew about Oxford, apart from the fact that you had to be seriously bright to go to the uni, was that Inspector Morse had hung out there. I began to spot places that had featured in the series. I was musing quietly on Oxford's unbelievably high murder figures when I noticed that the road we were travelling down, which was lined with huge Victorian villas, ended at a roundabout and on the other side of that was open country.

'How far is it now?' I asked.

'About half an hour,' said Hugh.

'Tell me about Teddy.'

'He's a lovely little chap. Very friendly.'

That didn't tell me a huge amount, but I'd find out more for myself soon enough.

'So he'll be going to a nursery school soon?'

'He already goes to the playgroup in the village a couple of mornings a week.'

I was slightly surprised. I had half expected he'd go off to some swanky private establishment. 'That's handy,' I said.

Hugh laughed. 'Not really. You'll need the car to get there. It's not walking distance.'

Of course. Stately piles like Arden Hall had acres of grounds. My dream of living in the heart of the country was about to come true – with knobs on.

'So what does an estate manager do, Hugh? Apart,' I added so as not to look completely dim, 'from managing the estate.'

'That's about it, really. I make sure the grounds are kept in order, and organise things like getting the hedges cut. I liaise with the tenant farmers and get the contractors in for the big jobs like the harvest. All the stuff like maintaining the roads on the estate, paying the workers' wages, keeping tabs on the budget for the gardens.' He shrugged. 'All pretty dull, really.'

'Not at all.'

'I enjoy it.'

And then he told me about the other staff at the Hall: the ones who cleaned the whole house before the visitors pitched up, the ones who worked in the private apartments, the ground staff, the gardeners, the administrators, the event organisers, the tour guides . . . I couldn't believe how many there were. Everywhere else I'd worked had had a cleaner, one house had paid a bloke to do the garden occasionally and another had employed someone to do the ironing, but no one had had staff like this. It was like something out of a costume drama.

'So how many people do work at the Hall?' I had to ask.

'About thirty, with about sixty part-timers on top. And I haven't even begun on the maintenance staff and the farm hands.'

Blimey, I thought, *Upstairs, Downstairs* here I come. While I wondered about what life in such an establishment was going to be like, Hugh drove along the road that led west from Oxford, through countryside that was beginning to green up in the early spring sunshine. This was exactly what I had always imagined life outside London would be like – chequerboard fields, livestock grazing, tractors working, trees all at different stages of coming into leaf and blossom splashing the hedges with white. All very *Trumpton* or *Postman Pat*.

Hugh swung off the main road and down a narrow winding lane. I began to pay even more attention. We must be getting close. I could see a brown sign pointing straight ahead with the distance to the Hall. Hugh turned again.

'This is a short cut,' he said. 'We don't encourage the paying punters to come this way. Can you imagine the traffic jams?'

Just as he said that a tractor pulled out of a farm gate ahead of us, towing a vicious-looking piece of machinery that was caked in mud and goodness only knew what else. A fairly strong whiff of something agricultural instantly permeated the car. Clods of mud and muck flew off the wheels and splattered the road, and occasionally our windscreen, until the tractor turned off the road again and into a farmyard. I opened the window and let some fresh air circulate.

'Still keen on the country?' said Hugh.

'Whatever that smell was,' I answered, 'it was still a whole lot nicer than the Tube in the rush hour.' And I meant it.

Ahead of us was a long wall. This was a wall that had been built to tell the local yokels that someone of quality lived on the other side, and he didn't want them getting too familiar. There was no doubt that it belonged to a time when everyone knew their place. The locals' place was this side of the wall and the other side was his – and they weren't welcome. As status symbols went, the wall was pretty impressive, but not half as impressive as the enormous pair of wrought-iron gates that Hugh swung the car between.

'And this is the tradesmen's entrance,' he said when I commented. 'You should see the ones at the front.'

I just managed not to say 'Fuck' out loud, which was my instinctive response, and not a good one for a nanny in charge of young and impressionable kids.

Once inside the gates we left behind the farm livestock and hedges and fields of crops and entered a beautifully landscaped park. Magnificent old trees had been carefully planted to show off their shape and foliage to maximum advantage. The ground was covered in lush grass, and in the distance grazed a herd of deer.

'Oh,' I exclaimed. 'Aren't they pretty? Like Bambi.'

'They're fallow deer. There are some red deer too, somewhere. Bigger than these and with no spots,' said Hugh.

'Thanks for that. I haven't a clue about any of this stuff.'

'Can't imagine there are many deer in London.'

I said, 'No deer where I live but squillions of foxes. And I see squirrels in Hyde Park.'

'Which I bet you think are cute and cuddly.'

I nodded. 'They are rather.'

'Not an opinion to hold round here. The locals will tell you that they're just rats with good PR.'

I laughed. 'Bloody good PR it is then. No one could ever describe a rat as cuddly. Well, not the sort you get in London, at any rate.'

The car rumbled over a cattle grid and through a peculiar wall. Well, it was more like a terrace really as it divided two areas of land of different heights.

'That,' explained Hugh, 'is a ha-ha. The idea is that it stops the deer, or any other livestock for that matter, from getting into the formal gardens without any messy fences to spoil the view from the house.'

I was impressed. 'Does it work?'

'It does for the deer. But the rabbits . . .'

'I imagine I'm not supposed to like them either, now.'

'That's right. You're catching on. They're not cute, they're not cuddly, they're vermin.'

Poor old Thumper, I thought. I'd look at him in a different light from here on in. Still, at least his mate Bambi seemed to be socially acceptable.

Ahead I could see the house. It was stunning in the pale lemony afternoon sunshine. The huge numbers of windows glinted and the grey-gold stone glowed while the lake in front of it sparkled and glittered as the gentle breeze ruffled the surface of the water. A couple of swans glided across it to complete the picture of a perfect stately home. Around the Hall were immaculate lawns and a creamy sweep of gravel that led from the front door, divided to go round both sides of the lake and then rejoined to go arrow-straight through an avenue of trees to the main gates. Or, at least, that's where I assumed it went as the gates were nowhere in sight and the drive disappeared over a slight rise in the land, somewhere in the middle distance.

Of course, being staff, we didn't pull up at the front of the house but followed the road round to the side. At the back of the house was an enormous arch leading into a courtyard.

'Leave your case,' said Hugh. 'I'll get someone to bring it up later.' But of course. One of the staff. 'Let's go in and introduce you to Teddy.'

I was expecting to meet the Earl first but maybe he was away. Maybe he had no interest in his only child's new nanny, but I found that a little hard to believe. Never mind.

I was led down yards of stone-flagged passages, through a number of functional fire doors and then through a panelled wooden one marked *Strictly private*.

We emerged in a large hall with a chequered marble floor and a large staircase which swept elegantly upwards in an oval spiral. Oil paintings hung on heavy chains on the walls and in the centre was a large oval table bearing a huge silver bowl the size of a baby bath. This wasn't the servants' quarters, that was for sure.

Hugh led me upstairs. 'The nursery is this way,' he said. The stairs might have been wide and shallow and beautifully carpeted but we still had to go up three storeys. By the time we got to the top I was panting. 'I told you there were a lot of stairs in the place,' he said. 'But you'll get used to it.'

I wasn't so sure but was too breathless to disagree.

He opened a door at the end of the landing and there was Annie.

'Hello again,' I said.

'Hello, my dear,' she said cheerfully. 'Welcome to Arden Hall.' She held the door wide for me and I stepped into my new work place. I was vaguely aware of Hugh behind me, telling Annie that he was going to get my belongings brought up, but I was engrossed in taking stock of an aristocratic nursery.

Until now I'd worked for all sorts but none of the families were what would once have been called 'old money'. One family had five kids and needed me just to be able to cope. Another of my families had both parents in incredibly high-flying jobs which meant they were cash rich but time poor. And then there had been my lovely Americans who had decided that they wanted their kids to be brought up with proper English manners. (Just as well they didn't see what depths most kids' manners in the Old Country had descended to!) But this was the first time I'd been employed by the aristocracy and, as I stepped into their world, I realised just what 'old money' meant.

The nursery was amazing. Full of wonderful toys from a beautiful old rocking horse with proper rockers to a wooden fort complete with whole battalions of soldiers. On the rug in front of the fire (not lit, but giving every impression of a proper coal one we could toast crumpets in front of) lay Teddy, quietly engrossed in some sort of game that involved a wooden railway set and a group of soft toys.

To my immediate right was a long, low window with a

window seat – perfect for reading stories together on wet afternoons. I noticed it had bars screwed across it to prevent accidents. I peered out. The view, across the park, was spectacular. I was taking it in when I was aware of something tugging at the hem of my jacket.

'Are you Miss Carter?' said a solemn voice.

I looked down. A small face with big brown eyes, framed by pale blond hair, was gazing up at me with a serious intensity. I crouched down to be on his level. My first thought was that there was absolutely no doubting who his father was – he was the spit of the Earl of Arden.

'Hello,' I said. 'Yes, I am. But I think it would be easier if you called me Lucy. You must be Teddy.'

'Yes. Annie says you're going to look after me.'

'I am. And I'm looking forward to it.'

'Do you ride horses like Mummy did?'

I shook my head. 'No, I don't.'

'Oh.' He stared at me for a minute, then walked away across the nursery.

Oh dear, I thought, was my lack of riding skill a serious fault in his eyes? Teddy had his back to me and was rummaging in a cupboard. I felt as if, by ignoring me, he was expressing his displeasure. 'Was that the wrong answer?' I asked Annie.

'Lord knows,' said Annie cheerfully. 'Who knows how the mind of a three year old works?'

Her sensible answer put me at ease. I nodded. 'It's good to see you again,' I said with feeling.

Annie smiled at me. 'Let me show you your rooms and then we can have a nice cup of tea.'

I was just contemplating exactly how nice a cup of tea would be when Teddy appeared at my side and tugged at my skirt again. In his hand was an old wooden hobby horse.

'I've got a real horse too. This is my indoor horse.'

'And a very fine horse he is too,' I said, kneeling down to get a better look. 'Does he have a name?'

'Arkle.'

'Arkle?'

'He was Daddy's horse first. Daddy called him Arkle after a famous racehorse.'

'Did he?' Not that I knew anything about horses. The only ones I'd ever heard of were Desert Orchid and Shergar.

'So does your Arkle do races?'

Teddy stared at me, then shook his head slowly. 'Don't be silly,' he said. 'He's only a toy.'

Well, that was me put in my place. And by a three year old.

Teddy laid the wooden horse on the ground. 'Can I show you my other toys?'

'Yes, please.'

He took my hand and pulled me across to the other end of the room. There I was introduced to his favourite robot, his pirate ship and his building bricks. He explained in simple language, to make sure I understood, the rules that he'd laid down for the game he was playing with his teddies and his railway. He showed me his fort, which had once belonged to his father, and the toy soldiers, which hadn't.

'Lead paint,' explained Annie.

The toy soldiers were obviously engaged in a battle against some robots; battle lines had been drawn up along the bookcase. Both sides had further strongholds made out of Duplo and, by the looks of things, the toy soldiers were about to be reinforced by a Playmobil pirate ship. In the corner of the room was Teddy's bed made up with sheets and blankets and an old-fashioned candlewick bedspread. Around the nursery were more bookshelves filled with picture books and old *Boy's Own* annuals. None of the titles looked the least bit modern. I suspected that a great many of the toys and books had done service for decades.

'And where do I sleep, Teddy?'

Again I was pulled across the carpet and through another door.

'Here,' he said, letting me go and running over to a bed and climbing on to it.

I looked about me. Quaint but cosy. The ceiling sloped but built into it was a dormer window framed with pretty chintz curtains. Along one wall were a wardrobe, a dressing table and a writing desk and along the other was my bed with Teddy sitting quietly on the edge, his feet dangling above the rug. By the writing desk was another door. I opened it and found myself in a bathroom that looked as if it had been designed by one of the Noah family. The bath was vast and had feet like claws, heating was provided by an oil-filled electric radiator and the loo had a cistern up by the ceiling and a chain handle to flush it with. There was another door by the loo. I peeked through it – it led back into Teddy's room.

When I returned to my bedroom Annie had removed Teddy from my bed and was straightening the covers.

'Your kitchen and sitting room are over there,' she said. I spotted a door on the other side of the room, hidden behind the wardrobe, and took a look through it. There was a large room with a gas fire, two armchairs, a table with the promised set of car keys on it and some dining chairs round it and a small TV and then another door through which I could see a small but adequately equipped kitchen.

'This is fantastic,' I said, turning round. 'All this space. Just for me.'

'And me,' said Teddy. 'I live here with you.'

'Indeed you do,' I agreed.

'You like it?' said Annie.

'What's not to like? It's splendid.'

Annie bustled over to the kitchen, followed by Teddy. 'Oh no you don't,' she admonished as he put a foot over the threshold.

Teddy turned to face me. 'I'm not allowed in there,' he said gravely. 'Dangerous.'

'It certainly is. Why don't you show me some more of your toys while Annie makes some tea?' His face brightened and he smiled, but only fleetingly. Grabbing my hand again he towed me back into his nursery. I was struck by how solemn all his actions were. For a three year old he was terribly subdued and serious, but maybe it was just shyness.

A few minutes later, when I'd had the intricacies of the battle for the fort explained to me, Annie returned with a tray laden with tea for the adults, a mug of milk for Teddy and a plate of shortbread for everyone. We sat round the nursery table and Annie explained Teddy's routine. I was just beginning to feel as though I wasn't going to be able to take in any more information when there was a knock at the nursery door.

'That'll be Hugh with your luggage,' said Annie, getting up from the table. She opened the door to reveal a man-mountain bearing my big case.

'Ma'am.' The hulk nodded at me as he dumped it on the floor by my bed.

'This is Jed,' said Annie. 'He used to be one of the Countess's grooms.'

Jed stared at me, slightly slack-jawed. 'She's pretty.' He shuffled his feet awkwardly.

I wasn't sure if he was referring to the Countess or to me. I didn't know what to say.

'That's enough, Jed,' said Annie firmly, in the same tone of voice she'd used on Teddy. 'Run along.' Jed departed and Hugh entered bringing my backpack. He looked pretty bushed. Jed, I'd noticed, might have been carrying feathers for all the effect lugging my stuff had had on him.

Annie sighed. 'Jed's a sweet lad, but not the brightest.'

'But brilliant with horses,' said Hugh, panting.

'Oh, yes. He can cope with horses,' said Annie. 'It's just his own kind he can't relate to. Now then, Lucy, I expect you'll want to get unpacked and settle in. I'll take Teddy off for a walk and leave you in peace. I'll give him his supper tonight at my place before bringing him back to sleep here, then tomorrow you can take over.'

I nodded and thanked her. Teddy seemed a bit put out that I wouldn't be going with him on his walk but I promised to read a bedtime story to him later on and that seemed to pacify him. When Annie and Teddy had left I set about exploring my flat. The kitchen cupboards were well stocked with tins and pasta and other dry goods. The fridge contained most essentials that I could want and in the freezer beneath it someone had put a variety of frozen vegetables, some chicken pieces and a bag of minced beef. I decided that I'd make myself spag bol when Teddy was tucked up.

Having checked out my quarters I set about unpacking. I'd about finished when Teddy trotted back into the nursery brandishing a stick as a sword. A short time later Annie followed, puffing rather from the three flights of stairs.

'How are you getting on?' she asked.

'Almost there,' I replied, gesturing to my almost empty case.

Teddy clambered on to my bed. 'Annie made me scrambled eggs for supper. And then I had apple pie and custard,' he informed me.

'Lucky you.' I tipped the last of my clothes on to the bed beside Teddy and flipped shut the case.

'I'll get your bags taken to the box room,' said Annie. 'Meantime you could leave them on the landing so's they don't get in your way.'

She took Teddy off to give him his bath while I hung up the last few items. I could hear splashes and soft chatter as Teddy played in the huge tub. I reckoned it was almost big enough to teach him how to swim. I joined them in the bathroom just as Teddy was being hauled out of the water all pink and shiny and looking quite delicious.

He sat on Annie's ample lap as she rubbed him dry and got him into his pyjamas. He gazed up at me from the cocoon of his towel as if he were sizing me up. I smiled at him and was rewarded with a brief flicker from him in return.

'Teeth, Teddy,' Annie ordered as she hung up the towel. 'Right then, Lucy, if you'd like to take over. I need to get back to give my boys their supper. I'll come over first thing to show you around properly and introduce you to some of the staff.'

'Thanks.'

'Night night, Teddy,' she said. 'Give Annie a kiss, there's a good boy.'

Teddy rushed over to her and gave her an enormous hug.

After Annie had gone Teddy and I chose a story and he snuggled down under his covers, to lie sucking his thumb while I sat beside him and read the chosen picture book. He was almost asleep when I finished so I dropped a kiss on his soft clean hair, switched on the night light and tiptoed out of the room.

As I began to cook supper for myself I felt strangely lonely in this big house. Were there other staff who lived in? Or were Teddy and I on our own? I hadn't asked and now I wished I knew.

In all my other posts the houses had always been busy and bustling with family life; the kids with computers or

TVs on, usually someone practising a musical instrument, perhaps some bickering between siblings and the parents coming home ready to grab a glass of wine and discuss their day at work. I found this quiet rather unnerving. And, not for the first time, I wondered when I was going to meet Teddy's father.

I switched on the TV for company and all I got was a hiss of static and fuzz. I checked the aerial, which was plugged in. I pushed the button to retune it automatically but the picture didn't improve. I fiddled with knobs and controls. Nothing. I sighed and switched it off. Bum. I ate my supper in silence with just a few tired thoughts drifting around my overloaded brain for company. Around me the house ticked and creaked and because I was aware of the sheer size and history of the place I found the noises unsettling and, to be frank, rather spooky. Normally I don't have a problem with being alone in a house (or virtually alone, as I didn't think Teddy, bless him, would be much of a help in a tight spot) but the noises were getting to me. I really wished I had something to cover them up and distract me till I was tired enough to fall asleep despite them. But, as my mother loved saying, 'If wishes were horses, beggars would ride,' so with nothing else to do I decided I might as well have a bath and hit the sack. It was only as I was climbing into bed that I noticed that someone had put a copy of *Swallows and Amazons* on the bedside table. I was seriously touched by this thoughtful gesture and at least, I thought as I opened it, it might stop me worrying about ghosts or intruders.

The next day, as good as her word, Annie arrived to take me on a guided tour.

'Sorry it's a bit early,' she said, bustling into the kitchen, rolling up her sleeves and cutting Teddy's toast into soldiers while I dropped his boiled egg into a cup – solid silver, I noticed. 'It'll be a lot easier if we get round the house before it opens to the public at ten thirty.'

'I understand.' I turned my attention back to Teddy. 'And are you going to help Annie show me where you live?' I said as I cut the top off his boiled egg and carried it to the nursery table.

Teddy nodded earnestly. 'Can I bring Arkle?' He scrambled on to his chair and tucked into his egg.

'Perhaps not,' said Annie. 'But after we've shown Lucy the house, we'll take her to see the stables and the gardens and Arkle can come with us then.'

'Daddy's away,' volunteered Teddy, changing the subject, his mouth full of egg.

'That's right, sweetie. He's got business to do,' said Annie.

I wondered how long he was gone for.

'He's been away a lot recently,' explained Annie. 'You know, since . . .'

Since Becca's death. I could imagine why. I supposed that if it wasn't for his son he would probably have no wish to come back to this place at all. With all his money I guessed he had several other houses he could go to; houses that wouldn't contain quite so many memories of his late wife. The poor man must be heartbroken. How, I wondered, did you get over something like that?

'Anyway,' said Annie, more brightly, 'Teddy has lots of people looking after him here and plenty to do.'

The mention of all the people who looked after Teddy prompted me to enquire about who exactly lived in. It seemed that everyone, with the exception of me and Mrs Porter, the housekeeper, lived in cottages in the grounds or the village. And even Mrs Porter didn't live in the family wing but in a suite of rooms in the main house. It seemed I was right; Teddy and I were on our own in this bit – well, till the Earl got back. But even with him around it was hardly going to be packed.

'I go to playschool,' Teddy announced apropos of nothing at all, in the way small children will.

'Gosh,' I said. 'I bet that's fun.'

'Yes,' said Teddy. 'And Miss Wilson is just the best.'

'But you haven't got playschool today. Today we're going to show Lucy where you live.'

'And it'll take ages and ages,' said Teddy, looking at me as if he was wondering whether I was up to it.

I thought I might just about cope.

*

Half an hour later, with Teddy washed, brushed and combed, Annie led me and him through a door and into the public part of the house. If I'd thought the family wing was grand I was completely gobsmacked when I saw the main hall. It went right up to the roof and was so big you could have got my mother's entire house into it and, I thought as I gazed around it, the houses on either side. High up, above an enormous fresco of nude women being fed grapes by hordes of equally nude cherubs that went round all four walls, were about a dozen huge windows that made me wonder how on earth they heated the hall in the winter. The bills for this place must be phenomenal, I thought. The walls beneath the frieze were red and hung with vast paintings, all of which seemed to figure even more nudes gorging on a variety of delicacies.

I felt a small warm hand slip into mine. I was pleased that he seemed to like me; even more so this time because Annie, whom he had obviously known all his life, was around. The Teddy seal of approval? I hoped so.

I looked down at him and smiled and then returned my gaze to the ceiling.

'Look at all the willies,' said Teddy, as if he were some sort of art critic pointing out the finer points of the paintings.

Indeed, I thought. Just look at them! Willies and boobs by the dozen.

'Heavens,' I exclaimed. 'You'd think they'd catch their deaths, having a picnic with no clothes on.' That made Teddy giggle, the first I'd heard, I noted. His solemnity worried me a little, but he'd had a tough time for a kid aged only three.

Seeing the house for real was more overwhelming than I'd expected. I knew it was big and I knew it was grand, but to see it in the flesh was awesome.

Annie seemed quite unperturbed about the whole place. She was used to it I supposed, and I wondered if I would ever become equally blasé. I looked about at all the gold leaf and echoing spaces and wonderful pictures and wondered what it would be like to be able to call such a place 'home'. All I'd ever known was a terraced house in a bland bit of suburban London. How the other half live!

We made our way across the hall, with Annie pointing out some of the paintings, and telling me the names of painters that I'd heard about and assumed only existed in art galleries. Everything was obviously incredibly valuable and I found it hard to get my head round the fact that one day it would all belong to Teddy. The only object I possessed that might be considered a family heirloom was a vase that had once belonged to my grandmother. It was electroplated and I always thought of it as the family silver. I smiled to myself as I looked about me and saw Teddy's family silver. It was like comparing a primary school football team with Manchester United.

We reached one of the main rooms of the house and despite my loosening my grip on Teddy's pudgy little hand he kept his fingers firmly locked in mine. This, apparently, was the Chinese salon. Then we entered the red drawing room. Annie took me through room upon room stuffed with beautiful carpets, precious clocks, wonderful paintings and priceless antiques. Oh, and yet more family silver. By about the seventh huge room Teddy decided that I could be trusted to walk on my own and dodged under the thick red rope that controlled the access of the paying punters.

Expecting alarms to sound and searchlights to spring to life I stepped over it to bring him back, although why I worried was beyond me as everything in the house was going to be his one day.

'Come to the window,' I said, holding my hand out to him, 'and show me the good places to play outside.' Even for a serious child like Teddy I could see that the house tour was becoming tedious. He clambered on to the window seat of one of the tall sash windows that ran along one wall. I followed and stood behind him. Outside stretched acres of grass with trees dotted about at intervals. A herd of deer grazed in the distance – the spotty ones I'd seen the day before. Had Hugh called them fallow deer? I could see the drive stretching into the distance. I realised that I couldn't see to the edge of the estate. Blimey, how much land did the Earl own?

I pointed out a tree with a low sweeping branch that almost touched the grass which would be ideal for climbing, but Teddy looked at me with such wide-eyed horror at the idea that I made a mental note not to try anything more exciting than ball games for a while.

We walked to the next room.

'The ballroom,' announced Annie.

'Wow.' I had never seen so much polished parquet in my life. Acres of it stretched ahead. Round the walls were huge mirrors which made the room look even bigger. I tried to imagine the balls and parties that had taken place there over the centuries: the ladies in their gorgeous gowns, the men in uniforms, the candelabra flickering, eyes flashing over fans, dance cards being filled, musicians playing, the tinkle of polite chit-chat and laughter. Oh, I thought, how very Merchant Ivory!

The floor was as big and shiny as a skating rink – and just as tempting. I slipped off my shoes, took a few running steps and slid. I shot across the floor most satisfactorily.

'Come on, Teddy,' I called from the far side of the cavernous space, 'this is fun.'

Teddy stared at me from across the room. I ran and slid back towards him.

'Try it,' I coaxed, but he just stuck his thumb in his mouth and looked at me as if I'd completely lost it.

'Never mind,' I muttered, slipping my shoes on again. Teddy obviously had never done rough-and-tumble or just being plain silly. If I achieved nothing else while I looked after him I was determined he would learn how to have noisy, uncomplicated fun. I wondered what his life had been like with his previous nanny to make him end up so subdued and serious. Not normal for a three year old in my book, not normal at all.

'Onwards and upwards,' said Annie as we emerged into the hall once again. She led us upstairs and through the rooms on the first floor. Endless bedrooms, anterooms, dressing rooms and even an interactive display about how life used to be in the house in the old days. For the 'Upstairs' lot it would have been pretty pleasant apart from the serious lack of plumbing and heating. However, the lack of running water and warmth made all the difference to the poor staff lugging mountains of coal and buckets of hot water all over the place to keep the gentry happy. Not much fun being 'Downstairs' in the old days, I concluded – and only one half-day off a month. I thanked my lucky stars that I had been born when I had – I wouldn't have fancied a job in service in the old days.

For the third time in about an hour we were back in the grand hall.

'Last leg,' said Annie. 'We'll do the private wing and then take Teddy out for some fresh air.'

Thank God for that. I'd had more than enough culture to last me for a month of Sundays and I was surprised by how patient Teddy had been at being dragged round the house. I didn't reckon there were many three year olds who would have put up with it. Maybe it was different if it was your own place, but did he know that?

In some respects the private wing was quite like an ordinary house apart from the scale of the rooms and the number of priceless antiques around. There was a drawing room, a dining room, a study and a den on the ground floor, none of which we went into. The door to the den was wide open and I noticed, amongst other features, that it had a nice big TV in it. Maybe I would be able to get my *Sex and the City* fix after all.

Then Annie took me down into the basement. Cook was busy making lunch for the staff, working on a huge lump of dough on the kitchen table. Behind her were two underlings, one peeling a vast mound of spuds while the other was washing up a couple of vat-sized saucepans.

The kitchen was warm and noisy and smelled of frying onions and caramel and something else quite delicious. This was an environment, the first since I'd arrived at Arden Hall, in which I didn't feel completely intimidated. It might have been big and bustling but it was also homely and comforting. Teddy seemed to feel likewise as he clambered on to a kitchen chair, nicked a lump of discarded pastry from the edge of the board and began to mould it like plasticine.

Cook greeted me with a huge smile. 'You tell me what you want in the way of stores for the nursery and I'll see you get it. Let me have your list when you start to run low. Pop down here or tell me on the house phone,' she said amiably, as she flattened a huge lump of pastry with a rolling pin. She was exactly as I imagined a cook should look: ample-bosomed, floury and friendly with huge hands that flicked the pastry over the marble slab with deft expertise.

This place was doing my head in. I was never going to be able to remember all the stuff Annie had told me, or the names of the people I'd met, or my way about the place. What with all that on top of the stuff she'd told me about Teddy's local activities – Tumble Tots, playgroup and story time at the library – well, my brain was ready to explode. I just hoped that no one would mind too much if I cocked things up or forgot their names or took Teddy with the wrong kit to the wrong event for the first couple of weeks.

We left the kitchen and headed back upstairs again; past the first floor which housed the Earl's private apartments, some spare rooms, the box room and goodness only knew what else, on up to the familiarity of the nursery wing. However, at the top of the stairs we didn't head for my own territory. Annie opened a door on the other side of the landing and suddenly I was in a world I recognised: normal furniture not fabulous antiques, office equipment, a couple of desks, strip lighting and standard carpeting. And behind one of the desks was someone else I recognised – Hugh.

When he saw us, he stood up. His charming old-fashioned courtesy made me smile. First car doors, now this.

'Hello,' he said. 'Found your way to the engine room?'

'Annie and Teddy are showing me round.'

'Got sat nav?'

'I think I may invest in it.'

'You'll get used to it.'

Teddy headed for another door that led out of Hugh's office. 'This is where Daddy works,' he informed me over his shoulder.

I followed him into the inner office, which surprised me by its austerity. Sure, the minions weren't going to get swanky furnishings, but I expected a bit of luxury for the man at the top; at the very least I expected more paintings and gilding so I was quite surprised by the modern, functional room I found. Teddy had already clambered into the big leather swivel chair behind the desk and seemed to be practising being the Earl of Arden.

'Come along, Teddy,' I said brightly, to cover up my discomfiture at trespassing in my boss's inner sanctum without permission. 'Aren't you going to show me the stables? Weren't you going to take . . .' Shit, what was the name of that hobby horse? Arctic, Albatross, Angus?

'Arkle,' said Teddy with a look which seemed to convey his general disappointment in the quality of his personal staff.

'Arkle,' I repeated, feeling slightly nettled. Nettled! By a three year old.

Hugh must have overheard us.

'If Jed's there you could ask him to saddle up Teddy's pony,' he said as we went back into the general office. 'Teddy loves riding, don't you?' A smile flicked across Teddy's face and he nodded briefly. I wished he'd shown real enthusiasm or even joy. 'Besides, if Teddy doesn't ride Toy Town that animal will get even fatter.'

The idea of riding might have pushed Teddy's buttons – as much as they could be pushed – but the conversation was having the opposite effect on me. My God, a horse. A real one. I gulped. Teddy's wooden horse was one thing but being responsible for a child on a living, breathing one was something else entirely. My heart sank. This wasn't in the job spec. I was about to get found out and sent packing for being completely unsuited to a job in the country. Why wasn't my first test in this job something like negotiating my way on to a double-decker bus with several children and a buggy? I could do that, no sweat. But a horse! No way. This was an aspect of country living I hadn't been prepared for and wasn't going to be able to cope with.

Hugh must have seen the look on my face. 'You wouldn't mind doing that, would you? You're not scared of the brutes?'

'I don't think so,' I lied. 'I've never had much to do with horses.' Except that I should have said I've never had *anything* to do with horses.

'Well, see how you get on with Toy Town. He's pretty biddable.' He flashed me a grin. 'And he's very small, so no threat.'

'Right.' Since when had horses been small? I'd seen the ones in Hyde Park. Even when they were just ambling along they looked big and lumbering. And as for when they went faster and you could hear the hooves thundering from yards away . . . Hugh was trying to make me feel better but I wasn't swallowing it. Besides, what did I know about supervising a kid on a horse? Suppose he fell off ? I'd just have to make sure he didn't, that was all.

I was about to leave the office when a pretty girl about my age came in.

'Hi,' she said. 'You must be Lucy.' I nodded. 'I'm Jenny. I do the admin for the inside of the house: pay, holiday rotas, stuff like that. If you need anything on the HR side come to me. Are your rooms all right?'

'Perfect,' I said. 'I've never had so much space.'

'Like there's a shortage here.' She gave me a wide, welcoming smile. I liked her instantly. 'I'll drop by and see you one day soon. Tell you about the night life around here. What there is to do for kicks.'

Kicks? Out here in the sticks? I wondered what she had in mind. Darts? Bowls? Oooh, hold me back, what a wild night that would be. But I fixed a smile. 'I'd love that. Thanks.' I wanted to stay and talk but it wasn't going to happen today. Teddy was tugging silently at my skirt to remind me of my promise.

'Oh, and this is for you.' Jenny handed me a buff manila folder. 'It was put together by your predecessor – Jo. It's a list of the things Teddy does and where to find them, important numbers like the doctor's surgery, stuff you need to know about the Hall. She thought you might need some notes.'

I took the folder and flicked through it. From what I could see it looked wonderfully comprehensive. I was hugely grateful. Teddy was tugging more insistently. I was being unfair in putting off the moment. I looked down at him and smiled. 'Gotta fly,' I said.

Annie got up from a chair in the office. 'Let's give Teddy some fresh air,' she said. 'He's been such a good boy.'

Unnaturally good, in my opinion.

Quickly we fetched Arkle from the nursery and back down the stairs we went. Hugh had warned me about the stairs in this place. I was just beginning to see what he meant. And part of me wondered if there was anything else about life at Arden Hall that I should be warned about. From what I had seen, this place was about as far removed from normality as it was possible to get and still be on planet Earth.

With Teddy and Arkle leading the way Annie and I made our way out through the garden room door and round the back of the house. This bit wasn't open to visitors and we were able to stroll through the private gardens in peace and quiet.

We rounded a corner of the house and there was the stable block, but it was no row of wooden sheds with half-doors like I'd seen in pictures of racing stables and riding establishments. No, this was unbelievably swanky. A huge stone building with a row of round windows up near the roof and huge double doors at the end, thrown open. Inside I could see shafts of sunlight streaming through the windows and the dusty air to form golden pools in the middle of the cobbles that ran through the centre. On either side were wrought-iron and wooden partitions over which poked the horses' heads. There must have been about ten or a dozen of the beasts in there.

'The Countess's event horses,' said Annie.

'What? All of them?'

'Mostly. That one there is Billy Boy – the one she won her gold medal on.'

I supposed Billy Boy was seriously superior to the others but they all looked much the same to me. All glossy, all bright-eyed, all big and, now I was getting closer, all quite scary.

Someone was whistling in the depths of the stable. The three of us stepped into the cool gloom of the building and I was hit by the sweet smell of hay and the more pungent but not unpleasant one of horse muck. Teddy dropped Arkle with a clatter on to the cobbles, which caused Billy Boy to toss his head and roll his eyes, revealing the whites. I did *not* want to get any closer. The horse looked angry. I wondered if it had been Billy Boy who had killed the Countess, because one of these huge brutes had and he looked mean enough right now to be capable of anything.

Now I was in the same building as the horses Hugh's idea that I should take Teddy for a trot around on his pony didn't seem very enticing. Frankly I didn't want to get any nearer to any of them, however 'biddable' Toy Town might be.

'Jed,' shouted Annie.

'Hi, Ma,' he shouted back.

Ma? So Annie was his mum. Well, well. Although why should I be surprised? Arden Hall was in the middle of nowhere so it must be the biggest employer for miles around. I imagined there were whole generations of families who had worked here. I made a mental note to be careful not to pass comment about anyone to anyone. If I did I would probably upset half the local population.

Jed lumbered out of one of the stalls carrying a nasty, spiky-looking fork. 'Ma,' he said, smiling at Annie. Then he saw me. 'Miss,' he acknowledged. The way he said it I almost expected him to tug his forelock.

Teddy ran to Jed and hung on to his leg.

Jed propped his fork against a wall and bent down. 'Hiya, little fella,' he said gently. Then he straightened and swung Teddy up in one giant ham-like hand. Teddy looked delighted. 'You come to see Toy Town?' He dropped Teddy over his shoulder so the boy was in a reverse fireman's lift, his little smiling face alongside Jed's. The two grinned happily at each other.

'Yes, I have,' said Teddy, showing enthusiasm and animation for the first time since I'd met him. I almost felt relief, as I'd been beginning to wonder if he was capable of behaving like a real little boy.

'Could you saddle him up?' said Annie. 'Teddy would love a ride around.'

I felt a small surge of apprehension.

'Righto.' Jed made his way to the back of the stables, carrying Teddy, who was chortling happily and kicking his chubby legs in pleasure.

While they were doing whatever was necessary at the back of the stables I had another look at the horses. I kept firmly to the central, cobbled aisle, well out of range of teeth, hooves, swishing tails or any other bits that might pose a threat. God, they were huge. I couldn't imagine how high you'd feel up there on a saddle. And then jumping over some of the huge fences Becca had had to negotiate to win her medal. Blimey, the Countess deserved a gong for even attempting what she'd done. I felt scared just standing firmly on the ground and thinking about it.

Jed reappeared leading what I, at first, thought was a big dog by one hand and Teddy by the other. Then, as he got closer, I could see that it was the dinkiest pony I'd ever seen. Jed looked like a giant with the two tiny creatures flanking him. Toy Town seemed as broad as he was high and his head only reached my waist. The idea of him getting any fatter was a joke – it just wasn't possible. His coat was the colour of best-quality polished brown leather shoes and his mane and tail were pale blond. I handed Annie my folder of info and reached out my hand and fondled his ear. Toy Town tossed his head away.

'Let him smell your hand first,' said Jed. He took hold of my fingers and held them to the pony's nostrils. Warm breath and a few whiskers tickled my knuckles. Then he moved my hand up to the animal's nose and placed it between Toy Town's eyes. I scratched it. An appreciative snort was blown out. After a few seconds I ran my fingers up through his forelock to his fuzzy little ears. They were warm and velvety. Maybe I'd be able to cope after all.

Jed picked up Teddy, now resplendent in tiny riding helmet, and dropped him on to the saddle. Now he was on top of the pony he could almost look me in the eye. Suddenly he seemed more grown up than three.

'Can we go to the school?' he asked.

Jed nodded.

'School?' I knew Mary took a little lamb with her, but a pony?

Jed grabbed the reins and led Toy Town out of the building and into the bright sunshine of the yard.

Annie said she'd got things to do and she'd meet us

back in the nursery in about half an hour. It seemed like a good plan to me. Teddy waved at her cheerfully from his perch and I followed Jed and the two small creatures out of the stables. I blinked, dazzled. Teddy, Jed and the pony were heading straight across the yard to a similar building – a barn, I'd assumed, not that I'd given it much thought.

The huge double doors were open and the same cones of dusty light were shining down like heavenly rays in old biblical pictures, only this time, instead of being neatly divided up into stalls, the space was just one huge sandy floor, like a huge flower bed or sandpit, and around the side were letters of the alphabet.

Jed saw me looking around. 'This is the indoor school, miss; this is where we train the horses.' I was no wiser about the letters of the alphabet but I didn't have time to ask as Jed handed me the reins. Ohmigod. I was in charge of a pony.

'Want to walk Teddy round?' he asked.

I gulped. 'How?'

'Just hold the reins. Teddy won't fall off; he knows what he's doing.' I was glad one of us did. 'Little lamb, this pony.'

'Right,' I said, trying to sound confident.

'It's not hard,' he said.

No. Of course it wasn't. I began to walk forward. Toy Town didn't. 'Er, giddy up,' I said hopefully.

Jed, standing in the middle of the huge expanse of peaty sand, gave a shrill whistle. Toy Town instantly began to stroll round the perimeter at a leisurely pace. Given his speed and the shortness of his legs I could easily keep up.

Teddy, his feet firmly anchored in the stirrups and his back straight, swayed gently in time with the pony's gait. Feeling confident, I smiled at my charge. He smiled back.

'Can I go faster?' he asked.

Jed whistled again – a slightly different note this time. Toy Town broke into a trot. So did I. It was a long time since I'd done any jogging, although looking after children means you're always on the go so I thought I was quite fit. However, by the second circuit of the indoor school I was fast running out of puff.

'Jed,' I pleaded, using up what little breath I had left, 'can ... we ... slow ... down? Please,' I added in desperation. Another of his strange whistles and Toy Town slowed to a walk.

'Faster,' pleaded Teddy.

I shook my head. 'Not till I get my breath back, sweetheart.' I looked imploringly at Jed. Please God, he sided with me and not Teddy.

Another bird-like whistle and Toy Town ground to a halt. Judging by the way his sides were heaving he was as thankful to stop as I was. We spent the next half-hour alternately walking and jogging until I decided that, even if Teddy wanted to go on, Toy Town and I had had enough – besides, Annie would be waiting for us.

'Was that fun?' I asked Teddy. He didn't have to answer; his smile said it all. Maybe this was the key to this serious little kid; riding seemed to unlock his more normal side. 'We can do this again another day,' I said, surprising even myself, but I was too chuffed that he had shown signs of really enjoying himself to regret the rash promise. I glanced at Jed. 'That is if Jed doesn't mind.' Jed shook his head.

'You just tell me when you want Toy Town ready, miss, and I'll see that he is.'

This was like something out of a historical novel. I felt I ought to be done up in a velvet riding habit and riding side-saddle rather than wearing jeans and a sweater and puffing around an indoor school beside a pony that was straight out of a Thelwell cartoon.

'Thank you, Jed,' I said, handing him the reins of the little pony and lifting Teddy down. 'Come on, young man,' I said. 'Lunchtime.'

When we got back to the nursery Annie was already there.

'I'll get off back to the farm, if that's okay with you,' said Annie. 'If you want anything, or there's something I haven't told you, my number's on the list by the house phone in your sitting room, but this file seems to cover everything. Dial nine and you'll get an outside line.' She gave Teddy a peck on the cheek and got ready to leave.

'Just one thing. When is the Earl due back?'

'Don't rightly know, Lucy. End of the week, maybe. Hugh may know.'

I was compiling a list of things I had to ask Hugh, when was the Earl due to return and what to do about my defunct TV being two of them. The third was how much time off I might expect – if any. I certainly wasn't going to get any till Teddy's dad returned home, which wasn't a problem in the short term, but I did need to get things sorted out; I had a life to lead too.

I made Teddy and me some pasta and salad which he ate tidily and with impeccable manners while telling me about the various horses in the stables. The names of the nags went in one ear and out of the other without so much as breaking step. I wondered how long it would be before the novelty of my new post wore off and I began to feel at ease and at home.

After lunch Teddy had a rest on his bed and I tackled Jo's file. I stuck the page listing the things Teddy did on various days of the week on the fridge. I decided that after his rest we would find the car I'd been allocated and drive around the local area to find all the places I'd be required to take him. It seemed like a good plan. And when we got back, if the weather was still fine, we might have a run around in the grounds before tea, bath and bed.

As I sat in one of the armchairs in my sitting room, which I'd positioned so I could see through my bedroom and into the nursery where Teddy was sleeping, I began to think about the lack of one or two other things, as well as the TV, which might make life tricky for me. I realised there was no washing machine or iron. So how was I supposed to look after his clothes? Maybe there were facilities somewhere else in the house. And I didn't have any cleaning equipment. Perhaps I was expected to fetch the Hoover from the basement. The thought of lugging it up those millions of stairs didn't appeal. In a place this size there must be more than one vacuum cleaner and if so, surely one could be spared for me. Perhaps, I decided, before we went for a drive, Teddy and I would nip down to the kitchens and have a word with Cook about the housekeeping.

When Teddy woke up, I gave him a few minutes to rub the sleep out of his eyes, have a wee and generally do the things all small boys do as part of waking up: let off a series of tiny farts, scratch his crotch, shove one finger up his nose to see if anything of interest had arrived in his sleep and another down his trousers, presumably for the same reason. I gently removed his hands from both areas and suggested we ought to go and see Cook before going out in the car.

'Goody,' said Teddy. 'She usually has biscuits,' he added wistfully.

We made our way out of the nursery and down the huge shallow staircase to the main hall of the family wing. As I held firmly on to Teddy with one hand and the banister with the other, I gazed about at the splendour around me. I could hardly believe that I was really living here; that my clothes were unpacked and hanging in a wardrobe in this house. I looked at the family portraits gazing back at me, at the wonderful bits of silver and china casually displayed on even more wonderful antiques, and felt completely overawed. Would I ever get used to this? I couldn't imagine becoming blasé about such surroundings but I supposed that if, like the Earl, you'd never known anything different, maybe you would.

We got to the ground floor and I managed to recall which of the doors was the one that led to the basement. I pulled it open and Teddy and I descended yet more stairs.

Boy, I was going to have leg muscles like a body-builder's by the time I finished here.

We pushed open the door to the kitchen and were greeted by a completely different sight from the morning one. Gone were the smells and the warmth. Instead it was all swabbed down, cold and clinical. It was hard to believe that this was the same place I'd visited just a few hours earlier. And instead of Cook at the big central table there was a thin, serious-looking woman in a black business suit tapping away at a laptop, a pile of household bills, a mobile and the house phone on the table beside her.

She looked up sharply as Teddy and I barged through the door. She looked me up and down, her lips tight and disapproving. Teddy inched behind me.

'You must be the girl from Pinner,' she said. No greeting, no friendliness, not even a smile for Teddy. And she made Pinner sound like some sort of sexually transmitted disease. I felt instantly cowed by her. There was something about her that was faintly familiar, but my memory banks couldn't quite work it out.

I could feel myself blushing and my small stock of confidence draining out of my toes as fast as the blood was rushing to my face.

I swallowed. 'Yes. I came to see Cook.'

'She's taken the rest of the day off. With the Earl away she doesn't have to prepare dinner. I'm Mrs Porter, the housekeeper.'

'Lucy Carter,' I replied. Then I got it; she'd brought in the coffee tray at my interview.

'I know.' There was a small silence, and she glanced at

her laptop. I was obviously interrupting her. 'So can I help you or did you want to speak to Cook in particular?'

'I don't know. I don't know who I should approach.'

'What's the problem?' She sounded like a schoolteacher when confronted by a particularly stupid pupil; the sort of tone I remembered only too well.

I plucked up the courage to grasp the nettle. 'I was wondering if there is a washing machine I could use. And there aren't any cleaning things in the nursery.'

'Is the nursery not up to standard? Have you a problem with the cleanliness?'

'No . . . I . . .' I felt foolish. Somehow I was aware I was making a faux pas but I didn't know what it was.

'Because if there is, I need to know.'

'No, the nursery is fine. Honest.'

Mrs Porter looked at me as if I was completely mad. 'Even so. If Maria doesn't carry out her duties properly, you must tell me.'

Maria? Who the hell was Maria? 'I don't understand.'

Mrs Porter sighed. 'Maria is responsible for the upstairs rooms of the private wing. She cleans the nursery and your flat twice a week and the bathroom daily.'

'So I don't have to—'

'Cleaning isn't part of your duties as nanny here.'

'Oh.' I felt quite foolish, but also indignant. How was I to know? 'Well, that's very nice,' I said lamely, 'but what about the washing?'

'The laundry maid sees to that.' Again she gave me that look, as if I was an imbecile. 'There's a laundry bin in your bathroom. If you leave your dirty linen in there it will be dealt with.'

I wasn't sure I really wanted some stranger dealing with my grubby knickers. I was fine about someone washing Teddy's things but I wasn't happy about mine. I think my face must have reflected my thoughts.

'The last nanny had no problem with this arrangement.'

I wanted to say 'Well, bully for her', but my courage deserted me.

'Is there anything else?'

'The television in my room doesn't work.'

A sigh. 'What seems to be the matter?'

'I don't know. There's no picture. I've checked the aerial and the tuning,' I added. I didn't want to give Mrs Porter any more reasons to think I was incompetent.

'I see. I'll arrange to get someone in to have a look at it.' She looked at her laptop again. Obviously doing the accounts, or whatever, was much more interesting than talking to me.

'Is there a spare one I could borrow in the meantime?'

She thought for a moment. 'I don't know about moving sets around the house. Without his lordship's permission . . . There's one in the den downstairs. With his lordship being absent I don't suppose it would matter if you used it.'

'But I won't be able to hear Teddy.'

'As far as I know there's a baby alarm. When your predecessor had time off I believe his lordship used it.'

'Thank you.'

A small voice came from beside my thigh. 'Can I have a biscuit now?'

I bent down to him. 'I don't think that's possible with Cook not here. Let's go for that drive and then we'll make some upstairs to have with our supper.'

'Promise.'

'Cross my heart.' I stopped before I got to the 'and hope to die' bit. Not appropriate considering the recent family history.

'Your car is parked in the courtyard,' said Mrs Porter, still crisp and efficient and not very friendly. 'It's the green Corsa.'

'Thank you,' I said. 'Come along, Teddy.' We left the kitchen together. I didn't say goodbye to her. I didn't think she and I were going to be bosom buddies and obviously she was way above me in the pecking order. I rather hoped our paths wouldn't cross too much.

I was glad to get out of the house. Teddy seemed to have forgotten about the lack of biscuits and pottered over to the car without complaint. He tugged on the door till I unlocked it and then climbed into the child seat in the back. I got him clipped in and, local map to hand, was soon bowling down the long driveway to the front gate, which was about half a mile from the centre of the village. I drove carefully along the unfamiliar route, squeezing the car along the narrow roads until I reached the tiny village square.

I glanced at the map as I pulled the handbrake on. This place was even smaller than I had expected. Around the square were marked the village hall, the pub and the library. As two of those venues hosted several of Teddy's activities I could see that getting lost was going to be tough, even for me.

I helped Teddy out of the car and held his hand as we walked across to the village hall, where I peered in through the glazed door.

'Can I help you?'

I jumped and spun round, feeling unaccountably guilty. Maybe I was trespassing.

'Sorry . . .'

'Miss Wilson,' said Teddy. He gave a little wriggle of pleasure. Whoever this was she obviously rated very highly in Teddy's world.

'Hello, Teddy.' A young girl with blond curly hair, a pretty face and an engaging smile was beaming at my charge. She crouched down beside him. 'How are you?'

'I'm fine. Lucy wants to see where my playgroup is,' Teddy explained gravely.

The girl looked up at me. 'Hello.' She stood up again and held her hand out, smiling.

My feeling of guilt dissipated as I took it. 'Lucy Carter. Teddy's new nanny.'

'Mandy Wilson. I help out at the playgroup. What do you want to know about it?'

'Nothing, really.' I explained that I was just exploring the village so I knew my way around.

'I don't blame you. Easy to get completely lost in this place. I don't know how people manage. All these streets, the hustle, the bustle . . .'

'You may laugh, but I've spent the morning going round the Hall. I'm going to need maps, compass and sat nav just to get out of the front door each day.'

Teddy looked confused. 'But I can show you the way.'

'And what happens when you're at playgroup? How is Lucy going to cope then?' said Mandy.

Teddy frowned at Mandy. 'Well, Hugh can help her,' he said slowly, as if he were explaining the solution to someone with learning difficulties. First Mrs Porter and now Teddy – I tried not to giggle.

'Look, why don't we go to the tea room and I can fill you in on what the local facilities and amenities are?'

It sounded like a good plan to me and before I knew it Teddy and I were sitting opposite Mandy in an archetypal tea room complete with the smell of baking and gingham curtains and having ordered tea and cake.

'Have you lived here long?' I asked.

'All my life. My mum was born here. My nan was in service up at the house. Half the village is like that. Of course, the other half are all incomers. Still,' she said cheerfully, 'the gene pool was a bit limited before they arrived so it's probably just as well.'

I grinned. 'I've noticed this place is hardly multicultural. Not like where I come from.'

Mandy raised her eyebrows in question so I told her about life in Pinner.

'Blimey. This must be a bit of a shock then. The most we get in the way of ethnic influence is cook-in curry sauce in the shop.'

I laughed. 'I'll cope. And I love the country. I love the peace and quiet.'

'Come off it. It's like living in a morgue.'

I shook my head. 'No sirens, no smell of fumes, no crowds . . .'

'No shops, no clubs, no fun, no jobs unless you're into farming.'

'You've got a job.'

'Yeah, and I love it, but there's no chance of any advancement and nothing much else on offer unless I move away. And I can't afford that.'

Teddy finished his cake and held up his hands, which were covered in crumbs and fudge icing. I wiped them, then turned my attention to his mouth.

'There's loads I'd like to ask you,' I said to Mandy. 'How about we meet for a drink?'

We exchanged mobile numbers and promised to ring each other in a few days to make arrangements. After my rather scary encounter with Mrs Porter my spirits began to lift again. Mandy seemed like fun and maybe with her and Jenny around living in the country wouldn't be so dull.

'See you tomorrow, Teddy,' said Mandy as we left.

I remembered that the next day was a playgroup morning. With no washing to do or nursery to clean I wondered how I would pass the time without Teddy to look after. No doubt I would think of something.

When Teddy had been fed and bathed and was playing quietly in the nursery I found the baby alarm and checked that it worked. I wouldn't go downstairs to the den until Teddy was sound asleep but it would be nice to chill in front of the box for an hour or so. It had been a long day, my brain was mushy from all the information it had had crammed into it and I felt like vegging out for a bit.

After I'd read Teddy his bedtime story I drifted around quietly until I was sure he was sound asleep; then, with the radio baby alarm clasped in my hand, I tiptoed out on to the landing. The light from the nursery nightlight was minimal, casting little more than a faint glow in a triangle out of the door. I put up the stairgate to stop Teddy wandering out of the nursery should he get up and come looking for me, then began to make my way to the head of the stairs. As I went my fingers brushed along the wall, feeling for a light switch. Nothing. Surely there would be one somewhere. I stopped where I could just see the top step and peered into the gloom, but still couldn't find the switch. Gingerly I felt my way carefully down the treads in the near darkness. There had to be a light somewhere. Maybe on the next landing. The darkness got deeper as I got further from the dim glow of the nursery. I ran the flat of my hand along the wall beside me – partly as support, but mainly to try to locate a switch. There had to be one, but these were big walls and I was stuffed if I could find it.

By the time I reached the ground floor the darkness seemed total. I could make out the faint gleam of polished furniture and the vague pattern of the tiled floor but other than that I was effectively blind. High above me, at the top of the stairwell, I could see the comforting glow coming from the nursery but the light didn't penetrate to these depths so, apart from telling me how to get back to my sanctuary, it was useless. Part of me wanted to forget the TV and return to the security it promised, but if I did, what would I do to pass the evening? Tuck myself up in bed with *Swallows and Amazons*? Blimey, it wasn't even eight o'clock. Tired as I was, I couldn't face bedtime *that* early. How sad would that be?

In the gloom, the house seemed even bigger than before and I felt like a burglar as I crept through the dim hall and along the corridor towards the den. I was sure a member of staff was about to leap out at me and accuse me of trespass, or that some alarm would be triggered at the local cop shop and a posse of burly policemen would crash through the door, hurling tear gas canisters and abuse. Guilt and nerves flooded through me and I felt a huge sense of wrong-doing.

I tried telling myself that this was ridiculous. I tried telling myself that I'd watched too many episodes of *The*

*Bill*. I tried telling myself that this was my home now and I had every right to leave my rooms and watch TV downstairs but, despite my bracing words to myself, my heart was still thumping and my breathing shallow with misgiving as I edged across the floor. As I went I felt along the walls trying to find a switch, but my fingers just found moulding and pictures – not an electrical fitting to be had anywhere. I knew it was ridiculous, I knew the house had electricity and the switches had to be around somewhere, but I was buggered if I could find them. Going slowly, terrified of bumping into something valuable and breakable, I stumbled my way along the corridor until I reached what I assumed was my destination. In the gloom I could see the glow of a red stand-by light. The TV, surely.

My memory told me that there was a table near the door with a huge Chinese lamp on it. My fingers fluttered in front of me. I encountered a big parchment shade. Yesss! And a switch. Fantastic.

Light flooded the room. Now I could see, my apprehension vanished like the darkness. I shut the door to block out the huge expanse of house. I wanted to feel cosy and with all that gloomy space lurking outside the room it was going to be impossible unless I put a barrier between me and it.

With a sigh of relief I made my way to one of the big squashy armchairs, grabbing the remote and a TV listings guide off the coffee table as I went. The room was pretty sumptuous by ordinary standards but compared to nearly all the other rooms at the Hall, other than the offices and my little section, the den was practically stark. Instead of antiques the furniture consisted of a beautifully covered three-piece suite, a couple of occasional tables, some pretty watercolours on the wall, a big mirror over the fireplace, a very swanky flat-screen TV and a few side tables with vases of flowers and family snaps. Almost homely, I thought as I looked around. Well, homely if you discounted the height of the ceiling and the size of the windows, now hidden behind some seriously expensive-looking curtains. It wasn't precisely my idea of a den, but in this house it was as close as it was going to get.

Idly I flicked through the pages of the guide and then the channels until I found something sufficiently banal to satisfy me. I turned the volume down low so I could hear the whiffings and stirrings of my charge over the radio alarm.

In the near silence I was acutely aware of the ticking and creaking of the old house as it settled and found it as spooky and unnerving as I had the previous night. I tried to tell myself that all houses moved slightly and made noises when it was quiet enough to hear them, and that Teddy and I were perfectly safe. I also tried to convince myself that London was a far more dangerous place than this neck of the woods, but still the hairs on my neck refused to quieten down. I found that I had only the faintest idea of what was going on in the programme I was watching. All my concentration was focused on the ticks, clunks and other faint noises of the night.

A door slammed. No way was that the sound of the house settling. I almost leapt to my feet. My heart thundered and I held my breath. I hit the mute button on the remote. Silence. Perhaps I'd imagined it. A second or two later there was a series of smaller bangs. I wasn't imagining them. They sounded as if they were in the house itself. But there was only me and Teddy. And this noise definitely came from the back of the house. My heart rate shot up and I held my breath to make sure I didn't miss the least sound. Maybe the noise wasn't from inside the house at all. I crept to the door and pressed my ear against it. Nothing. Whatever had been making the bangs had stopped now. Maybe it was a fox, I told myself. I knew about foxes. Foxes we had in abundance in Pinner and I knew about the way they could upend rubbish bins and the dreadful screams, like someone being murdered, that they made while mating. Yes, a fox. That was surely it.

Then the light and the TV died.

I nearly yelped with fright. Maybe I should call the police, but my mobile was up in my room. Shakily I groped my way through the pitch dark to the door and put my hand on the knob. There was another noise. Closer this time. Feeling sick with fright I bit back a scream. My God, what was going on? And what about Teddy?

Teddy! He was alone and vulnerable upstairs. If there was an intruder he needed me to protect him. My breath was ragged with fear and I could feel my knees trembling. My legs felt as if they were about to give way beneath me, they were so shaky. I leaned against the door for support while I tried to work out what I should do. But there really wasn't a choice. I had to get to Teddy and make sure he was safe. And Teddy was upstairs. Could I slip out of the den and get to the stairs without being spotted?

I turned the knob as gently as I could. Inch by inch,

praying that it didn't creak, I eased the den door open. The corridor that led to it from the main hall was so black I could make nothing out. Thanking any god that was listening that I was wearing soft shoes, I tiptoed along the corridor.

Ahead, in the main hall, I heard someone cough quietly and swear under their breath. It was at this point that I realised I still had the remote in my hand. I stuffed it in my pocket. If I had to fight I wanted both hands to punch and scratch. Feeling helpless, and gagging with nerves, I crept forward. Every cell in my body was on edge. Every nerve, every muscle, every blood corpuscle was rigid with fear but I had to get to the stairs, Teddy and a phone before the intruder did. A shoe squeaked on the marble floor. Not mine.

My nerves, which had been taut with fear, stretched so much I thought I might faint. But Teddy was upstairs. I couldn't abandon him. I had to think of him and not me.

Keeping to the side of the passage, I crept forward some more. My eyes adjusted to make out shades and shapes in the black. I could see where the corridor from the den met the hall. I could see the vague outline of the big table and the huge silver tureen. I tried not to think about the possibility that there was a mad axe-murderer just feet from me.

'Oh, for fuck's sake,' I heard a man's voice mutter sotto voce.

I wanted to scream. I swallowed the bubble of noise back down.

I reached the point where the corridor joined the hall.

I peered round the edge of the wall. Nothing. But he was here. I knew it, but I couldn't see him. Across the other side of the hall were the stairs. But the expanse of marble floor between me and that first tread might just as well have been the English Channel. I could see my destination but no way could I get there.

I stood at the corner and scanned the hall. Where was he? I heard a shuffle. My eyes locked on to the source of the noise like a missile on a target. There – I could see a shape.

Whoever it was, he was standing near the door to the basement stairs. I could see something like an open cupboard door, and concentrated on the scene. I could just make out that he was doing something in the cupboard.

Shit. Maybe it wasn't a cupboard, perhaps it was a safe. Or maybe it was the alarm system for the house. Or maybe it was the key pad. Anyway, it didn't matter; he had no business to be doing whatever it was he was up to.

Taking a slow, deep, soundless breath I pulled the remote from my pocket, slipped my shoes off and inched my way across the cold marble floor. Then, holding the remote firmly in my right hand, I brought it down as hard as I could on the back of the intruder's head.

There was an unnerving second when I thought I'd completely cocked up, and the man didn't move. Then there was an agonised groan as he slumped to his knees clutching his head. I fled across the hall and sprinted up the stairs, taking them at least two at a time, my bare feet making no sound on the thick carpet. At the top I hurdled the stairgate and slammed the nursery door. On the other side, from somewhere down the stairwell, I heard angry shouting. I didn't bother to try to make out the words. Trembling, panting and still utterly terrified I hit the light switch. Nothing. Fuck, of course not.

I dumped the remote I was still clutching, grabbed the phone that was just visible in the dim moonlight coming through the nursery window and dialled 999. Nothing. I tried a second time, more carefully. Silence. Oh, my God, he'd cut the electricity *and* the phone lines. I was nearly sobbing by now. I dived across the nursery, cursing as I trod on a stray piece of Lego and a jolt of pain shot through my bare foot. My handbag was on the chair by my bed and in it was my mobile. I crashed into my bedroom. In the darkness I couldn't find my bag. I was sure it had been by my bed. I fumbled around for it, feeling over my bed, on the floor, across the table. I knocked over the lamp, and the book fell to the floor with a soft flump. Then I remembered – duh! – the bag was on my dressing table.

I ran round the bed, stubbing my toe on the leg and almost yelling with another sharp pain. I found the dressing table by the simple expedient of careering into it. There was my bag. I flipped it open and felt around for my phone.

Then I froze.

I heard the click and squeak of the nursery door.

I dropped my bag. I had to protect Teddy.

'Leave him alone,' I yelled. Or at least I meant to yell but it came out as a strangled, inarticulate squeak.

'I beg your pardon,' said a shocked but low voice from the next room.

I could hear Teddy stirring. Our exchange must have

penetrated his sleep. I moved slowly back into the nursery. Self-preservation made me want to run away but I couldn't abandon Teddy. I needed to put myself between this monster and him.

'Please,' I said. I could hear the start of a sob in my voice. 'Please . . .'

'And just who the fuck are you?' The voice sounded angry and cold. Dangerous, even.

I swallowed. 'The nanny.'

There was a dreadful silence. 'Downstairs, did you just hit me?'

If I admitted it would it make things worse? I almost laughed. How could things be worse? 'Yes. And,' I added defiantly, 'I'm sorry I didn't lay you out cold.'

'You bloody nearly did.'

'Good.'

'Is that why you had to find a new job?'

What? My defiance was stopped in its tracks. This wasn't right.

'Do you make a habit of braining your employer?'

Oh, shit. I swallowed again. 'Employer,' I repeated stupidly. A hideous, cold, creeping realisation was crawling up my body.

I heard a heavy sigh from across the room.

'That's right. Not the greeting I expected when I got home, but what it lacked in warmth was more than compensated for by enthusiasm and surprise.'

'Home?' Oh, shit, how wrong had I been?

'Oh, for God's sake, girl, do you have to repeat everything?'

At this point Teddy stirred and mumbled, 'Daddy?'

'Hiya, big fella,' said the intruder gently. 'Yes, Daddy's home.'

'Daddy,' said Teddy sleepily but happily. That seemed to clinch my intruder's identity. Fuck again! I felt saggy with the awfulness of what I'd done. I'd just clobbered the Earl.

'That's right,' said the Earl. 'Now you go back to sleep again and I'll come and see you first thing.'

'Night, Daddy,' said a small voice, partly muffled by a thumb.

'Night, Teds. See you in the morning.'

Silhouetted against the window I saw the Earl move back towards the nursery door. I followed, stifling a yelp as I trod on that sodding piece of Lego a second time. I went out on to the landing and shut the door behind me.

Now what? What did I say to my employer, the man I'd just hit? I felt completely foolish, guilt-ridden, stupid and ashamed, all of which emotions overrode any relief that I might otherwise have enjoyed from knowing I wasn't about to be killed – or worse. Actually, what could be worse than being killed?

'I suppose I should congratulate you on your vigilance and bravery,' he said.

'I'm sorry,' I stammered. How the hell did you apologise for hitting an innocent man? *Sorry* was the best I could manage.

'You're sorry? Well, that makes everything okay, doesn't it? Just peachy.'

It was the sarcasm that made me lose it – something I

had never done before in my life. I'd fucked up totally, I'd thought I was about to die and my foot was complete agony. All that adrenalin had to find a vent somewhere and out it all poured. Besides, what had I got to lose? My job was probably a goner already.

'Peachy? *Peachy?*' I yelled. 'What the hell has that got to do with it? I thought I was in terrible danger, not to mention your son, and I did my best to protect him and the house. I was terrified out of my wits. Look.' I held my shaking hand out but in the near darkness the gesture was wasted. I snatched my hand back again. 'I think you should be giving me a medal for what I did, not ripping the piss out of me for making a mistake. Besides, if you will insist on sneaking around in the dark, behaving exactly like a burglar or a murderer, what the hell do you expect?' I stopped, panting slightly from my outburst and scarily aware that the sudden confidence I'd found had disappeared again. Back whooshed all the guilt and shame. I stood there wondering if I ought to offer to pack my bags there and then.

There was a slight pause. I thought the Earl was probably wondering just how fast he could get me out of his house. 'Well, I didn't expect to get brained while I was trying to fix the sodding fuse, that's for sure,' he said.

'Fuse?'

'That's right. That's why I was working in the dark.'

I swallowed again. I'd done a lot of that in the last ten minutes. 'You weren't safe-breaking.'

'Safe-breaking?' I could hear the incredulity in the Earl's voice. 'Oh, dear God, I've got a nanny who thinks I keep the family jewels in the fuse cupboard. I must tell the insurers that.' He started to laugh.

'Well, how am I to know where your blasted jewellery is kept?' I wailed, feeling close to tears. 'I hardly know where anything is yet.'

'Sssh, you'll wake Teddy,' he snapped quietly.

'Sorry.' Tears of remorse and relief and God only knew what else were very close. Maybe it was apparent in my voice.

'Let's go downstairs,' he said, less aggressively. 'For a start I need to get the lights working again and secondly I want a stiff drink. You sound as if you could do with one too.'

'I don't drink when I'm on duty,' I said, trying to hold myself together.

'Well, come off duty then. I'm here now.' He turned and began to go downstairs.

My choice was quite simple: I could go to my room and lie there wondering about the repercussions of bashing my boss on the head and whether I was going to have to leave in the morning. Or I could follow the Earl, have a drink and pray that I could grovel sufficiently to keep my job. I followed. Lying in my room feeling sorry for myself wasn't going to help anyone. Grovelling might just do it. And besides, I had hit him awfully hard. His head must hurt like buggery.

I stood in the hall like a spare part while my boss rummaged around in the cupboard again. Finally, after several bouts of impressive swearing, the light in the den flicked into life and spilled out into the corridor. Two seconds later the Earl strode across the hall and switched on several more lights. The light switches, I noticed, were below the dado rail, whereas I had been searching for them at shoulder height – where they are in modern houses.

And there I was, face to face with the man I had just tried to deck. He was, quite simply, the most beautiful bloke I'd ever clapped eyes on. Unbelievably handsome, what with big brown eyes framed by long dark lashes, fantastic cheekbones and a cleft in his chin that made him look like a cross between Gregory Peck and David Beckham.

'Hi,' I said awkwardly. 'I'm Lucy.'

He raised an eyebrow. 'I think I've gathered that. Edward.' He must have seen my flicker of surprise. 'Please, call me Edward. It's easier all round and I can't bear toadies.'

'Oh, right. Nice to meet you, um, Edward.'

'You didn't think so a few minutes ago.'

'No . . . well . . .'

'So, about that drink.'

'Thank you, that would be very nice.'

He walked past me and headed towards the den. I followed. With the lights on I could see loads of light switches. It was a pity I hadn't found them earlier and left a couple of lights burning. Then the Earl would have known I was in and might have called out a greeting as he entered the house. It would have saved me some minutes of total terror and him a nasty bang on the head.

When we got to the den he pulled open part of the panelling and revealed a small cupboard filled with bottles and glasses. Just as well I hadn't known about that before our encounter. I might have clonked him with a bottle, not the TV remote. And a bottle might have done some really serious damage. I decided not to think about it.

'What will you have?' he offered. I hesitated. I fancied a glass of wine but I didn't want him opening a bottle just for me. 'I'm having a large brandy,' he said, 'and by the look of you you ought to have one too.'

I glanced at my reflection in the overmantel. I was sheet-white. My eyes were huge and staring. I still looked terrified. 'Thanks. Maybe I ought.'

The Earl . . . Edward . . . poured two huge slugs into a couple of brandy balloons the size of goldfish bowls.

'Here.' He handed me one of the glasses, then took his own and flopped into a chair, wincing as he did so. In the corner the big TV, which had come on with the restoration of power but was still on mute, silently cast a flat light into the room. I stared at it rather than Edward.

'You know, I thought *you* were a burglar. I mean, it's not every day you get bashed over the head in your own home. So naturally I assumed I'd startled an intruder. Luckily for you, I suppose, you hit me so hard that I was too stunned to catch you.'

'I'm sorry,' I said again. 'Does it hurt very much?'

'What do you think?' There was more than a hint of anger in his voice.

'I really am sorry,' I said quietly.

'I suppose,' he said, taking a sip of his drink, 'I ought to thank you. I imagine that tackling someone you thought was a burglar took a bit of courage. However, you were a little fool to do so. You might have ended up hurt – or worse.' He rubbed his head, which only served to underline just who had got hurt.

I shifted my gaze from the TV to my drink. Being called a fool stung – even if it was true. 'I know. And if I'd thought that the burglar was just pinching paintings I'd have probably let him get on with it.'

'Precisely. They're only things. Their loss, though it would have been a blow to me, wouldn't make a jot of difference to anyone else in the world.'

And he knew all about the loss of more than just *things*.

'I wasn't thinking about your things,' I said, still staring at my drink. 'I was thinking about Teddy.'

'Which is admirable.' There was no warmth in his voice. I suppose I'd just displayed the sort of loyalty that he expected as standard from his staff.

And I noticed that he still hadn't said a proper thank you. He'd said he *ought* to thank me, but that wasn't quite the same as actually doing it. I was aware I'd hurt him physically, but his attitude to me seemed unforgiving, which I found upsetting. I had no right to expect him to fall on my neck in gratitude but it was an honest mistake that I'd made.

'Where's the remote?' he said. 'It isn't as if either of us wants to watch this crap.'

'Upstairs,' I mumbled.

'Upstairs? What the hell is it doing there?'

My fault again. Obviously I could do nothing right. I took a sip of the brandy. It made my eyes water as it hit my throat. Suddenly the awfulness of the previous few minutes, the horror of what might have been, was too much for me. I felt tears well up – proper ones, not just a response to the strength of the brandy. I felt even more of a fool. I was overreacting to a farcical mistake and now I was crying.

I stared at my lap. I didn't dare sniff or reach for a hanky; Edward would spot what was going on. I had to hope I'd be able to pull myself together before that happened. I felt a tear roll, unchecked, down my cheek.

I was aware that he was staring at me. I studied my brandy even more intently. I had to explain about the remote.

'I had it in my hand when I . . . when you . . .'

'Is that what you hit me with?'

I nodded. I didn't look up, knowing my face was wet. I couldn't answer him; I didn't trust my voice not to give me away.

'Are you all right?' he asked.

I shrugged, glad there were several yards between us and the light wasn't too bright. Maybe he wouldn't spot I was blubbing.

'I'm sorry I gave you such a fright.' He sounded kinder. Maybe he was regretting behaving like such a brute to me. 'And I can sort of guess how you felt. You gave me one hell of a scare too.'

'Sorry,' I mumbled yet again.

'I thought the house was empty.'

How could he have thought the house would be empty? What about his son? Had he forgotten him? 'Didn't you expect Teddy to be in the nursery?' I blurted out.

'He's been staying at Annie's a lot recently. It's been . . . tricky. And I forgot you were due to start around now.'

So much for thinking I was a valued member of staff. I was so low on the scale as to be completely forgettable. Not a new concept for my self-esteem to cope with but a blow none the less. Thanks a bunch.

'So I came in through the garden door, fell over some junk that had been left lying around there, and switched on the light, but the bulb blew and took the fuse with it. That's the problem with these old houses: the electrics are a nightmare. I made my way to the fuse box and the next thing I know is I get a whack on the back of my head.'

'Sorry,' I said.

'So you keep saying. I shall believe you soon.'

Forgetting myself, I looked up. I saw his eyes widen slightly as he took in my wet cheeks.

'Look, you've had a dreadful evening and a horrid fright. I'm sorry I gave you such a scare. Really. Drink some of your brandy. It'll make you feel better.'

His sudden change of attitude surprised me. Perhaps I'd misjudged him. Or maybe he'd just been bad-tempered because his head was still hurting. I drank my brandy. This time it warmed, rather than burned, as it went down my throat and I found it much more pleasant. I couldn't remember drinking neat brandy before. I thought I could get to like it. When I put my glass down I saw that Edward was offering me his hanky.

'It's quite clean. Honest.'

The gesture made me want to cry again. I blinked back the tears, put my glass on the nearby table and went over to take the hanky. I blew my nose and wiped my face.

'Better?'

'A bit.' I offered him his hanky back.

'Keep it. I've got dozens.'

I tucked it up my sleeve and went back to my seat.

'Tell me about yourself,' he said.

'It's all on my CV.'

'That's not what I meant.'

Perhaps he hadn't read it. Maybe he'd left the whole process of hiring a nanny to Annie. I gave him a brief résumé of my life; that I was the only child of a single parent, that I had seven cousins, all much younger than me, and I'd spent an awful lot of my teenage years willingly looking after them. Then I'd got a job as a nursery nurse and had finally amassed all the various qualifications and NVQs to become a proper nanny. I missed out the bit about my mother's bloke Dave and the reasons why I had wanted to get away from home as soon as I could.

'So you like children,' he said when I'd finished.

I wondered, for a second, if he was taking the piss. I felt like cracking the old joke about loving them but not being able to manage a whole one for lunch. My face must have given me away.

'Joke,' he said, with a sigh. This man kept making me feel a complete idiot. 'How do you like Teddy?'

'He's lovely,' I said honestly, glad to be on safe ground, but deciding not to mention that I thought he was extraordinarily subdued and it worried me. 'I think we're going to get along just fine.' As I said that I heard faint stirrings over the radio baby alarm. 'I think I'd better go and check on him. Then maybe I'll turn in too.' I drained my brandy. 'It's been an eventful day.'

'I'll come up with you.'

'There's no need.' Did he feel the need to keep an eye on me?

'I want to fetch the remote.'

'Oh.' Another wrong conclusion. How much more stupid could I get?

We made our way towards the stairs.

'Just one thing,' said Edward as we got to the foot of them. 'I don't mind, couldn't care less in fact, but why weren't you watching the TV in your own room?'

I explained.

'Then we must make arrangements for you to have another one till yours is fixed.'

As I climbed the stairs, I hoped that would be sooner rather than later. I didn't think I could take too much of being made to feel a complete idiot every few minutes.

Edward came into the nursery the next morning just as Teddy was settling down to a scrambled egg. 'Hello, big fella,' he said.

Teddy got down off his chair and toddled over to his father. Edward scooped him up under his arms and gave him a hug.

'Did you miss me?'

'Yes,' breathed Teddy. 'I dreamed about you, Daddy. I dreamed you were here.'

'But I was. I saw you in bed last night, and I said hello.'

Just after you'd scared the shit out of me, I thought. But I fixed a smile to my face and looked happy about the reunion.

Teddy nodded as he realised it hadn't just been a dream.

'So what are you doing today, Teds?'

'I've got playgroup.'

'Then you must finish your breakfast and get ready.'

Teddy looked instantly thoughtful. I could see he was torn; time with his father or time with his adored Miss Wilson. Such a tough choice.

'Miss Wilson will be very upset if you're not there today,' I reminded him.

That seemed to solve his dilemma. He brightened and told his father about our outing to the tea room the day before.

'Well, that sounds like fun. And chocolate fudge cake – my favourite. So Lucy found her way to the village all right. Clever her.'

I was still rather raw at the way he'd made me feel a complete idiot several times the night before so I wasn't in the mood to be patronised again. Annoyance began to well up inside. I sat at the table and concentrated on buttering my toast. 'Come on, Teddy, your egg will be getting cold. Come and sit down. You can tell Daddy everything later.'

'Quite right,' said Edward. 'You mustn't upset Nanny.' He looked at me and raised his eyebrows. I got the distinct impression he was laughing at me. I ignored it.

'I'll see you before you go. Come and say goodbye to me, Teddy.'

Teddy ran back across to the table and finished his breakfast tidily and efficiently. I took him to the bathroom to supervise cleaning his teeth and combing his hair and then let him play with his toys for a few minutes while I quickly washed up the breakfast things and tidied around.

'Can we go and see Daddy now?' said Teddy when he saw I was finished.

'If you know where to find him.'

'He'll be in the office.'

At least I knew I could find that – and it didn't involve climbing stairs.

To be honest I wasn't that keen on another encounter with Edward. I already felt as if I'd seen quite enough of him to last me the whole day. Besides, I was certain he'd only patronise me, or make me feel stupid again, or both.

We entered Hugh and Jenny's office and Teddy made a beeline for Edward's inner sanctum.

'I hear you had an exciting evening yesterday,' said Jenny.

I sighed. So the other staff already knew. Maybe he'd put a notice on the Internet. Great. I wondered exactly what he'd told them; that the new nanny was too dim to find light switches and thought that the fuse cupboard was a wall safe.

'He said you were really brave,' added Hugh. 'I don't think I'd have tackled someone who had broken in.'

I felt slightly taken aback. I hadn't expected praise.

'Did you really hit him?' asked Jenny.

I nodded again.

'God, you are such a hero. I'd have phoned the police and then hidden.'

'I tried to call them when I got to the nursery but the line was dead.'

'Dead?' said Hugh and Jenny together.

Then Jenny said, 'You remembered to dial nine first to get an outside line? So it would be four nines, not three.'

Shit. I sighed and shook my head. Maybe I would get it right in an emergency next time. But under the circumstances it was just as well. How much more embarrassing would the whole incident have been if I'd had a bunch of burly coppers turning up on top of everything else?

'You must have been terrified. I'd have peed myself,' said Jenny.

'Well . . . it was close,' I admitted.

'What was close?' said Edward. He'd suddenly appeared in the doorway between the two offices.

'Nothing,' I mumbled, feeling my face blazing. Edward overhearing that last comment was all I bloody needed. Maybe he hadn't; I wasn't going to ask and find out.

'Would you like me to take Teddy to playgroup this morning?' said Edward.

I shrugged. I didn't have anything else to do; no washing, no nursery to clean. But what the hell would I do instead?

'You could come with us. I'll show you around on the way back.'

I didn't want to sound churlish but I wasn't sure I really wanted to spend the morning – or any part of it – in Edward's company, not the way he kept making me feel stupid. 'I saw over the house yesterday, but thanks.'

'I meant showing you the outside, the estate.'

'Oh. Well, that would be lovely,' I lied. I'd only look rude if I turned him down.

'Jenny, would you call Mrs Porter and remind her that Lucy's TV needs looking at? And ask her if we've got a spare one anywhere. Surely there's another one around the house somewhere.'

I was faintly flattered that he'd remembered – but as the lump on his head was the direct upshot of my not having a working TV in my room I supposed it might be hard for him to forget.

The three of us, Teddy, Edward and I, went downstairs and out of the garden room door. I could see the things that Edward had tripped over the night before – a couple of pairs of wellies and a chair in need of mending. Or maybe it only needed mending because he'd tripped over it. Either way, it was in a sorry state.

'There's an alarm on the door. I'll give you the code on the way back. Please memorise it rather than write it down. If you do and we get burgled my insurers won't be happy.' He grinned at me. 'Although once word gets round the criminal underworld about how fierce you are I imagine no robber will come near the place.'

I tried to grin back but once again I felt just a tiny bit patronised.

'Lucy isn't fierce,' said Teddy loyally. 'She's lovely.'

'No, you're right,' said Edward. 'Of course she isn't a bit fierce.'

We went outside to the private courtyard where Edward headed towards a battered Land Rover. It wasn't what I was expecting, to be honest. Okay, maybe I didn't think he swanned around in a chauffeur-driven Roller, but this was a bit of a comedown.

'Jump in.'

It wasn't locked. Even I could see it wasn't worth it. No thief in his right mind would dream of nicking it, not when there were half a dozen much nicer and smarter cars to choose from. Teddy scrambled into the back and climbed into his car seat. Edward sorted out his straps and then we were off. It was noisy and draughty but I supposed it was practical if you were a landowner.

We pulled up in the village some minutes later, Teddy jabbering excitedly about his plans for the morning at playgroup. I jumped out of the Rover, got Teddy out of his seat and took him across the road to the village hall. Already the place was full of children, tearing around excitedly. I helped Teddy out of his coat and watched him disappear into the throng.

'His peg is just here,' said a voice by my shoulder. I turned and saw Mandy. She was pointing to a low rail of coat hooks, each with a carefully written name stuck beside it, and a picture. Not surprisingly, Teddy's name had a bear by it. I hung his jacket up.

'Thanks.'

'Do I see his dad's Land Rover outside?'

I nodded. 'He got home last night.' I told her about our encounter. Mandy's eyes widened, then she burst out laughing.

'It wasn't funny,' I protested. 'I was terrified.'

'It must have been awful at the time. But you've got to admit now . . .'

'Yeah, well, maybe I'll see the funny side one day. I'd better let you get on. I'll give you a ring soon and we'll fix up that drink. I'm off the hook in the evenings now the Earl is back.'

'Great, that'd be fun.' A wail came from deep in the hall. 'Got to dash. Bye.'

I left Mandy and the cacophony of several dozen high-spirited children plus one very unhappy one and Teddy (who didn't seem to fall into either category) and returned to the Land Rover.

'Right,' said Edward. 'Ready for the magical mystery tour?'

'Fine.'

He swung the vehicle round in the little street and set off back to the estate. He waved cheerfully at the guy in the toll booth at the gate as we roared past it. Almost instantly he turned the wheel again and set off down a side road that I hadn't noticed before, so we were running parallel with the main wall round the grounds. We passed a herd of deer. These must be the red deer that Hugh had told me about – no spots, bigger than and not half as pretty as the fallow deer I'd seen the day I arrived.

'Do you like venison?' asked Edward.

'I don't know,' I said, slightly shocked. I hadn't thought of the deer as a food source.

'You'll have to try some. Very nice and very healthy. Low fat. Not that you need to worry.' He shot me a grin.

I felt I ought to smile back, so I did. But I wasn't sure that I wanted to try it, however healthy and low fat it was. It would still be like eating Bambi.

Ahead I could see the end of the parkland around the house. There was a hedge and, across the road, a cattle grid. Edward slowed the vehicle down to make it less bouncy as we crossed it.

'And now we're on Home Farm. The estate owns it but Annie and Mike run it. You know Annie, don't you?'

I nodded. 'She's lovely. Teddy adores her.'

'She's been like a mother to him since . . . And especially after the last nanny had to go in such a hurry.'

'It must have been difficult,' I said, meaning the

disruption of losing my predecessor with hardly any notice, but Edward misunderstood me.

'I don't think Teddy really understood about his mother. He was too little.'

'No. Well . . .' I didn't know what to say. I hadn't anticipated that the subject of Becca would come up. But it had and it was my fault. Another brick dropped. I lapsed into an embarrassed silence.

Beside a clump of trees I could see a pretty house with tall chimneys, a central front door and ivy covering the brickwork. It looked like a picture-book farmhouse, all snug and welcoming – exactly as a farmhouse should. To the side were a muddly collection of barns and outbuildings and a huge yard with a wall round it. Edward pulled up by the gate to the yard.

'Would you do the honours?' he asked.

I jumped out of the Rover and lifted the latch. Edward drove through and I shut the gate again. A sheep dog came bounding out of a kennel in the corner. It gave me a perfunctory sniff and then rushed over to the Earl, tail wagging, barking excitedly.

'Hello, Patch,' he said, rubbing the dog's ears. The animal wriggled with pleasure.

The back door opened, and there was Annie.

'Kettle's on,' she said in greeting. 'Mike's just called to say he's on his way back from the top meadow. He'll be here in a minute.'

'Good,' said Edward. 'I need to talk to him about spraying.' He turned to me. 'Come on, Lucy, come and say hello to Patch.'

I walked across the yard to join him.

'Hi, Patch,' I said as I got closer.

I heard Edward say, 'And I need to congratulate you, Annie, on your choice of nanny. Not only is Lucy here a hit with Teds but she's a fantastic security guard too.'

I closed my eyes and sighed. I knew what was coming next. As we went into the huge, warm and wonderful farmhouse kitchen Edward regaled Annie with the story of the previous night's events.

'My my,' said Annie, looking at me with wide eyes. 'I'd never have thought you had it in you. And you're such a slip of a thing.'

She bustled about the big room, filling a massive teapot with boiling water, getting plates off the dresser and a big fruitcake out of a tin. Without asking if we'd like any she set about cutting vast slices from it, slapped them on to the plates and pushed them across the table to us.

'Tuck in.' It was more of an order than an invitation. I took a bite. The cake was amazing.

'This is delicious,' I said with my mouth full.

Annie nodded. 'My mother's recipe.' She started to fill some mugs with tea. 'Sugar?' I shook my head. 'That's why you're so skinny,' she said as she shovelled three heaped spoons into her own mug. 'We'll have to feed you up while you're here.'

The door opened again, letting in a quick blast of cold March air. I turned round to see who had come in. This had to be her husband – it was certainly Jed's dad, for the likeness was astounding. I was introduced and then he and Edward began to discuss farming matters, which they punctuated with noisy slurps of tea and big mouthfuls of cake.

'So, apart from the excitement of last night, how are you getting on?' asked Annie.

I gave her a full rundown of events so far.

'It's a lot to get used to,' she said when I told her about not knowing about the laundry maid and the cleaner.

'I don't know what I'll do with all my free time when Teddy's not around. In my other jobs there was always stuff I had to do for the children – washing their clothes and tidying their rooms.'

'You'll find something to do. Ask Jed to teach you to ride.'

Good grief, no. I could cope with Toy Town but I didn't fancy getting close to anything bigger. I shook my head.

'Perhaps Teddy doesn't need another horsewoman in his life,' said Annie quietly, glancing across the table at the two men. They were completely taken up with their discussion and paid no attention to her comment. Even so, I thought it wasn't completely tactful.

'Anyway,' I said, wanting to move on to safer ground, 'I'm not here to enjoy myself.'

'You can always come over here. If it's washing and tidying you're going to miss I can find plenty for you to do.'

Edward pushed his plate and mug away.

'Have you finished?' he said, looking at me. I nodded. 'Then let's get out of these people's hair.'

I thanked Annie for the tea and the cake.

'Just remember, you're welcome here any time,' she

replied. 'And I promise I was joking about the housework.' I grinned at her. 'Unless you insist,' she added. 'And be sure to bring Teddy to see me again soon.'

I promised I would and went out to the Land Rover with Edward. I did the gate again and jumped in as soon as he'd driven through.

'Lovely couple,' said Edward.

'Have they always lived there?' I asked.

'Mike's been there all his life. He was born there. Annie's mum worked at the Hall when I was a nipper. Annie used to look after me sometimes; she taught me to swim in the lake, and to ride a bike.'

No wonder Edward treated her like part of the family. I suppose she was, to all intents and purposes.

'My parents spent a lot of time in London. Well, my mother did. My father went there on business quite often but was always busy with estate work when he was home,' he continued as we drove back over the cattle grid. 'And being an only child I suppose I could have been lonely, but Annie always had ideas for things to do. She was lovely to me when I was young; just as she is to Teddy.'

'Didn't you have a nanny?' I thought people like him always did.

'I did when I was very little. She'd been my dad's nanny before me. But she died when I was about five and I was considered too old for one by then. Anyway, it wasn't long after that I was sent off to boarding school.'

'Is that what you've got planned for Teddy?'

The Earl shot me a glance. 'Good heavens, no. What

sort of parent do you think I am? I had a loathsome time. Hated every minute of it. Teddy will go to a day school. There are plenty of good ones around here.'

He sounded annoyed by my comment. Would I never get anything right with him, I wondered, somewhat sadly.

We turned on to the main drive towards the Hall. After a couple of minutes Edward drove off the road and on to the grass, heading for a stand of trees I could see in the middle distance. We skirted the copse and behind it was a huge lake.

'This is where I learned to swim,' he said, leaning forward on the steering wheel and gazing at the calm water, which was partly covered with lily pads. 'Over there, in the trees, there's a boat house.' He turned to me. 'Can you row?' I shook my head. 'Not much call for that in Pinner, I suppose.'

A minute ago I'd annoyed him, and now he was being nice to me again. I couldn't get over this blowing hot and cold. I couldn't work out if he liked me or not. But did it matter? After all, I was only a member of staff; I wasn't there to be liked but to do a job of work. I turned my attention to Edward and the question I'd been asked.

'Not a lot,' I agreed.

'I'll teach you. Then you can take Teddy across to the island and have picnics and make campfires. I'm afraid I can't supply you with a sailing dinghy and rowing is quite hard work, but would you like to do it anyway?'

'Yes,' I said. 'I'd absolutely love to.' Then a thought struck me. 'Did you put *Swallows and Amazons* in my room?'

'Annie told me it had been your dream. That's why you got the job.'

Oh, goodness. I felt incredibly touched. 'Thank you.' Maybe I'd only felt like a dunce because I'd been reading him wrong. Maybe I just misunderstood him.

'Just make sure Teddy wears a life jacket whenever you go on the water.'

'Of course.'

'Good.' He reversed the car away from the lake and turned it round to head back towards the house. When we reached the courtyard a small red sports car was parked there.

'Bugger,' he said under his breath.

I looked at him.

'Zoë,' he said. 'She and Becca were friends. She offered me a lot of help after the accident.' But then he added, almost under his breath, 'But now she won't give up.' I looked at him but he was ignoring me again. 'She just won't take no for a fucking answer.'

'I'm sorry?'

'She wants to buy Billy Boy. I've said she can't.'

Now I knew who Zoë was. Zoë McMahon – an eventer like Becca. She and Becca pretty well divvied up the major prizes between them, although as I recalled Becca usually took first and Zoë second.

'Buy Billy Boy? I see.'

'You probably don't,' he said quite rudely, 'but it doesn't matter.'

That was a snub. No mistake. I'd crossed some unseen line and now I was back in my rightful place. Obviously, teaching me to row was so I could take Teddy boating, not because it might fulfil some childhood dream of mine. I really had to stop deluding myself that he was being kind to me because he liked me. I sighed heavily and got out of the vehicle.

'Still, I suppose I'd better be nice to her now she's here,' I heard him mutter as he strode off.

'Thanks for the tour,' I called after him. 'I'll let you get on.' But Edward was already almost in the house and I don't think he heard me. I'd been dismissed.

'That's all right, Lucy,' I muttered angrily. 'It was a pleasure. I enjoyed your company.' I slammed the door shut and followed him into the house.

Feeling out of sorts and foolish I stomped up to the nursery. I could hear the sound of vacuuming coming from my bedroom. The girl pushing the Hoover over the carpet hit the off switch when she saw me come in.

'Hi,' she said. 'You must be the new nanny. I'm Maria.' She held out her hand.

'Lucy,' I said.

'Thanks for tidying up. Makes my life a lot easier if I don't have to pick up all Teddy's toys.'

'No sweat. To be honest it made me feel as if I'm earning my money. What with all the staff in this house I feel a bit redundant.'

The phone began to ring. Since Edward was home I waited from him to pick it up, wherever he was.

'Aren't you going to answer that?' said Maria.

Well, no one else seemed to be doing so. I walked through to the nursery and picked up the receiver. 'Hello?' I said in my best voice. 'Arden Hall.'

There was a pause. 'Miss Carter?'

'Yes.'

'This is Mrs Porter, on the house phone.' Of course. I

hoped desperately that Maria hadn't heard my gaffe. I could just imagine yet more tales of the new nanny's stupidity winging their way around the other staff. 'I'm ringing about your television.'

'Oh, right. Thanks.'

'One of the men has had a look at it for you and thinks there's a problem with your aerial connection. A technician has been contacted but he can't come out here for a day or two. In the meantime there's a TV in the study you are very welcome to use.'

'Thank you,' I said. 'What about the Earl? Won't I be in his way?'

'It was his suggestion. Besides, he mostly uses the one in the den.'

'Okay.' I thanked her for letting me know and hung up.

I went back into my bedroom. 'Remind me where the study is,' I said to Maria.

'At the bottom of the stairs. The door on the right. Why? No one ever uses it.'

I explained about the TV.

'The one in there is a nice big one,' said Maria, 'but I hope yours gets fixed soon. I wouldn't want to spend too many of my evenings in that room.'

'Why?'

'You'll see.'

I decided that I'd go and take a look. After all, I had nothing else to do and Maria wanted to get on with cleaning my little empire so I'd be doing her a favour by getting out of her hair. I went back down the stairs to the ground floor. I half wondered where Zoë and Edward were because, apart from the sound of distant vacuuming coming from the nursery, the private wing seemed completely deserted.

I opened the door to the study and peeped round. My God, it was like a shrine to Becca. No wonder Maria thought it was a bit spooky. Around the walls were cabinets containing her trophies, medals and cups. Photos of her and her horses were everywhere, and two big paintings of her hung on the walls, one above the fireplace and one over the big desk opposite. By the desk was a large cabinet with double doors, which I assumed held the television, since there was no sign of one anywhere else in the room. I moved across the floor and flipped it open. I was right. Not quite as big and swanky as the TV in the den, but a pretty fantastic set even so. Under it were a DVD player and a VCR – my every whim would be catered for. I cast around to see if there were any films I might be able to watch if I didn't want to be bored rigid by endless makeover, gardening and cookery programmes. There was a drawer in the base of the cabinet. I slid it open and found it was full of tapes and discs. I checked out the titles: 'Training 2004' and 'Hanover 2003' were the first two I clocked. I scanned the other labels stuck to the spines of the tapes and the penny began to drop. Burleigh, Badminton . . . these were recordings made by Becca about her horses.

I glanced at my watch. I still had nearly an hour before I had to collect Teddy. I picked out a couple of tapes at random and slid the first into the VCR. Then I switched on the TV, hit the play button and sat on the sofa to watch. It was weird hearing Becca's voice through the loudspeakers. It was hard to remember that she was actually dead. In fact it was a really spooky feeling, sitting on a sofa that she must have sat on, in her house, watching a tape that she had made, listening to her commenting on the horse she was filming and the process by which she intended to get it to improve – while all the time she was in a coffin in the churchyard nearby. It gave me the creeps and I nearly switched the tape off but somehow I was mesmerised by it.

The next shots were of the indoor school, with Jed getting the horse to perform at the end of a long rein. It seemed to be doing things perfectly but Becca obviously wasn't happy. She made Jed put the horse through the same manoeuvre time and time again. Each time he did it he gave the commands with those strange chirruping whistles he'd given Toy Town, only with Becca's horses he'd used a proper whistle – I could see it clamped between his teeth in the video – whereas now he just pursed his lips. I watched as the horse did the same thing over and over to the same whistled commands. So that was how you became a world champion and a gold medallist: endless patience and practice.

'I didn't know you were interested in horses.'

I jumped, partly with surprise at being crept up on, but also out of guilt. I had no right to be looking at these tapes. I jammed the second one behind a cushion and twisted round to face Edward. I could feel my face flooding with colour.

'I'm sorry,' I stammered. 'I was just . . .'

'Curious?'

I nodded.

'You know what it did for the cat, don't you?'

I nodded again, feeling utterly embarrassed. What was the matter with me and this job? I seemed to be incapable of getting anything right.

'I'd forgotten we had all those tapes. They're no good to anyone now. I'll get Mrs Porter to take them away.'

I felt mortified. I hit the off button on the remote and the TV screen went blank. The last thing Edward needed were these reminders of his dead wife. And if this room – this shrine – was anything to go by, he still adored her.

'You needn't . . . I won't watch . . .' I dried up. 'Thanks for saying I could use this TV till my one is fixed,' I finished lamely, standing up.

'That's fine. I rarely use this room. You'll probably be happier not to have to worry about other people when you want to relax.'

I could see he certainly didn't want me cluttering up the den in the evenings, being a nuisance, getting in the way. Much better if I was hived off to a place on my own where I was least likely to annoy or upset him.

'Well, don't let me keep you,' he said.

I edged towards the door and Edward stood to one side to let me through.

'Zoë will be staying for a few days,' he told me as I passed him.

I didn't know why on earth he thought I ought to know. His private life was nothing to do with me, although apparently 'being nice to her now she was here' meant offering her bed and board.

'Right,' I said.

'Maybe Teddy could have dinner with us one day this week instead of nursery supper. You'd be welcome to eat with us too, of course.'

'Oh.' The thought filled me with horror. 'Maybe dinner is a bit late for him. I don't think we ought to wreck his routine.' I was using Teddy's bedtime as an excuse for being entirely selfish; I was certain that Teddy would have been over the moon to be downstairs with his dad rather than in bed at the normal time.

'Once in a while wouldn't hurt.'

'No, of course not.' He was right, and anyway Teddy was his child so the decision was ultimately his. And why shouldn't Teddy have supper with his father? I'd have to brace up.

'Perhaps Friday, when he doesn't have playgroup the next day.'

'Of course.' I looked at my watch. Time was getting on and there was something else I wanted to do before it was time to get Teddy. 'Let me know for definite and we'll be there.' Although I didn't fancy an evening of trying to make polite conversation to a man who clearly thought I was stupid. Maybe he'd ignore me and just pay attention to Teddy. But if he did I'd have to talk to Zoë, and what on earth would she and I have in common? The whole idea was a nightmare, but there was no way I could see to get out of it. I made my escape and headed for the stables. I wanted to see if Jed would get Toy Town ready for Teddy after lunch.

I didn't see Jed about when I got to the stables, so I

called his name. I heard footsteps approaching from the rear of the building but it wasn't Jed who came out of the room at the back but a very beautiful blonde in unbelievably tight breeches, a crisp white shirt and fabulous leather boots. She looked every inch the champion horsewoman that she was – Zoë McMahon.

'And you are?' she said, as if she owned the stables.

I told her. She eyed me up and down as if I was a bit of horseflesh at a market and she was working out what I was worth.

'I see,' she said. 'Firefly's cast a shoe. Jed is off dealing with him.'

I assumed Firefly was one of the horses. 'Will he be long?'

'Half an hour. Maybe less. Why?'

Not that it was any of her business but I told her anyway.

'I'll tell him,' she said.

I felt as if I'd been dismissed. I slunk out of the stables wondering why I couldn't be more assertive – after all, I had as much right to be there as her. More even – I lived in the house. I sighed. I really needed to brace up and stop being such a wimp.

The rest of the day passed much as I'd planned; I collected Teddy, he had his lunch and then we spent some quiet time in the nursery. I told him he might be having supper with his father at the end of the week. He just gazed at me and nodded; no expression of enthusiasm, no complaint, just acceptance. I'd never come across a small boy quite like it.

At about three we went down to the stables and he had a ride on Toy Town, with Jed again doing his odd, whistled commands. During a lull while Toy Town and I got our breath back after a particularly vigorous bit of trotting I asked Jed why he had stopped using the proper whistle.

'I lost it,' he said. 'I was dead upset. It were my grandfer's. Pretty it was, shaped like a little bird. A little wren. My grandfer carved it and he give it to me. But then I lost it.'

'That's a shame. But maybe it'll turn up one day.'

'Maybe,' said Jed. 'But it's been gone over a year now. Since before she died.'

I glanced at Teddy but thankfully he seemed oblivious of this casual mention of his late mother.

After Teddy's ride it was back up to our rooms for some playtime, a spot of children's TV, supper, bath and bed. All in all we had a lovely time together and I felt quite relaxed when I had finished all my chores for the day, although I still worried about his solemnity and lack of emotional display. It made him an easy charge to look after, but I would have to think up some fun activities that might help bring him out of himself a little.

I was just thinking about going to watch some TV, as I had absolutely nothing better to do – which was boring – when my mobile rang. I checked to see who was calling. *Mandy*, said the screen.

'Hiya,' she said. 'How do you fancy coming to the pub for a drink tonight?'

It was exactly what I fancied but I thought I'd better check it was going to be okay with Edward first. For all I knew he and Zoë had plans to go out. I told Mandy I'd ring her back as soon as I'd confirmed I was free to go.

I left the nursery and made my way down the stairs. Unlike the last time I'd done this, the house was ablaze with lights. I got to the ground floor and listened for voices. I heard a tinkling laugh coming from the den. It had to be Zoë. I went to the door and knocked.

'Come in,' yelled Edward.

I poked my head round the door.

'Oh, it's you,' he said.

He really knew how to make a girl feel good.

'Sorry to bother you,' I said tightly, 'but do you mind if I go out tonight?'

'Of course not. Is the baby alarm around?'

I pointed to it lying on the table and went over to switch it on. Instantly the faint whisper of the sound of a sleeping child was transmitted into the room.

'Off you go, then.'

'About getting back in,' I said.

'You've got a key, I take it?' I nodded. 'The alarm is by the coat rack in the garden room. The code is 1945. Can you remember that?' I nodded again. 'Punch in the numbers and then the hash key.'

I'd had to deal with alarms before. I knew the form.

'Have a nice time. Going anywhere exciting?'

'The pub with Mandy Wilson.'

'Then the answer to my question is no.' He smiled. 'But enjoy yourself anyway.'

There! He'd done it again; he was being nice to me. But then I knew he didn't like Zoë much and he was being nice to her too. Perhaps it was just a question of good manners. I gave up. I didn't understand this bloke at all.

I looked at Zoë, as if the solution lay with her, but she was just staring at me with narrowed eyes. She, unlike Edward, obviously didn't do manners and her expression didn't make me like her any more than I had earlier. Meanly, I hoped Teddy woke up and disturbed their cosy evening. Then, feeling legitimately free, I rang Mandy and skipped out of the house and into my car. Before I knew it I was sitting in a corner of the pub with Mandy, two glasses of chilled white wine in front of us.

'There are more exciting places around,' said Mandy, gazing at the darts match going on in one corner and then swivelling her eyes to take in the elderly couple playing cribbage at a nearby table, 'but this is the closest to home.'

I held my hands up. 'Am I complaining? I'm out of the house, I'm off duty and I've got a drink.'

'How is it going?'

'Better. At least I haven't hit Edward again.'

'Edward?'

'He says it's easier than calling him "my lord" all the time.'

'You're in there, then.'

I laughed at the ridiculous idea. 'Don't be daft. Who on earth could match up to Becca? Anyway, he's still besotted with her.' I told Mandy about the shrine in the study.

'Yeah, but he'll have to move on some time. It's been over a year.'

I shook my head and said, 'As if he's going to move on

to me. For a start he's miles older than I am, secondly I don't fancy him and thirdly he thinks I'm a moron. Oh, and fourthly . . .'

'Fourthly? How long is this list?'

'Fourthly,' I continued, ignoring her, 'Zoë McMahon is staying and need I say more. If he's contemplating moving on – which I doubt – he's far more likely to be interested in her than me. I mean, she *is* a looker.'

'Well, as I haven't seen this woman in the flesh I couldn't possibly say, but already I can tell that your judgement is shit.'

'How?' I said, a little nettled. I mean, Mandy hardly knew me. Surely this assessment was a bit harsh?

'You said you don't fancy the Earl. Either you're fibbing or you're blind. So which is it?'

'Well, you're right, he *is* fanciable, but only in a Daniel Craig or Johnny Depp sort of way. I mean, it doesn't matter how much I fancy either of them, nothing is ever going to happen, is it?'

'But you're never likely to meet either of those two, whereas you're already living with the Earl.'

I splorted my drink. 'Don't put it like that! It makes it sound as if . . .'

Mandy raised an eyebrow and shrugged. 'Well, you are! How else can I put it? And you never know – I mean, you're pretty stunning too.'

'Now who's got crap judgement?' I said after I'd wiped up the wine on the table with my sleeve.

'Oh, for God's sake. I really can't be doing with false modesty.'

I gave Mandy a long stare before I replied. 'I've got mirrors in my flat, you know.'

'Yeah, and I've got eyes. I saw the way the two blokes playing darts and the barman all looked at you when you walked in. You've got a fantastic figure, you've got huge great eyes and amazing bone structure. For fuck's sake – you've got cheekbones, what more do you want?'

Considering it was Mandy with her doll-like prettiness saying this, I felt a bit confused.

'My boobs are too big, my hair is the colour of straw and my eyes are the colour of sludge.'

Mandy shook her head. 'Wrong, you're a curvaceous, hazel-eyed blonde. Who put those other ideas into your head?'

I wasn't going to tell her that it was my mum's shitty boyfriend; family loyalty and all that, although why I felt any sort of loyalty to Dave absolutely defeated me. Life at home had been very cosy with just my mum and me until I was about twelve, and then Dave had appeared on the scene and everything had changed. Mum suddenly didn't have as much time for me and I felt pushed out. I really hated him for that. Loathed him for coming along and muscling in on our lives.

Looking back I know I was obnoxious, but he was too. We were equally vile to each other. My excuse was that I was a teenager and it was my world that he was crashing into. Obviously I felt that my relationship with my mother was threatened and tried to protect it. Being stroppy was my way of coping. But what was his excuse? He was a grown-up and should have known better. He should have realised that the way he was always having a go at me, all those constant digs, all those snide remarks, were bound to have an effect on me. So I was rude to him and he was foul back. The trouble was, my comments just bounced off him – the ones he made back to me hit home every time. Whether it was just the vulnerability of my hormones or whether it was that he was cleverer with words I wasn't sure, but either way, after a few years, he'd managed to completely undermine my self-esteem.

And since I'd left home, which I did as soon as I could just to get away from him, I hadn't been in a situation where my confidence could be rebuilt. Perhaps a lovely boyfriend might have done the trick, but the trouble with being a nanny is that you don't get to meet a lot of unattached men. Dave said that I was only a nanny because I was too dim, too dull and too unattractive to do anything but work with kids who wouldn't be able to object to sharing their lives with a reject.

You know, if you get told something often enough, it seeps into you and you end up believing it. And I believed Dave.

I glanced at my reflection in the dark window, trying to reconcile what I saw with what Mandy had just said. Maybe I wasn't completely hideous, but I couldn't believe I was a beauty either. Not like Zoë or Becca. Besides, what did it matter? I wasn't after a bloke, and a fling with my employer was definitely not an option.

On Friday, Teddy and I, washed, brushed and in clean clothes, made our way down the long flight of stairs to the ground floor.

'Seven thirty,' Edward had said in his perfunctory phone call to me the previous evening to confirm the arrangement. He was going to be in London all day and wasn't expecting to be back before seven; obviously, informing me about his wishes for supper was just another hassle to be slotted into his busy schedule. I didn't manage to ask what we should wear. Big mistake. I mean, I didn't think that I was expected to rush out and buy a long frock but should I wear my ordinary work clothes, or a dress, or what? Anyway, before I'd worked out how to frame the question Edward had rung off. I thought about asking Maria but I felt shy about my ignorance. Mrs Porter was just too scary to approach so I rang Annie.

'Lord knows,' she said. 'I never got invited to the house for a meal. Of course I went to all the staff parties and the like. They threw a big one when Becca won her gold medal. I think that must have been about the last time I was there for something like that. But I was never invited to dinner.'

'Oh,' I said, embarrassed at having made the assumption. 'Anyway, it's not dinner, it's just supper,' I added.

'But Edward isn't one for a load of fuss. Just change into something clean and tidy.'

Clean and tidy. That could cover just about anything. When Teddy was in bed on Thursday night I went through my wardrobe, feeling more and more despondent as I riffled through the hangers. A sour voice from my past echoed through my head.

'I don't know why you're worrying,' I heard Dave say in my head. 'Who the fuck is going to look at you?'

He was right, of course: why was I concerned? I was only being invited to help Teddy and make sure he behaved. There was no way Edward was inviting me for the pleasure of my company. That thought decided me on a neat, navy skirt and plain white blouse. Teddy I put in a clean checked shirt and a pair of brown cords. He looked delectable in his smart clothes.

At the bottom of the stairs I met a new member of the household.

'Hello, Master Teddy,' said a middle-aged man in a smart business suit.

'Hello, Smith,' said Teddy confidently.

'I'm Smith, miss,' the man said to me. Not 'Mr Smith', I noticed. Yet another member of staff and, if I wasn't mistaken, a real live butler!

'Lucy Carter,' I mumbled.

'His lordship asked me to tell you that he's in the den. And to ask you what you would like to drink.'

Shit – what did I want to drink? I whizzed through my memory banks for a socially acceptable non-alcoholic aperitif. 'Tomato juice, please.' I couldn't bring myself to call him just 'Smith', but I felt that if I called him 'Mr' it would be a black mark – again. I wished this sort of stuff came naturally to me.

'Certainly, miss,' he said. 'And what about Master Teddy?'

'Master Teddy will have orange juice,' I said, suppressing an irrational urge to giggle at all this formality. I expected Smith to disappear but he preceded me down the corridor and threw open the door to the den.

'Miss Carter and Master Teddy,' he announced.

Teddy and I stepped into the room and instantly I realised this wasn't just family supper but something much more formal and hideous. I stopped in my tracks, holding tight to Teddy's hand. The room seemed full of people – all staring at us, all done up in smart suits and dresses, with lacquered hair and jewellery and . . . What the hell was going on?

Instantly I assumed I'd made a mistake, got the wrong day, got the wrong end of the stick. It was just the sort of thing I was capable of. After all, no one in their right mind would invite a three year old to a formal dinner when they had a nanny to take care of the child.

'Come in, come in,' said Edward jovially. I noticed that Zoë, dressed up and beautiful, was standing right beside him, as if she owned him. I also noticed that she didn't seem thrilled to see me or Teddy. In fact, I got the distinct impression that if she had her way we'd be back up in the nursery where she so obviously thought we belonged. And to be honest, it's where I felt I belonged too.

However, even while I was trying to work out quite what Teddy and I were supposed to do, I noticed that Edward's welcome sounded as if he was expecting us. On his past form, if he hadn't been, he would have been quite capable of asking me what the hell I thought I was doing. This was getting worse. If he was expecting Teddy and me, why hadn't he warned me that it wasn't just family supper we were joining him for? If I'd known I'd have worn something more suitable, a frock at the very least. As it was I looked exactly like the maid who was drifting around the room offering a tray of canapés. But then I was only hired help too, so perhaps being dressed like this was okay.

I gripped Teddy's hand tighter as I bent down to him. 'Best behaviour now, sweetheart,' I reminded him. 'And if you feel tired, just tell me and I'll take you back upstairs to bed.'

Teddy grinned up at me, looking full of beans and not the least bit sleepy. Bugger, I thought. I was relying on him for my emergency escape plan. I was handed our drinks. I noticed Teddy's orange juice was served in a cut glass tumbler like mine, which was hardly a suitable drinking vessel for a child of his age. I could just see the whole lot ending up down his smart shirt. Holding his hand firmly, I took him off to a chaise longue at the side of the room. Teddy clambered on to it and then, when he was safely settled, I handed him his drink. Concentrating on making sure that Teddy didn't make a mess, I didn't spot Edward approaching.

'I'm sorry about all this.'

I looked up at him. 'All what?'

'These people,' he said quietly. 'It wasn't my idea.'

I shrugged. Well, considering this was his home I couldn't think for the life of me who else's idea it would be. Oh, of course, one of the maids had dreamed it up. Silly me.

'That's okay,' I said, trying to suppress my feelings of anger and embarrassment.

'Zoë wanted to meet some of the neighbours.'

'That's nice,' I said. Zoë seemed to be very much at home here, I thought, arranging his social life, wanting to get to know his friends. I wondered what her relationship with Edward was. Or maybe this was all part of his having to be nice to her now she was here. Not that it was any of my business.

Edward looked at me. I took a sip of my drink.

'I knew nothing of the change of plan till I got back just now.'

'Really.' I wasn't inclined to give too much ground. He could still have warned me. I could have worn something more suitable. Hell, Teddy and I could have had beans on toast in the nursery. Making a child of his age sit through a grown-up dinner party was just ridiculous. And I wasn't going to enjoy it either. I fixed Edward with a hard stare.

'Are we going to have supper soon?' Teddy asked.

'I hope so,' said his father, turning his attention to his son. 'Are you hungry?'

Teddy nodded solemnly.

'How hungry?' said Edward.

'I could eat a horse,' Teddy answered.

'Toy Town?' asked his father in mock shock.

Teddy stared at him, wide-eyed. 'Don't be silly, Daddy,' he said.

Edward smiled at his son and ruffled his hair. 'I'll get someone to bring you some crisps to keep you going.' He went off to circulate and I was left wondering whether it might not be a good idea if we disappeared as soon as everyone went into the dining room. Surely none of his guests would notice us disappear. Most of them hadn't noticed us appear in the first place, I thought as I watched them flock around the beautiful Zoë, who was obviously the star attraction.

'Hel-*lo*,' said a man who had suddenly loomed up in front of us.

The hairs on the back of my neck stood on end. 'Hello,' I said back as coolly as I could. I had no idea who this bloke was but there was something about him that I found unattractive and rather threatening. And what's more he looked smarmy, with that upper-crust veneer of complete self-confidence. I disliked him instantly.

'I haven't seen you around here before.' He leered at me, or rather at my tits.

'That would be because I've just arrived.' I helped Teddy to take a sip of his drink and prayed whoever he was would just go away.

'I've got it, you're the new nanny.'

I looked at him. 'Yes. That's right.'

'I'm Justin, Justin Naylor.' He looked at me expectantly.

I knew the name, of course I did; he was another of the winning Olympic equestrian team, but I wasn't going to give him the satisfaction of letting him know that I recognised it. He looked quite bumptious enough without any help from me. 'Lucy,' I replied.

'What a pretty name. Goes with a pretty face.' Although how he knew that defeated me as he'd looked nowhere but at my bust since he'd pitched up.

From the way he was slurring his words I realised that he was already fairly plastered. I imagined he must have turned up like that. I ignored him and turned my attention to Teddy, who was looking bemused by the stranger's behaviour.

Justin plonked himself down beside me on the chaise longue. He was far too close. I felt my flesh creep. 'I say, I don't suppose you fancy reading me a bedtime story one night, do you, Lucy?'

I felt myself cringe. I was right out of my depth now. I had no idea what to do or how to handle this situation. I didn't think telling one of the Earl's guests – and, for all I knew, one of his best friends too – to piss off would go down a storm. I could feel my face going brick red. I stared at my drink and wished he would just go away.

'Lucy,' said Edward. 'Would you like another drink?'

I looked up at him, gratitude washing through me. A knight in shining armour. Well, an Earl in a lounge suit but hey – the principle was the same. I shook my head – one tomato juice was quite enough – and hoped that Edward would see how uncomfortable I was about being the focus of attention of one of his guests, and a drunken one at that.

'No? Justin?'

Predictably, Justin nodded, although I felt there was some sort of atmosphere between the two men. Or maybe I was imagining it. After all, weren't these Edward's friends?

'And while we find you that drink let me drag you away from my nanny' – did I imagine that Edward emphasised the words 'my nanny' to make him sound quite proprietorial? – 'as there's someone I'd like you to meet. You don't mind, do you Lucy?'

I almost wept with relief. 'No, drag away,' I said.

Edward gave me a smile as he took Justin by the elbow and steered him to the far side of the room. But a minute or two later I caught a glimpse of Edward's face as he moved away from Justin and the 'someone', and I thought that something had just really upset him. He looked thunderous. Then suddenly it was almost as if a mask was removed and the usual Edward was revealed, all charm and smiles. Perhaps I had imagined it.

While Teddy and I sipped our drinks, ignored now by the other occupants of the room, I made up names for the people in the portraits round the walls. He actually laughed out loud when I christened one of the horsier-faced ladies 'Lady Hermione Wobblebum'. His giggle made Edward look round. He stared at me and for a moment I thought he disapproved of Teddy's outburst, but then he gave me an approving nod. Then he turned his attention back to his other guests and Teddy and I resumed our cloak of invisibility. I thought about making up names for the guests too but decided it was too risky; Teddy might repeat them. Although, given the size of some of the bosoms, the loudness of the braying voices and the stuffiness of the stuffed shirts, it was horribly tempting.

It wasn't too much later that Smith (I still thought of him as Mr Smith; lack of the right sort of education I suppose) announced that dinner was served. My heart and spirits nosedived with dread at the potential pitfalls ahead for a three year old at a formal meal. My apprehension wasn't lessened when Edward joined us. No escape now.

'Let me show you the way,' he said, taking Teddy's and my glasses away and handing them to a passing maid. Over his shoulder I noticed that Justin was now leering at Zoë and ignoring me. Lucky Zoë, I thought.

I voiced my concerns to Edward as we waited for the other guests to leave the den.

'Nonsense,' he said briskly. 'Teddy will be fine. But I promise you that as soon as he gets bored you can make your escape. Deal?'

Reluctantly I agreed that his solution didn't sound impossible.

We all trooped into the dining room, Edward, Teddy and I going last. When we walked through the door it was like entering some sort of movie set. Flickering candles in three huge silver candelabra lit the room, the crystal glasses sparkled, the china gleamed and the silver cutlery massed in ranks beside each place looked utterly daunting.

The twenty or so guests had all found their places when we arrived and were busy hauling out their chairs and making themselves comfortable. Zoë, I noticed, was at the foot of the table and I wondered if that had been Becca's place. I also wondered if she had plans to move into other places that had been Becca's. I noticed that Justin was beside her. Snakily I thought that they probably deserved each other, and at least, if they were together, other people were being spared their dubious company.

Then I noticed that the only two free seats were to Edward's left.

He held my chair out for me. 'You won't know a soul so I put you next to me. Under the circumstances it was the least I could do.'

'Under what circumstances?'

'Having this hideous charade foisted on you.' As he said this in a low voice to me he was smiling and nodding at the guests around him. 'I couldn't cancel Zoë's arrangements; it was too short notice when I got back, so we'll just have to make the best of it.' More gracious smiling and nodding. 'Anyway, just do your best to keep Teddy happy. I'm sure it'll all be fine.'

I gazed down the table to Zoë, who flashed me a look of sheer venom. Maybe, I thought, that when she'd taken the Countess's place she hadn't planned on Edward's sitting me next to him. I didn't think it was likely to endear me to her.

I turned my attention to Teddy, who was already starting to fiddle with the ranks of cutlery arrayed before him. Swiftly I picked it all up except for a knife, a fork and a spoon and piled it in front of me. A maid shot over.

'Is everything all right, ma'am?'

'Can you get rid of this extra stuff?' I asked. 'And while you're at it, Teddy only needs one glass.'

A flunky appeared with a tray.

'Isn't it a shame,' said a loud voice, floating over the hubbub of the other guests, 'that children don't know how to behave properly at table any more.'

I felt myself going beetroot. Getting rid of the superfluous cutlery was obviously the wrong thing to do.

'I rather wish,' said Edward loudly, 'that we used wooden platters and daggers and threw the leftovers on the floor for the dogs. So much less fuss. And think of the insurance savings on this lot.' He gestured at all the silverware on the table and dropped me a discreet wink.

'Well, of course manners are a modern invention,' the old bat agreed, completely changing her tune. 'Like fish forks,' she added with an audible simper.

Fish forks?

The first course was rolled out: pâté and melba toast. I told Teddy that it was meat paste and he tucked in heartily. In the spaces between courses I kept him amused by making puppets out of my napkin and inventing stories involving yet more of his relations' portraits hanging round about us. Occasionally I risked a glance in Edward's direction and each time I looked I found he was watching me. Waiting for me to drop another brick, I thought.

The main course was a wonderful chicken casserole with lashings of fluffy mash. Another course that Teddy enjoyed, for which I thanked God and Cook.

The woman on Teddy's left decided to pay him some attention. She asked him about his riding and Toy Town and then, not listening to his answer, proceeded to tell him all about her own horses. Predictably Teddy's attention wavered and he began to get quite wriggly.

'Goodness, I just don't know where people get the patience to deal with small children,' she said to those near her in general, but me in particular.

'So you don't have any?' I asked.

'Spawned four,' she said with an overloud laugh. 'Had a nanny till they went away to prep school. That's the way to do it, in my opinion. Of course, now they've all buggered off. Job done and I can get back to breeding horses.' She gazed at me, looking supremely self-satisfied.

I gazed back, wondering why on earth she'd bothered with motherhood at all. Did she have any idea about all the wonderful moments she had denied herself? Luckily I was spared having to answer her as a chorus of like-minded opinions reinforced hers. Among this set it seemed children were something you had to have to safeguard the inheritance, but you didn't really want the bother of looking after them any longer than was absolutely necessary – which seemed to be about a fortnight each summer when the nanny had a holiday. Then I noticed that the woman opposite – miles away across the shining acres of mahogany – was looking at me with a huge grin on her face. She dropped me a wink and I nearly burst out laughing. Maybe not *everyone* in this set was more interested in their livestock than their kids. I grinned back.

I returned my attention to Teddy, deciding his conversation was infinitely more to my taste than most of what I was overhearing.

Pudding appeared – crème brûlée. I showed Teddy how to break the toffee crust and get to the creamy custard beneath. He adored it and eventually I had to remove the little bowl to save the pattern.

Around us Edward's guests were knocking back the wine, getting noisier and more raucous and looking as though they were there for the duration. Time for us to depart. Quit while we were ahead, and all that. Under the circumstances I thought Teddy had been amazing.

I leaned towards Edward to whisper my plans. He leaned back towards me and I found his nearness unsettling.

'Um . . . um . . .' My mind blanked.

He smiled at me, as if he understood his effect. 'Yes?' he said encouragingly.

I snapped myself out of my stupor. 'I'm going to take Teddy upstairs. He's been so good and I don't want to push it.'

'He's been amazing. But it was all down to you. Thank you.' His dark brown gaze was fixed on my face and made my insides go mushy, but I wondered if he was judging me through a haze of wine. Certainly most of his other guests were well on the way to getting pissed – or were behaving as if they were – and Justin appeared almost paralytic. So much for good breeding, I thought. If lads on a street corner behaved like this the police would be rounding them up in a second. If rank had its privileges then so did class.

'It was nothing,' I protested. 'Just doing my job.' I gathered up Teddy, who was beginning to flag. As the pudding plates were cleared and the cheese boards began to appear we quietly left the room.

Teddy was so knackered, poor little scrap, that I ended up carrying him up the last flight of stairs, so by the time I got him to the nursery we were both on our knees. I dumped him on his bed – spark out – and sagged on to the candlewick bedspread beside him, panting as if I'd just run a mile. After about five minutes I'd recovered enough to start hauling a sleeping Teddy out of his clothes. Despite the fact that he was only a very little boy it took some manhandling to get him into his pyjamas. And then came the tricky matter of trying to shove him under the covers.

At this point he woke slightly, stirring and mumbling but sufficiently conscious for me to get him to cooperate. Finally I had him tucked up and I collapsed with relief on to the floor beside his bed.

'Are you all right?'

I looked up. Edward was standing by the nursery door, looking at me with concern.

I nodded. 'Fine, honest,' I replied in a low voice, glad that the dim nursery light would hide my blush of embarrassment at being caught lying down on the job. I stood up and twitched Teddy's covers straight. 'Long day,' I explained.

'I just popped up to say goodnight and thanks.' He moved further into the room and stood beside Teddy's bed. He ruffled his sleeping son's hair and removed his thumb from his mouth. Instantly Teddy plugged it straight back in again. Edward looked at me and grinned. 'You did a terrific job of keeping him entertained at the table. I can't think what Zoë was thinking of, changing the arrangements like that.'

Well, I could. I'd seen exactly what she was playing at. She'd been demonstrating to Edward how good she would be as Becca's replacement.

'Anyway, I came for this.' Edward picked up the roving half of the baby alarm from the nursery table. 'You have a lie-in in the morning, you deserve it. I'll deal with Teddy, so don't you worry.'

'Oh. Okay.'

He turned to go. 'And before I leave you to get some sleep, I need to aplogise about Justin.'

'You don't have to.'

'Yes I do. He was a guest in my house and he behaved appallingly. He was pissed, lecherous and boring.' Edward's face darkened. 'I'm sorry. He's a bastard. If I'd known Zoë planned on inviting him I would have vetoed it. However . . .' He stopped suddenly and sighed as if he was bringing himself under control. 'Well, as I said, the arrangements were all a bit of a surprise. I hope he wasn't too rude to you.'

'He wasn't rude, just a bit . . . obvious. And he made

me feel a bit awkward.' Almost as awkward as I felt now with Edward up here in the nursery with me and ignoring his guests downstairs.

'So, sorry, and thanks again.'

'It was nothing. Justin wasn't too dreadful and Teddy's an angel.' I felt curiously shy. 'You'd better get back to your guests. They'll be wondering where you've got to.'

He shrugged and shoved his hands in his pockets. 'You're right, I ought to be there.' He stared at me again before he muttered goodnight and left.

I switched the lights off and made my way to bed where I opened my book but didn't see the words on the pages in front of me. I was asleep in minutes.

Quiet scuffles woke me the next morning. I got out of bed and opened the connecting door, expecting to see Teddy playing with his toys or heading for the loo for an early-morning pee, and instead I came face to face with Edward.

I jumped, acutely aware that I was only in my nightie; quite decently chaste, not flimsy or seductive, but a nightie none the less.

'Go back to bed,' he whispered. 'You're supposed to be having a lie-in.'

I remembered, but I was awake now. And I wanted a cup of tea.

'I'm going to make myself a cuppa. You want one?'

Edward nodded. 'Please.'

I padded back through my bedroom to the kitchen, grabbing my dressing gown off the back of the door as I went. I shrugged myself into it as I filled the kettle and plugged it in.

'Milk and sugar?' I called quietly as I took a couple of mugs out of the cupboard.

'Just milk,' he replied, right behind me. I jumped again. I hadn't expected him to follow me.

'I'd forgotten how cosy this little flat is,' he mused, staring around at my minuscule kitchen. 'It's years since I've been in here.'

Not since he'd had a nanny, I imagined. I pootled around, finding tea bags, getting the milk out of the fridge, and Edward hooked a stool out from under the counter and plonked himself down on it. He gazed around him, looking as if he was immersed in memories. I left him to it. Besides, I was still too full of sleep to chat intelligently. It was as much as I could cope with to make the tea.

'You got slippers?' he asked after a couple of minutes.

'Yes. Why?' I handed him a steaming mug.

'I'll tell you in a mo. Back in a tick.' He put his mug down on the table and hurried out of the kitchen and the nursery. I watched him go and wondered what on earth he was up to.

A couple of minutes later I was in my slippers and he was back in the kitchen brandishing the baby alarm.

'What?' I asked, completely confused.

'Bring your tea and come with me.' He stuffed the alarm in his trouser pocket. 'I've got something to show you.' He must have seen the expression on my face, because he laughed. 'Don't worry, it isn't etchings or anything nasty. You'll like it. Honestly.'

Yeah, right. But I followed him all the same. Curiosity is a very compelling thing. And anyway, it was a bit of a thrill to be invited – just me, on my own – to accompany him on this jaunt, whatever it was. When he wasn't making me feel like a moron he had this knack, I'd noticed, of making me feel quite special. And right now he was doing the latter.

We tiptoed through the nursery, past a sleeping Teddy, and out on to the top landing. We were heading towards the estate offices when Edward stopped and tugged at a tiny knob I hadn't noticed before. There was a concealed door in the wall.

'Wow,' I said, even more intrigued.

Edward pulled the door open to reveal a flight of steps. 'These,' he explained, 'were so the maids could do all their work, lugging coal and water and so on, without getting under the feet of the likes of us.'

'Us?'

'Well, me, I suppose. But nannies were a bit like governesses. You know, not really servants.'

'But not family, either.'

'Almost,' said Edward, giving me a smile. 'Anyway, there're loads of these stairs all over the house so the poor little maids could scuttle about like mice behind the wainscoting.'

I peered into the gloom of the stairwell. The steps were precipitous and uncarpeted stone. They looked lethal. Health and safety would have something to say about them these days, I thought.

'Come on,' said Edward as he led the way through the

door and up the stairs. And there was me thinking we were on the top floor.

Clasping my cup of tea and glad my dressing gown was thick I left the warmth of the main house and headed up the cold, dimly lit stairs. At the top there was a tiny landing with two doors. Edward opened one of them.

'Welcome to Housemaids' Heights.'

I stepped into the large room. Bare boards, a couple of small grimy windows, a tiny fireplace and one tap were all I could see.

'Time was when twenty or so of the poor kids slept here. There's another room just like this on the far side of the house for the footmen. Couldn't have them fraternising. Lord knows what they'd have got up to. The more senior staff had the bedspaces by the fire. Very senior staff, the butler and the housekeeper, got their own rooms elsewhere.' He looked around the room. 'Grim, isn't it?'

Grim didn't come close. I thought of all the luxury downstairs, and the fact that this house had been no different from hundreds of others up and down the country. It was a wonder the lower classes hadn't risen up and murdered the nobility in their beds. I said as much. Edward laughed and pointed out that they had in France and Russia.

'But I didn't bring you up here for a lesson in social history.'

He turned round and opened the other door. Behind it was a set of even steeper stairs – almost a ladder. He handed me his mug and shinned up it. Light and a draught of freezing air flooded down as he opened a trap door at the top.

His legs disappeared from view, then he leaned back through the ceiling and told me to pass him both mugs and join him on the roof.

I followed cautiously, not sure how safe the whole business was. As I got near the top of the stairs my head popped into fresh air. All around me was a vast expanse of grey, lead- and slate-covered roof, all different levels and gradients with huge chimneys popping up at intervals all over it. I half expected to be confronted by Dick Van Dyke and a crowd of unlikely chimney sweeps performing a song-and-dance routine. But no cabaret seemed to be forthcoming so I scrambled out over the sill and did my dressing gown up tighter. The still air was perishing but the view was spectacular.

'Wow!' I breathed again.

'Isn't it?' said Edward, handing me back my mug. I wrapped my hands round it, grateful for the warmth. 'See, I told you you'd like this.' He grinned at me, pleased that his treat was being so well received.

Around me were the acres of parkland that surrounded the house, a translucent turquoise sky arched above us and on the horizon, to the east, was the golden glow of the sun, just rising. The grassland had fingers and trails of milky mist across it, the hedges and the trees rising out of it. It was like fairyland. I traced with my eyes the line of the main drive, invisible under the mist but the line it took clearly defined by the crowns of the avenue of trees that flanked it. At the end the tops of the great golden gates glistened in the low early rays of the sun. Beyond the park wall were the higgledy-piggledy roofs of the village that sheltered behind it. Wisps of smoke rose vertically from some of the chimneys into the still air, adding to the dream-like quality of the scene.

A flash of light in the distance caught my attention. A train was zipping towards the distant horizon, the carriage windows catching the dawn sun. I wondered for a second where it was heading before I turned my attention back to the estate. I picked out the gates again and the main drive, and then found the road that led to Annie and Mike's farm. Just beyond the park and the hedge I spotted it, looking more like a picture out of a Beatrix Potter book than a real place. I could make out the motley collection of barns and outhouses beside the house and as I looked I saw a tractor set out and trundle along a track. I wondered who was driving it.

'Look,' said Edward. 'There's a balloon.'

'Where?'

He stood behind me with his hand on my shoulder and I was acutely aware of his face next to mine as he pointed it out. 'There.'

I could see the balloon now but I didn't care about it, despite its graceful, colourful beauty as it bobbed up into the sky. All I was aware of was Edward's proximity. I could smell the clean tangy smell of the soap he used. I could feel his breath on my skin. If I moved my head a fraction I could lay my cheek against his. I wondered . . .

'See it?'

I nodded, not wanting to break the spell.

He moved away. The magic moment evaporated, and reality reasserted its presence. I shivered.

'We ought to go down. You're cold.'

'No, not really.' I was lying. I was frozen, but I didn't want this intimacy, this moment of just him and me and no one else, to end. 'Teddy must love this place.'

'I've not brought him here yet. I'm waiting till he's a bit older. But I expect he'll find the back stairs and the roof on his own. I did.'

I thought about the pleasure of exploring a house as big as this, of playing hide and seek with friends, of the endless fun to be had by creeping round the back stairs and popping up in unexpected places – or just using them as ways to avoid boring adults.

'It must have been such fun growing up here,' I said, turning to him.

'Curate's egg,' he answered.

'Sorry?'

'Good in parts.'

I remembered his hatred of his boarding school. 'It must have been horrid to have to leave all this to go away to school.'

He nodded. 'It wasn't just that. It was also coming back and finding that something else had had to be sold to keep the place going, and there still wasn't enough money left for anything fun to happen. Well, I told you that my mother wasn't around much – always up in London partying. I think she hated this place. And my father . . .' There was a pause. I waited from him to continue. 'Well, my father was much more concerned about preserving the place for his heirs than he was about the heir himself.'

I didn't know what to say. What with that and his horrid school, his childhood sounded as though it had been a pretty miserable affair.

'Enough of that. Let's get back in the warm.' He sent me down the stairs first and then followed and locked the trap shut. I couldn't help wondering why on earth he had shown me the roof. Maybe he took loads of people up there. But I'd somehow got the impression that the place was special to him.

When we got back to the nursery Teddy was just stirring. I went into my room to get dressed and left Edward to greet his son. When I returned the nursery was empty. I felt strangely abandoned.

I drifted around my flat for a while, doing some odd chores for myself, made some breakfast, listened to music and got bored out of my skull. I caught sight of the car keys sitting on the mantelpiece and decided that as it was a beautiful day I should get out and explore the countryside.

At the top of the drive I had a choice, Oxford and shops or the countryside. I decided to save the shops for a wet day and turned left on to the road that led through the village to the unknown. And the unknown proved to be stunning: rolling hills, beautiful views, picture postcard villages with greens and pubs and thatched roofs, lambs frolicking in the fields and everywhere looking green and fresh and clean. All those years in London thinking Hyde Park was a big open space had not prepared me for this. I switched on the car radio, found Radio One and whizzed along the peaceful roads singing happily but tunelessly to myself.

After about half an hour I came to a little town. I decided to explore so I found a space to park my car and set off down the steep main street, which was flanked by interesting-looking shops. No Woolies, no Smiths, no Tesco, but a deli, a couple of dress shops, a real butcher, a bookshop and about a dozen places selling souvenirs, trinkets and gifts. Outside one of them was a rack of postcards including a view of Arden Hall. On a whim I bought one to send to my mum. Next to the shop was a tea room, so I popped in there to have a cup of coffee while I wrote it.

I had the postcard written, addressed and stamped by the time my order arrived so I had nothing but my thoughts to occupy me while I drank my coffee and chomped away at a vast scone with cream and jam. Going back over the events of the morning, I relived those moments on the roof and felt another little shiver of pleasure just thinking about it. He must have taken Becca up there, I thought, and Zoë. Perhaps all the staff were shown his empire from that vantage point. So why, I wondered, had it felt so intimate? Was it just that he touched me when he'd pointed out the balloon? I sighed as I mulled it over, and decided that it was just me wishing it to be more than it was. I might like to think that it had been a special moment but it had probably meant nothing to Edward. Why should it? But I had to admit to myself that Edward was beginning to invade my thoughts more and more.

I paid my bill and picked up my postcard. Next stop the post office. I found it eventually down a little side street, next to a real toy shop with a window display of lovely old-fashioned toys: spinning tops and hula hoops, teddy bears and dolls' tea sets. I shoved my card in the box on the pavement and went into the toy shop. An old-fashioned bell pinged as I shut the door. There was a wonderful mix of stock. I bought a number of small gifts for my cousins ready for when birthdays cropped up – as they did with startling frequency – and was just about to leave the shop when I spotted a kite. Teddy would love it, I thought, and as far as I knew he didn't have one. On impulse I bought it.

I mooched around the town for a bit longer, but there were no shops designed to appeal to a twenty-something London girl. If I'd been into silk head squares with pictures of horses on them, or waxed jackets, cords and sensible shoes, I'd have been in seventh heaven, but nothing took my eye.

I returned to the Hall. Maybe Teddy would be around and we could try out his kite. But Teddy wasn't there and my TV still hadn't been fixed. The weather was too nice to waste it by loafing around, although there were some clouds building up in the distance. I thought I'd take myself off for a walk in the grounds, perhaps explore the lake.

I was just crossing the big stable yard when I heard Jed whistling – not a tune, but the signals he gave to the horses. I decided to take a look at what he was doing. I wandered over to the indoor school and slipped in through the big open door. Jed had his back to me and I didn't want to disturb him, so I sat down on a straw bale in the shadows.

Through the dusty air I watched him exercising one of Becca's horses. He was making it do wonderful things and the animal moved like a dancer. First it trotted but in a very slow controlled way, holding each hoof off the ground for much longer than normal. Then he made it trot so that it moved diagonally, crossing its hooves. Finally he got it to prance along, changing the leading hoof every other pace. It was amazing. I couldn't believe how clever and graceful it all was. I'd seen dressage on the box. Like half the country I'd watched Becca strutting her stuff at the Olympics, willing her and the team to win, and I'd watched that bit of her training video, but seeing a horse do it for real was something else.

Jed whistled and the horse came to a standstill. Then he used a signal I'd not heard before, a long, piercing, steady note. I watched in amazement as the horse hunched down on its hindquarters and then jumped into the air, kicking out its back legs as it did so. It was an astounding move. I clapped and Jed spun round.

'Who's that?' he called, squinting against the light flooding in through the big door.

'Only me,' I said, standing up and moving forward so he could see me.

'Miss Lucy,' he said, recognising me.

'That was fantastic. The horse is wonderful. You are so clever being able to make it do all those things.' I could see Jed blushing. 'So which horse is this?'

'Billy Boy,' he said.

'Oh, is that the one—' I was going to say 'that she rode in the Olympics', but before I could get the words out Jed interrupted.

'I wasn't there when he killed her. The police didn't

believe me but I wasn't. Miss Becca was working alone with Billy Boy. I wasn't there.'

'I'm sorry, Jed, but you've lost me.' I was confused; then the penny dropped. 'You mean it was Billy Boy that killed the Countess.'

'She was with him here when it happened, but I was in the stable.'

'Of course you were.' I could see Jed was getting quite agitated. I hoped I sounded soothing.

'His lordship believed me. He told the police.'

'Of course he believed you.'

'They said I was lying, but I wasn't, Miss Lucy, I wasn't.'

'Of course you weren't,' I said, wondering what it would take to calm him down.

'It's wrong to lie. I know that.'

'Quite right.'

'My mum would tan my hide if she thought I was lying.' He looked at me earnestly.

The light in the indoor school suddenly changed. The sun had gone in. I glanced at my watch.

'Goodness, is that the time? I've got to get going.' I didn't, of course, but I could see that Jed was working himself into a state and I reckoned if I left he'd calm down again.

'What time is it?'

'Nearly one. I don't know about you but I need some lunch. I expect your mum'll be wondering where you are.'

Jed nodded. 'Yeah.' He shuffled his feet. 'You believe me, don't you, miss?'

'Of course I do,' I replied. And I did. He didn't have the guile to lie, but I felt somehow unsettled by what he'd said. I knew that the police had been called in to investigate her death but surely that had just been a formality. Didn't they do that with every sudden death? Had they suspected there was more to it than just Billy Boy lashing out? The thought gave me the creeps and I shivered, and then I dismissed it. If there had been more to it the police would have found out. I was just being stupid – again.

Jed led Billy Boy out of the indoor school and as I watched the animal go I wondered why on earth Edward was so keen to keep the horse. If it had killed someone I loved I'd probably have got rid of it; sold it or given it away or anything not to have it around any more. I shook my head in bewilderment. It all seemed a bit . . . odd.

By the time I'd grabbed some lunch it was obvious that the sun wasn't going to make another appearance and as I stared morosely out at the gloomy sky a fat drop of rain hit the window. I sighed. Now what? I thought about snuggling down on the sofa with *Swallows and Amazons* but I wasn't in the mood for reading. I'd done all my washing (I wasn't having the laundry maid sneering at the quality or cleanliness of my knickers), my rooms were tidy, and I was at a total loss. Maybe there was something worth watching on the telly.

I strolled down the stairs. The silence was absolute. Not a sound anywhere. I wondered where all the staff were. I couldn't believe that none of them were on duty. Surely some of them had to be lurking about somewhere in case Edward wanted something. Not that it was any of my business. It was just odd to be all alone in the place in daylight.

At the bottom of the stairs I stopped and listened. Not a sound, so I took myself into the study and picked up the remote for the TV. Idly I flicked through the channels. Rugby – no. I zapped to the next channel. Ice skating – zap. Show jumping – za— My finger hovered over the button as the camera shot cut to the commentator and Zoë.

'With me is Zoë McMahon,' said the commentator. 'So, Zoë, what do you think of the talent we've got coming through at the moment?'

Zoë smiled at the camera. 'Just fantastic. Some of these young kids are doing really well in a tough sport.'

'And how about you, Zoë? Have you found a replacement for Beelzebub?'

I remembered Beelzebub. Well, I remembered the accident. It had been splashed all over the front pages of just about every paper in the land when the poor animal had gone headlong over a fence at some three-day event and broken its neck. The pictures had all been of Zoë being led away from the scene in floods of tears. The trouble was, there had been a sneaking suspicion, which had subsequently been voiced in some of the redtops, that she'd been crying because she'd just blown her chances of winning some big event and not because of the horse. And having met her I could see just how that rumour would start.

Zoë's smile faded as she tried to look sad. 'Beelzebub

was such a star. He's horribly hard to replace, but I have some good young horses coming along and I've got my eye on a fantastic new one.'

'Really? Tell me about it.'

'Sorry, but I can't, not until I've done the deal.' She laughed. 'Anyway, it may not happen, but I'm really hoping. It's such a special horse.'

And I knew she was talking about Billy Boy.

The camera zoomed in on the commentator's face. 'Thank you, Zoë, for that. Now back to the competition, where . . .' No, I couldn't face eventing. Zap. Football – zap. Oh, for God's sake! Not everyone wanted to spend their wet Saturdays watching sport.

A black and white movie appeared on the screen. For want of anything better I began to watch it. It didn't look as if it was really my thing but hell, it was better than nothing. I shoved the cushions on the sofa into a more comfortable position and flopped back on to them.

'Ow!' Something hard was digging into the small of my back. Annoyed, I scrabbled around and pulled out a video. I stared at it and then I remembered. It was the tape I'd hidden when I'd been caught red-handed watching one of Becca's other training videos. I slid over to the drawer where the other ones were kept, but when I pulled it open it was empty. Edward, as good as his word, had told Mrs Porter to clear them away and she had. Above the drawer was the slot of the VCR. My hand, holding the tape, moved towards it. I knew Edward probably wouldn't want me to watch it, I knew I was about to do wrong, but like Alice in Wonderland, when she was confronted by little cakes and bottles labelled 'eat me' and 'drink me' and knew she was taking a risk by doing so, I still went right on ahead and was prepared to face the consequences. I mean, training videos weren't really that private, were they? I wasn't prying into any secrets or anything. I knew what I was doing couldn't really be justified, but . . . The tape slid smoothly into the recorder and was swallowed up.

I flicked the TV on to the video channel and there was Becca at the Olympics. And there was Billy Boy going through similar manoeuvres to those I had just seen him practising in the indoor school. They both looked fantastic; he was as shiny as a conker and Becca looked fabulous in top hat and tails, her long dark hair in a glossy chignon which looked simple but had probably taken an age to create. I pressed fast forward and skipped to Becca doing the cross-country. Now she was dressed more like a jockey competing in the Grand National. I watched her thunder round the course at breakneck speed, she and Billy Boy hurtling over huge fences, through water, and down precipitous slopes, while the clock ticked at the corner of the screen. I knew that she got a perfect time, I knew that she was in the lead after this phase, but I still found myself on the edge of my seat willing her to cross the line just as the clock hit zero and feeling intensely relieved when she did. When it had happened a few years back the whole nation had breathed a sigh of relief, only to have to hold its collective breath again the next day when she competed in the show jumping.

I watched that phase next as, in yet another set of

snazzy clothes, this time black riding jacket, snowy-white breeches and hard hat, she completed a faultless clear round. She looked wonderfully beautiful and poised as she cantered Billy Boy round the ring, patting his neck in appreciation of what he had done. The recording stopped. I pressed the button to rewind it but it took me a couple of seconds to realise that I had hit the wrong control and the tape was fast-forwarding instead. I stopped it and it automatically began to play again. A picture appeared on the screen. I recognised where it had been filmed. We were back in the indoor school, only this time I was watching a completely different Becca. Now she wasn't beautiful and poised. In this bit of film she looked like a she-devil and she was lashing at a horse with her riding crop. I watched in horrified fascination as Jed threw himself between her and the animal – not Billy Boy, another horse – begging her to leave it alone, and she turned her fury on him, catching him a vicious blow across the face. It was ghastly. Then the film stopped. The tape after that was a blank.

I was stunned by her display of temper. My God, had Edward known she could be like that? Of course he must have. But she had been awful, hideous, a monster. And he'd still worshipped her? Or maybe he'd loved her so very much he had been prepared to forgive her anything – even that temper.

I sat on the sofa too shattered to move. I just gaped at the blank screen for several seconds before I pulled myself together again. Unbelievable, I thought as I hit the rewind button. With a whiz the tape spooled back to the beginning and then ejected itself from the machine. I pulled it out of the slot and hid it at the back of the drawer, hoping it would seem as if Mrs Porter had overlooked this one when she'd cleared the others out if it ever came to light.

With Edward again taking charge of Teddy, Sunday morning stretched before me as Saturday had, a prospect I found rather dispiriting. The country idyll was all very well but there wasn't a shedload of stuff to do. In London I used to spend my weekends with friends, trawling round the shops, taking in a movie, going out for a drink; it was all there on my doorstep. But here? It was miles to anywhere and apart from Annie, Mandy and some of the house staff, I didn't know a soul. It was a mile just to get to the gates and even then there wasn't much on the other side. I thought I might take myself to the village shop and buy some reading material and a bar of chocolate. If nothing else it would kill a few minutes, maybe half an hour.

I parked on the green and headed for the shop. I was just about to go in when I heard my name being called and spun round. It was Annie.

'Hi, Annie,' I said.

'How are you getting on?' she asked.

'Fine. Teddy's lovely and I'm managing not to get too lost in the house.'

'And how do you like living in the country?'

'Well, it's very different from London, that's for sure.' I told her about my trip out to a neighbouring town the day before. 'And I bought a kite for Teddy. I think he'll love it.'

'All kids love kites. Jed had one as a nipper and we had a lot of fun with it. There're plenty of places on the estate that're perfect for flying one. There's a hill up behind our farm that always seems to catch the breeze.'

'I'll check it out.'

'Ask Jed. He knows where I mean. He'll show you.'

I must have looked a bit sheepish. After upsetting Jed yesterday I was sure he wouldn't want anything to do with me again. I came clean to Annie.

'I wondered what had gone on. He was in a rare old mood when he came in for his dinner.'

'I didn't mean to, honest,' I said in my own defence. 'He jumped to the wrong conclusion when I asked him about Billy Boy.'

'That was a bad time he had. The police were convinced he did it. They accused him of training the horse to kick out at a given signal and then setting Becca up so she was in the way.'

'No!' That was a dreadful idea. Then a memory of Billy Boy performing that amazing leap into the air, his back legs kicking out, flitted into my mind. A memory that was just as swiftly followed by a picture of Becca, her face ugly with fury, lashing out at Jed and that other horse. But might he have hated her so much . . . No, surely not. Not Jed.

'They had him in for questioning for hours.' Annie shook her head. 'It was a bad do.'

I could imagine. No wonder Jed had got so upset, reliving that memory. 'I still don't reckon he'll be too keen on kite-flying with me and Teddy.'

'He'll have forgotten all about it in a day or two.'

Annie was his mother and knew him better than anyone, but I wasn't so sure. The memory was obviously painful and raw and I'd just picked at it again like a kid with a scab.

I went into the shop and bought a couple of magazines and a Sunday paper, then returned to my flat and faced the prospect of a whole day with nothing much to occupy it. I'd just settled down in an armchair, gas fire warming my toes and a cup of tea by my elbow, when I heard noises in the nursery. I went to investigate and found Teddy rummaging in a cupboard.

'Daddy says we can go to the zoo.' He turned his serious dark-brown gaze on me.

'Zoo?' I didn't know there was a zoo nearby.

'Daddy says it'll be fun. Do you want to come?'

'Lucy is having a well-earned day off,' said Edward from the door. 'The last thing she wants to do is hang around with you, young man.'

Actually a trip to the zoo sounded like fun, but I reckoned Edward didn't want me muscling in on his treat for his son.

'Oh, please come with us, Lucy,' said Teddy, slipping his hand into mine.

'You're very welcome to join us,' said Edward. 'I mean, if you've nothing better to do.'

But did he really mean it? Was this a polite offer or a

genuine one? 'Please, Lucy,' said Teddy earnestly.

I looked over Teddy's head, trying to judge Edward's mood. He was smiling at me but he didn't strike me as brimming with enthusiasm. But was he the sort of bloke to show his feelings, or was he being 'nice' again?

'You really would be welcome.'

'Well . . . I haven't . . . I mean . . .' I shrugged.

'You mean you can't think of a good reason to disappoint Teddy, is that it?' Edward grinned at me, and I found myself grinning back. 'You'd better wrap up warmly; the forecast is for it to get chilly later. Teddy and I have come back to get an extra jumper.'

I hurried into my bedroom and threw on a thick sweater and grabbed my jacket and gloves.

'All set?' asked Edward. I nodded.

The three of us hurried down the stairs and out through the garden room door to the courtyard. This time Edward walked past the old Land Rover and instead unlocked a battered Volvo.

'In you get,' he said. He started the engine, which coughed into a roar, and off we sped down the long drive, past the incoming tourists all driving vastly smarter cars.

It took us about half an hour to get to the zoo, during which time we sang along to some nursery rhyme CDs.

'It's all very well for you,' said Edward during a pause in the music. 'This is about the hundredth time I've had to endure this disc. It lost the novelty factor some months back.'

I could sympathise. 'My last family had some old

favourites too. I think I'll come out in hives if I ever hear them again.'

'The *Thomas the Tank Engine* theme has that effect on me.'

'And what about *Bob the Builder*?'

'Oh, don't.' Edward gave a mock cry of anguish.

'I can't hear the songs,' whined Teddy from behind us.

'Sorry,' we chorused. 'That told us,' I added.

Edward turned the music up a little louder. 'Hopefully, we can chat and he can sing along.' No complaint seemed to come from the back as he went on, 'So what did you get up to yesterday?'

I told him about my excursion into the Cotswolds. 'I couldn't believe how pretty it all is round here.'

'I've stopped noticing. Maybe I should come out with you. Maybe I'd see it with fresh eyes if I went with someone who wasn't bored by it all.'

'But how can you be bored' – I gestured to the passing scenery – 'with this?'

'Because I'm old and cynical.'

'Rubbish,' I snorted, forgetting who I was talking to.

Edward looked at me with raised eyebrows.

Shit. I'd forgotten my place. 'I'm sorry,' I mumbled. 'I don't know what came over me.'

'Don't be. Very refreshing.'

But I didn't think it would be a good idea to be so outspoken again. He might find it refreshing once but just rude if it happened again. In the silence I wondered how I could have forgotten myself and my position so much as to have said what I did. I stole a glance at him and saw a small smile on his lips. He just didn't behave the way I expected someone who was rich, upper class and a celebrity to. He seemed so . . . normal. And nice.

Well, obviously he was nice. I knew he could, and did, turn it on.

Edward swung the car into the car park and found a space. It was already quite crowded, which surprised me. At the ticket booth he refused to let me pay and we joined the other visitors, who seemed to consist mostly of families with young children. By lunchtime we'd seen all the animals and explored the gift shop, and Edward had bought Teddy a wicked rubber snake which Teddy said he was going to show Cook and Annie. Neither Edward nor I thought that either was going to be terribly thrilled but Teddy was adamant that they'd love it.

I thought that Teddy looked more lively and animated, more like a three year old, than he had since I'd arrived to look after him. I wondered if it was the fresh air or spending time with his father that had done the trick. Either way I was delighted that he seemed to be having fun.

'Right. Lunch, I think,' said Edward.

As he said it I realised that I was absolutely starving.

We drove away from the little zoo and out into the countryside. After a few miles we turned off the main road on to a narrow lane. On either side of the car the hedge stood on top of high banks and every hundred yards or so indentations had been cut into these to allow two cars to pass. Edward carried on, squeezing the big Volvo along the track until we came to a humpbacked bridge and a sign which announced a pub.

'Here we are. The best bacon sarnies in Gloucestershire,' he announced. Then he looked at me. 'Oh, lord. You do like bacon sarnies, don't you? I mean, everyone does. I never thought to ask.'

'I love them. Besides, even if I didn't I'm sure there'll be something else on the menu.'

In the car park, while Teddy and I waited for Edward to lock the car, I impulsively took both Teddy's hands and swung him round. For the first time I heard him squeal with genuine delight. Edward looked across at us and for a second I was worried he might not approve of such behaviour, but then I saw him smile.

We made our way into the bar. I was aware of several stares of recognition as we crossed the packed saloon and went into the dining room. As we took our place at an empty table I was aware of yet more. Edward, busy finding out what Teddy wanted to drink, getting menus and generally sorting out his little party, seemed oblivious. Teddy and I took our seats while Edward ordered our drinks from the bar: orange juice for Teddy, white wine for me and a pint for himself.

'I need a wee, Daddy,' announced Teddy on Edward's return.

'Come on then, big fella, let's find the Gents,' he said, putting a tray of brimming glasses in front of me and extracting several menus from under his arm.

They disappeared through a door and I picked up the menu to while away the minutes till their return. It was the mention of Becca's name that made me tune in to a conversation behind me.

'She doesn't look a bit like Becca,' I heard some woman say in what she obviously thought was a whisper. 'Quite different, really.'

'Yeah,' replied her male companion. 'But maybe Edward reckons she won't screw half the men in the county every time he turns his back.'

I froze and felt my face flood with colour. How could people be so insensitive? How could these people make such a personal comment about someone they probably never even met? And how hurtful. I felt angry on Edward's behalf, and I wondered what they would say about me when I was out of earshot. Might they speculate on what Edward was doing with such a mouse? The idea that I might be an object of public scrutiny (and, worse, compared to Becca) was quite unnerving.

I was still feeling acutely self-conscious when Edward and Teddy returned from the loo. I made myself behave as normally as possible and hoped to God Edward would put my flushed face down to the cosy warmth of the pub rather than embarrassment.

'It's nice here,' I said, looking around me in what I hoped was a relaxed and casual manner. And the pub *was* nice – there was a huge log fire burning brightly at one end, cheerful chintz curtains framing the windows and gleaming brass and copperware decorating the walls.

'I haven't been here for a while,' said Edward, taking a pull at his pint. 'I'm pleased to see it's much the same. Places round here have a habit of changing hands and then you find the pub you thought you liked has turned into some dreadful gastro-experience.'

'Makes it sound like a bad tummy upset.'

Edward laughed. 'Well, some of them turn my stomach.'

I took his advice about the bacon sandwiches while Teddy decided to have a home-made burger and chips. We chatted about our morning at the zoo till the food arrived, brought to our table by a florid, middle-aged man.

'Nice to see you again, my lord,' he said jovially. 'It's been a while since we've been able to welcome you here.'

'Yes, it's been a year or so, hasn't it? And how are you keeping, Alan?'

'Mustn't grumble,' said Alan. He looked at me, but Edward didn't offer to introduce us. Alan went off to get some knives and forks for us and a bottle of tomato ketchup for Teddy.

'And how are you, sir?' he said on his return.

'Like you, Alan. Not grumbling.'

'You know, it's a lot more than a year or two since you were here, sir. It must be six at least.'

'As much as that?' said Edward, although I could tell he knew it had been ages. Alan muttered something about seeing to his other customers and left us to our meal. Edward obviously didn't want to be the focus of attention.

Teddy chatted happily during the meal, often through large mouthfuls of burger, for which Edward and I made allowances. Finally, stuffed full of fresh air, lunch and memories, he snuggled on to his father's lap and let his eyelids droop.

'How about I get us some coffee while Teddy has a doze?' I suggested.

'That'd be grand.' Edward fumbled in a pocket. 'Let me give you some cash.'

I shook my head. 'I think I can run to a couple of cups of coffee – even on my wages.'

'As I know perfectly well how much I pay you, I should think you can.' Edward grinned at me.

At the bar I ordered ordinary coffee rather than one of the rather exotic variations on offer.

'Nice of his lordship to come here again,' said Alan.

'It's a nice pub,' I said.

'So is that his little boy?'

'Yes. That's Teddy.'

Alan busied himself getting cups off a shelf and pouring the filter coffee.

'Funny how he never brought the Countess here. He'd been a regular of ours since he was old enough to drink, but once she turned up . . . Well, I suppose she preferred fancier places, so we didn't see him again. Not till now, at any rate.' He looked at me as if I would know why Edward had had a change of heart and returned to his old haunt. I stared back, wondering whether to tell him that I was just the nanny. 'Two pounds fifty, please.'

I handed over the change and took the coffee back to our table, mulling over the snippets I'd learned about Becca recently: she had a vile temper, she didn't like country pubs and, if the overheard gossip was to be believed, she wasn't the most faithful of wives. It seemed our National Sporting Treasure had had more than just feet of clay.

But it was none of my business. I suddenly felt

ridiculous. Edward had loved her regardless of her faults; you only had to walk into the study to know that. And no wonder, with her magnetic beauty and amazing talent. Any idea I had had that he was the least bit interested in me was just ridiculous. He was being kind so that I felt welcome and didn't get bored and hanker after the bright lights of London again. Being friendly to the nanny would be a small price to pay to make sure she stuck around for Teddy. And the sooner I took that on board the better, I told myself sternly.

We managed to strap Teddy into his car seat without waking him.

'He'll be wide awake when we get back to the Hall,' I said. 'What have you got planned for the afternoon?'

'I'd hoped to crack on with some estate work while he had a rest, but . . .'

'I can take him out for a run around, if you'd like.'

'That's a very kind offer, but you're supposed to have weekends off.'

I shrugged. 'I've nothing better to do.'

Edward took his eyes off the road and looked at me. 'Bored with the countryside already?'

'Not at all,' I protested. 'But . . . well, I bought a kite yesterday. And the weather's perfect.'

'A kite! You know, I can't remember the last time I flew one.'

I could feel my face colouring at this unexpected approval. 'I saw it in a toy shop and I thought Teddy might like one.'

'But that's brilliant. What fun!'

'I bought it for Teddy.'

'Oh.' The disappointment was obvious in his voice. I hadn't meant it like that but the damage was done.

'I didn't mean you can't have a go. Come with us.'

'If you don't mind, I should go and see Mike.'

'On Sunday?'

'Farmers don't get days off, you know. The cows still need milking.'

'Suppose.' I felt that I'd pissed him off. He certainly sounded as if I had.

We drove in silence back to the Hall.

'Thanks for the lunch,' I said as I got out of the car.

Edward nodded, curtly, I thought. 'I hope Teddy likes the kite.' There was no warmth in his voice, just the flat statement.

I unstrapped Teddy from his car seat, not sure what to say to Edward to placate him. I was just about to suggest that he joined us as soon as he'd finished his business when he zoomed off. I was left holding Teddy and feeling as though I'd offended him over a kite. Then I noticed that Zoë's car was back and I felt a flicker of irritation. But maybe she would cheer Edward up. Being older and more sophisticated I had no doubt she could think of all sorts of better ways to amuse him than a spot of childish kite-flying.

I carried Teddy into the house and put him on the sofa in the den so he could wake up slowly. I was just undoing his jacket to make him more comfortable when I heard heels clacking on the marble floor. Zoë swept into the room.

'Oh. It's you,' she said.

I nodded. 'Sorry. Who did you expect?' Although why on earth I was apologising was beyond me. I had as much right to be in the house as she did.

'Edward. I thought I heard the car.'

'He dropped Teddy and me off. He's gone to Home Farm.'

'When will he be back?'

'I don't know.' Teddy began to stir, and I turned my attention to him. 'I saw you being interviewed on the telly yesterday,' I said over my shoulder. 'How exciting for you.'

'Not really,' she said coolly. 'It happens all the time.'

Which I suppose it did to the likes of her. 'I'd have found it exciting,' I said.

'Well, yes.' Her implication was perfectly plain.

'Could I ask you to do something for me?' Zoë looked at me as if I'd just accused her of something unpleasant. I carried on. 'I want to fetch something from the nursery. I won't be two ticks. Just keep an eye on Teddy for me.'

She sighed. 'If I must.'

I flashed her a smile and shot out of the room; I wasn't going to trust her with Teddy for a moment longer than I had to. Panting, I reached the nursery, found the kite, still in its paper bag, and was back downstairs before, I hoped, she could think of reasons to complain. I whizzed back into the den to find her sitting on a chair swinging one of her shoes on the end of her toe – the image of someone terminally bored.

'Good,' she said, standing up quickly as if I'd been gone two hours not two minutes. She swept out of the room again. I wondered how long she was going to be hanging around the Hall. Didn't she have a home of her own?

Teddy soon woke up and once he was fully conscious I told him about the kite.

'And Annie says there's a hill on the farm that would be perfect. Let's go and see her and ask her where it is.'

Teddy was more than happy to go along with my plan and I whisked him off to Annie's in my car for a spot of serious fun. Irrationally, when I walked into Annie's kitchen I was disappointed not to find Edward there. Annie gave me directions to the best hill, told me to leave the car in the yard and suggested that Patch, as a companion, would add to the fun. I took her advice.

I have to say, Teddy wasn't the best kite-flyer in the world, but what he lacked in technique he made up for in enthusiasm and we had a whale of a time. He proved his earlier burst of high spirits wasn't a one-off and after an hour of running about he'd squealed and shrieked quite enough to assure me he was normal. While he belted around trying to keep the kite airborne I threw sticks for Patch to chase until he got fed up and went off into a bramble thicket to snuffle around for rabbits.

The sun began to go down, a thin veil of cloud drew across the sky and the temperature dropped. Standing still, I was beginning to feel chilly.

'Come on, Teddy,' I called. 'I think we ought to be thinking about going home soon.'

'Must we?' he shouted back.

'Five more minutes,' I bargained.

I couldn't see Patch so I stuck my fingers in my mouth

and whistled. I called his name, too, but not a sign. I walked to the other side of the bramble thicket and tried again. From this side of the hill I could see two figures approaching – Mike and Edward. I whistled and called Patch a third time. Maybe my technique was poor or maybe Patch only responded to Mike's whistle because I heard a piercing trill from lower down the hill and Patch bounded out of the dense scrub and shot off to his master. Mike's whistle also attracted Teddy's attention and he came thundering round the thicket, dragging the kite along the ground behind him.

'Daddy,' he shrieked. 'Daddy, look!' He held up the kite.

'Wow!' Edward called back with enthusiasm.

Teddy ran down the slope but I remained where I was. If Edward was still annoyed with me I didn't want to spoil the atmosphere. I rubbed my hands to keep the circulation going while I waited for the little group to join me. I slapped a smile on and hoped Edward had forgiven me.

'Teddy's had a ball this afternoon,' he said as he approached.

'It's been my best day ever,' said Teddy, wriggling like a puppy.

'Our Jed used to fly kites up here when he was a nipper,' said Mike. 'Mind you, they were just paper and sticks, not a swanky job like this 'un.' He looked at the nylon 'wing' that was Teddy's kite.

'They're back in fashion,' I said. 'There're places around London where blokes fly kites so big they could lift you off the ground.' I saw Teddy's eyes widen at the wonderful thought.

Mike whistled. 'Really?'

'Honest,' I affirmed. I shivered. The air had now lost all its warmth and dusk was settling over the countryside. 'Come on, Teddy,' I said. 'Time we went home.'

He looked at his dad to see if he agreed with me. Edward nodded. 'Yup, definitely time to go.' He took Teddy's hand and began to lead him back towards the farmhouse. 'Maybe Annie can be persuaded to give us a cup of tea.'

'And a biscuit,' added Teddy hopefully.

I fell into step beside Mike, Patch trotting at his heel. 'Your dog didn't come when I whistled for him,' I said. 'Does he only answer to you?'

'Not normally. He's pretty good. He must have been on the scent of something really interesting.'

Edward turned round. 'I meant to say, that's a pretty impressive whistle you've got.'

'For a girl?'

'For anyone,' he said. 'Must've come in handy for hailing taxis in London.'

I didn't point out that my wages didn't allow for extravagances like taxis.

'I wish I could whistle,' he added.

I stopped in my tracks. 'You can't whistle?'

Edward shook his head. 'Nope. Hopeless.'

'But everyone can whistle.'

'Everyone except Edward,' said Mike. 'Annie'll tell you. She spent years trying to teach him but he never managed it.'

'Can you teach me to whistle, Lucy?' Teddy asked.

'I expect so. We'll have a go at bedtime.'

Teddy looked thrilled at the prospect.

'Let's hope you have more success with him than Annie did with me.'

I couldn't imagine that Teddy wouldn't manage the skill. Until Edward, I'd never met anyone who couldn't whistle.

Life at Arden Hall fell into a routine. I soon felt completely at home in my new flat, my TV was fixed, I got to know the other members of the household staff, and the days drifted past, soon turning into weeks. Mrs Porter was still scary but I'd learned that it was nothing personal and that she was just made that way. Edward seemed to be away on business a lot during the week and at the weekends he took over Teddy's care, so our paths rarely seemed to cross. Whether he was now visiting Zoë instead of her coming to the Hall I didn't know, but she seemed to have disappeared out of everyone's hair. No loss there.

Teddy had mastered the basics of whistling – breathy and tuneless but he'd cracked it. I promised when he was a bit older I'd teach him how to do it with fingers in his mouth.

It was well over a month later that Teddy and I, having had lunch, pottered around and made some biscuits, were trying to decide on an activity to pass the afternoon out in the fresh air.

'We could fly the kite,' he suggested.

I shook my head. 'It wouldn't work today. Look, there's no wind at all.'

Teddy scampered over to the nursery window to make sure that I was telling the truth. 'Are you sure?'

I checked the tree tops visible from our high window and they were completely lifeless. The sky was a uniform battleship grey and it was one of those quiet early spring days that are just damp and colourless. There was a hint that winter was almost past – the trees were in leaf, the gardens full of spring flowers – but the air lacked any real warmth if the sun didn't shine. Nearly time to get the summer clothes out but not quite.

'Sorry, lamb. Another day. Let's take a ball instead and play football.'

He seemed happy enough with that so I found one in the toy cupboard and together we made our way down to the garden room door. Near the bottom of the stairs Teddy stumbled and in order to stop him from falling I dropped the ball to steady him. The ball bounced down the last few steps and across the marble hall.

'Yours, I think.'

I looked up and there was Edward, balancing the ball on the palm of his hand, looking stony-faced.

'Normally we don't encourage ball games within Arden Hall. The insurers get upset.'

'I'm so sorry, I really am. I didn't mean to drop it.'

'Joke,' he said.

'Joke?' I repeated, faintly confused. He didn't look as if he were joking to me.

'You are *so* easy to wind up,' he said. 'It's not fair.'

My confusion turned to annoyance. 'Well, I'm glad to provide the comedy turn.' I stamped across the marble tiles and snatched the ball off him. 'Come on, Teddy, let's go and find somewhere for a kickabout where we won't be in the way.'

Teddy looked from his father to me and back again. 'Do you want to come and play with us?' he asked.

'I'm sure your father is far too busy,' I snapped.

'Not a bit of it,' Edward said easily. 'In fact, there's nothing I'd like better.'

'Really?' A slow smile spread across Teddy's face and he wriggled. I wondered if the promise of playtime with his father was a rarity.

In spite of my prickle of annoyance at being the butt of a joke I felt my ill-humour soften and I wondered whether it might not be better to leave them to play together without me getting in the way. I offered to leave them to it as we made our way out to the courtyard.

'Absolutely not,' said Edward. 'A game of football wouldn't be half so much fun without Lucy, would it?'

Teddy assured me that if I didn't play then he didn't want to either.

'Wait a mo,' said Edward, and he dived back into the garden room. A minute or two later he emerged with some battered old flowerpots. 'Goalposts,' he explained as he placed two at one end of the open space and then two at the other. 'Lucy and Teddy against me. Fair?'

Teddy thought it sounded perfect. Edward rolled the ball in front of Teddy, who kicked it gently back. I ran up to Edward and tackled him, winning the ball.

'Come on, Teddy,' I called as I charged up our makeshift pitch. Teddy didn't seem to know what to do. I kicked the ball to him. 'Come on, Teddy,' I encouraged him. 'Kick it at the goal.'

Teddy looked at me. I could see from the confused expression on his face that he didn't seem to know what to do. I ran between the flowerpots.

'Kick it towards me, Teddy.'

'Offside,' yelled Edward.

Teddy looked at his father and kicked the ball to him.

'Well done, son,' said Edward, running back the other way.

I thundered down the pitch. 'Help me, Teddy. Help me get the ball off your dad.' Teddy ran towards Edward. I could see that he was getting into the spirit of things. 'Go on, Teddy,' I yelled. 'Tackle him.'

Teddy hurled himself at his father's legs. Edward made an elaborate show of losing the ball to his tiny opponent. Gleefully Teddy set off again, followed by Edward, who pretended to run fast but took such small paces that Teddy was easily able to get away from him.

'Go on, Teddy,' I yelled. 'Go on, score.'

This time he got the idea and the ball trickled over the line between the flowerpots. I ran up to him, picked him up and whirled him round.

'What a champ,' I crowed. 'Michael Owen, eat your heart out.' Teddy grinned and chuckled as I celebrated our lead.

Edward restarted the game and swiftly scored a goal of his own.

'Right then, Teddy-me-lad,' I said. 'We can't let him beat us. Time for a team talk.' Teddy looked completely bewildered as I took him to one side. 'Right, Teddy,' I whispered. 'You go and tickle your dad while I get the ball. If he's laughing he won't be able to tackle me. Okay?'

'Okay,' agreed Teddy solemnly.

He ran over to Edward and thrust his hands up under Edward's sweater.

'That's right, Teddy,' I shouted. 'Tickle him.'

'Oi, ref,' said Edward. 'Tickling's not allowed.'

'Tickle? Tackle? There's hardly any difference,' I shouted back as I dribbled the ball between the flowerpots.

'Well, if we're going to play to those sorts of rules . . .' Edward grabbed Teddy and began to tickle him back. Teddy dissolved into shrieks and giggles, his whole body shaking with mirth. When his father finally let him go Teddy was pink with delight. He began to run over towards me but tripped over his own feet and fell headlong, his hands outstretched in front of him, skidding along the uneven paving of the courtyard.

His giggles instantly turned into loud, snotty sobs. Edward got to him first and picked him up. Teddy wailed while I examined the gritty grazes on the palms of his hands.

'Nothing too bad,' I said to Edward, who was looking concerned. 'It must sting a bit, but no lasting damage. How about a sweetie, Teddy? Would that make you feel better?' But Teddy just bawled more loudly. 'Why don't you bring him up to the nursery? I've got some Savlon and sticking plasters there. I expect a combination of the two will make our wounded soldier feel a bit braver.'

Edward headed for the house, his son in his arms. Teddy's sobs continued wetly, interspersed with the odd hiccough. I held the garden room door open, and then the door into the hall. As we were crossing the chequered tiles I saw Mrs Porter emerge from the basement.

'Oh dear dear,' she said, sounding disapproving rather than sympathetic. Old bat, I thought. I'd always had her down as one of the children-should-be-seen-and-not-heard brigade. Well, Teddy could certainly be heard at the moment – the visitors to the main house were probably getting an earful too.

'Just a graze,' said Edward. 'Nothing to worry about, Mrs Porter.' Not that I thought Mrs Porter was the least bit worried – unless she was concerned Teddy might drip on her pristine floor. 'We'll take Teddy up to the nursery and clean him there.'

'Very good, sir.' She watched us head up the stairs.

Once in the nursery I led the way into the bathroom and ran warm water into the basin. Edward sat on the cork-covered stool, cuddling Teddy, whose sobs had abated a little. I sploshed some mild disinfectant into the water and soaked a piece of gauze.

'Let me have a look at your poor sore hands, Teddy.'

He held them out. They were both scraped raw, with little specks of gritty dirt embedded in the grazes. I knew that cleaning them up was going to sting a bit but it would have to be done.

'I'll be very gentle,' I said to Teddy, miming to Edward that he should hold Teddy tight. Despite my best efforts poor little Teddy's sobs redoubled and I could see that it was upsetting Edward. I was as quick as I could be and in just a few minutes I'd finished, slathered on some soothing antiseptic cream and topped the whole thing off with a couple of large plasters. As I stuck the second one down on his grazed hand I looked over the top of his head to check how Edward was doing and found him staring straight into my eyes.

For a second, maybe it was longer, time seemed to stop as we stared at each other. A little bolt of shock and desire juddered through me. It threw me completely off balance. He was so unbelievably attractive this close and he seemed to be looking at me as if . . . Don't be stupid, I told myself. I dropped my gaze, vividly conscious of his proximity and my body's reaction. Mindlessly I carried on automatically smoothing down the plaster on Teddy's palm.

'Sorry to interrupt,' came a voice from the door. 'Mrs Porter said I'd find you here.'

Zoë again. What was she doing here? The spell was broken. I looked over towards her and was shocked when I saw her expression: she was staring at me with a look of undisguised dislike that verged on loathing.

Why? What had I done? Zoë couldn't possibly think that I was any sort of threat.

Edward swivelled round and the expression on her face metamorphosed into something more pleasant. I wondered if I had imagined everything – or maybe being this close to Edward had overheated my brain and I was misinterpreting everything as a result.

'Edward, darling.'

Darling?

'I've just had my agent on the phone and he's got this fantastic offer from my sponsor. It really is just spectacular. I couldn't wait to tell you. I think you'll be impressed.'

'Congratulations,' said Edward, sounding, I thought, distinctly unimpressed.

'The thing is, I need you to talk to him. He's going to ring back later this morning and I said I was sure that you wouldn't mind.'

'Did you now?' The sarcasm in his voice was obvious but Zoë just prattled on obliviously about the offer and what time her agent was going to call back.

'So you'll talk to him. It's about Billy Boy,' she added, almost as an afterthought.

Edward stood up, Teddy still in his arms. 'And I've told you where I stand and what my answer is.'

'But just say you'll talk to him. What harm can it do?'

Judging by the expression on Edward's face I thought that plenty of harm had already been done.

Edward swung Teddy on to his hip. 'I'm not discussing this,' he said frostily and strode out of the bathroom.

Zoë stared after him and then turned to me. I was still kneeling on the floor and she towered over me. I felt at an utter disadvantage. 'He's so unreasonable,' she said angrily. 'What good is that horse to him?'

'But it was Becca's horse.' I couldn't believe how insensitive she was.

'Precisely,' said Zoë. She turned to go and then changed her mind. 'Oh, and one other thing, sweetie. Don't get the idea that he fancies you.' I must have looked startled because she added, 'I saw the dewy look on your face just now. But let me tell you, he's not the least bit interested in you. Oh, he might fancy a shag, but it wouldn't be anything more than that. Men have needs and you're on the premises and probably available; a handy stopgap till something more suitable comes along.' She swept off.

Bitch.

But then a truly embarrassing thought speared through my brain, trailing the poison of Zoë's comment. If my thoughts had been that obvious to Zoë they must have been to Edward too! I felt my face flame red at the hideous thought. Oh, shit! How embarrassing. Now he wouldn't just think me a moron but a lovesick moron as well. How sickening was it that he now knew I had a crush on him? A wave of nausea rolled through my stomach.

Zoë took off in a swirl of gravel and exhaust fumes. I really hoped she'd got the message and was gone for good. Her nasty comment though, I knew, was going to linger for a long time.

The next day the phone rang in the nursery. It was Edward.

'I've just heard from Annie. One of her cats had kittens a few weeks ago. She was wondering if Teddy would like to come over and see them now they're old enough for visitors.'

I thought that was probably a no-brainer and said as much. 'I'll bring him downstairs, shall I?' I added, although I was suddenly acutely aware of Zoë's voice in my head.

'Why not?' he said.

I delivered Teddy to the foot of the stairs, wrapped up against the chill weather that the previous day's gloom had heralded. I found not only Edward but Jenny who was discussing something to do with the staffing levels of the main house. I was glad she was there as I felt I would be able to hand over Teddy and escape without looking rude. After all, they were busy and I didn't want to interrupt.

'Hiya, stranger,' she said when she saw me. 'I've hardly seen you for weeks. We ought to get together and have a good catch up.'

'There's no hurry,' I said. 'I'm not planning on going anywhere for a bit.'

'I thought you were coming with us to see the kittens,' said Edward.

'No . . . I thought you and Teddy . . . Surely you don't want me along,' I finished lamely. Besides, I didn't really want to go. The thought of spending more time in Edward's company was making me curl up with embarrassment.

'Of course we do. Don't we, Teddy?'

'Yes.' Teddy nodded enthusiastically.

Jenny laughed. 'Looks like our chat will have to wait.'

'Not if you'd rather,' said Edward.

I glanced from him to Jenny, desperately hoping she'd say something to give me an excuse to stay put.

'Go on,' said Jenny. 'The kittens will have grown up and gone to new homes before you can say Jack Robinson. We can chat any old time.' Not what I wanted to hear.

'Settled,' said Edward.

'But I haven't got a coat.' I was only in jeans and a sweater, quite unsuitable for venturing out on such a nippy day. 'You don't want to wait for me to get ready.'

He rolled his eyes. 'There's bound to be one hanging up in the garden room you can use. We'll kit you out on the way to the car.'

I was dragged off before I could procrastinate any longer. Edward found me an old waxed jacket hanging on a peg. He thrust it at me. 'Here, put this on. It'll keep you warm enough till we get to Annie's.'

As before, when we got to the farm I jumped out to open the gate and was greeted by Patch. Annie, hearing the engine and the barking, came to the farmhouse door and stood there smiling in welcome, her arms folded across her ample bosom.

'They're in the barn,' she said, knowing full well what the purpose of our visit was. Teddy clambered out of the vehicle and looked at Annie for permission to go in. She nodded and smiled encouragingly.

The open-sided barn was stacked full of hay bales and things like fence posts and bags of fertiliser. In one corner was parked an antique tractor and beside it was an ugly piece of equipment with lethal-looking spikes.

'Hold my hand, Teddy,' I commanded. Lord only knew what else might lurk under the piles of straw and hay bales. I looked into the dusty heights of the barn and saw huge cobwebs like chandeliers hanging from the beams. I wondered what other wildlife was around. I tried not to think about mice and rats and told myself they wouldn't be a bit like the ones in London. All the same, I wished I was wearing boots.

Annie joined us as we stared around the barn for signs of the kittens. By the tractor a bowl of food had been licked clean but other than that there was no trace of the mother or her young. We searched around, calling out and making encouraging noises, but apart from getting chilled to the bone from the nippy breeze that was blowing into the big building we achieved nothing. Just as Teddy was starting to get restless the mother cat appeared and wound herself round Annie's legs.

'Hello, Puss,' she said, bending down and picking her up. 'And where are the kids?' But Puss just lay in her arms looking smug and inscrutable. 'Come on,' Annie said to me. 'Let's leave the boys to look for the kittens. You and I can go back to the kitchen and have a cuppa. We'll bring one out to you too, shall we, Edward? And a glass of squash for Teddy?' Edward nodded and said he thought he and Teddy would give it five more minutes before they jacked it in and joined us. I was only too happy to give up the search and go and warm up.

Annie shut the kitchen door behind us and pushed the huge kettle over on to the hot plate of the Aga. 'Soon get that boiling,' she said as she bustled about getting out plates and mugs and the cake tin. 'I hear Zoë was around causing trouble again,' she added out of the blue.

'Um, yes. At least it seems like it. I think she and Edward had a bit of an argument over Billy Boy.'

Annie narrowed her eyes. 'She'll be back. It's a pity she lives close enough to even think about visiting. She's always around now – well, since Becca died. She's a minx for wanting that horse, and she knows it. Still, I don't suppose you get where she is without treading on toes and not minding it.'

'I suppose she feels that Billy Boy's talent is going to waste if he doesn't carry on competing.'

'That's as maybe, but I know for certain that Becca

wouldn't want Billy Boy to go to Zoë. Becca might have *said* Zoë was her friend but it wasn't like that. She wouldn't have given her the time of day, let alone her best horse. Mind you,' said Annie as she slopped boiling water from the kettle into her big brown teapot, 'there's a lot of people Becca wouldn't give the time of day to so Zoë wasn't special on that count.'

The image of Becca slashing at Jed with her riding crop flitted through my mind. 'I suppose they both had to be very determined, to get to their level,' I said quietly.

'Determined is one word for it,' said Annie. She stirred the tea, slapped the lid on the pot and put the cosy on. 'But in Becca's case the phrase "spoiled little madam" seems more appropriate if you ask me. Only daughter of a multimillionaire and the apple of his eye. There was nothing she ever wanted and didn't get – not if she set her heart on it.'

Maybe, I thought, Edward had been one of the things she had set her heart on.

Teddy ran into the kitchen. 'We've found the kittens,' he said. 'We've found them.' He bounced up and down with excitement, all smiles. He was a different chap from the solemn, silent child I'd met on my arrival. Annie stared at this new, animated Teddy and then gave me a smile full of approbation. I felt ridiculously pleased.

Teddy was never going to let me wait for my cup of tea so Annie promised to bring it out to me as I was dragged back to the chilly barn.

The kittens were very sweet. They'd got to the perfect age of being still incredibly tiny but also playful and tottery and adventurous. Teddy was in raptures, dragging bits of straw along the ground for them to pounce on and giggling when one or other of the three lost its balance or tripped over its own paws. The mother cat sat on a straw bale, safely out of the way, and took the opportunity of a lull in the business of motherhood to have a thorough wash. Being a full-time nanny, I understood.

Annie appeared with the tea just as I was wondering if it was possible to die of cold at this time of year and within sight of a centrally heated farmhouse. She handed the boys their drinks and told me to come back into the kitchen to thaw out.

'I can't think what you're thinking about, Edward,' she grumbled at him. 'Allowing poor Lucy out on a day like this without a proper coat. You know there's no warmth in a jacket like that. She'll catch her death and you'd only have yourself to blame.'

She hustled me inside and slammed the door against the cold. 'Come and warm yourself by the Aga,' she said, pointing to the battered old sofa right beside it. I didn't need telling twice. I sat there, basking in the warmth, with my hands clasped round my steaming mug, and what with that and the Aga I soon felt better. I wondered about Annie's attitude towards Becca but perhaps it wasn't so odd. After all, I reasoned, she'd obviously been like a mother – or maybe a much older sister – to Edward in his youth. It would be natural for her to have opinions about the girl he married. And if she felt that Becca had not been good enough for Edward . . . well.

And of course there was the business of Becca hitting

Jed with her riding crop. If Annie was like a she-wolf with Edward, who wasn't her flesh and blood, how much more defensive would she be about her own son? All in all it was understandable that she didn't have much time for Becca.

'Tell me more about Becca,' I said.

'Nothing much to tell, really,' said Annie as she sliced up great slabs of fruit cake. 'She met Edward at a hunt ball around here about six or seven years ago, and that was that. "Whirlwind romance", the papers said.'

'It was a fairy tale,' I said, remembering back to the headlines of the time.

Annie narrowed her eyes a little. 'I don't think real life is much like that, though, do you?' She handed me a plate of cake.

'Well, it's nice to dream. I could fancy being swept off my feet by a handsome prince.'

'I think that's what Becca fancied too, but as the only available ones in this country were either spoken for or too young she decided to settle for an earl instead. Poor Edward never had a chance. And dreams have a nasty habit of turning into night—'

The door flew open.

'We've had enough of the kittens,' said Edward, clumping in, followed by Teddy. 'Budge up,' he said. He plonked himself down beside me while Teddy scrambled in between us. Annie doled out big slices of cake and silence fell while everyone chewed.

I was chewing over more than cake, though. Had Annie really implied that Becca had chased Edward? And that last unfinished sentence? *Dreams have a nasty habit of turning into nightmares?* Was that what she was going to say? But surely Edward had adored Becca, despite all her faults? And why on earth wouldn't he? He would have had to be made of stone not to have been mesmerised by her, and maybe she only lost her temper rarely, when really provoked. Maybe, compared to all her other attributes, her temper didn't matter to him. Ultimately he'd worshipped her. The study, that shrine to her, was surely proof of that?

There was a note pushed under my door when I got back, inviting me for supper with Jenny.

*Come round to mine*, she'd written, and she gave an address in the village. *About eight o'clock*. She'd left a phone number too. I dialled, remembering to put a nine ahead of her number – unlike the night I'd tried to get hold of the police after I'd clobbered Edward.

'I'd love to. I'll just have to check that Edward is okay to babysit.'

'Surely he should take it as a given that you're off in the evenings, unless he arranges otherwise.'

'Well . . . I just don't like to assume.' And I didn't, but as I rarely went out during the week the question hardly arose. I rang Edward, who was surprised that I felt I needed to ask.

'I'll tell you when I would like you to babysit,' he said, which made me feel foolish for asking.

I got to Jenny's cottage in the village about ten minutes after eight. I had a bottle of wine with me, although as I was driving I wasn't planning on drinking much of it.

'Come in, come in,' she said when she opened the

door. Behind her was a low-ceilinged hall with dark panels and beams. I instantly envied her her cosy little house.

I handed over the bottle and followed her into the tiny living room. It was exactly how I had always imagined a country cottage to be, low beams, chintz curtains, a fire in the grate and bright rugs on the wooden floor. Curled up in one of the squashy armchairs was Mandy, who was already tucking into a glass of wine. She looked completely at home – but it would be difficult not to in such a lovely welcoming room.

We greeted each other with enthusiasm.

'I didn't know you were going to be here.'

'I didn't know myself until about half an hour ago,' she replied, 'but Jenny thought that as the only other person in the village with all their own teeth and not due a telegram from the queen, I ought to be included.'

Jenny handed me a glass of wine.

'So . . .' said Mandy. 'How's it all going?'

I told them. And when I'd gone over all the things I'd done with Teddy since I'd arrived, even I thought it was a fairly impressive list.

'I'd heard you'd been loafing around a lot,' said Jenny.

I was just about to rise to the bait when I saw the expression on her face.

She grinned. 'I've heard that Teddy's been having a ball since you arrived. Everyone around the Hall is saying so. They're also saying that he's a different child. A proper little boy, not a robot any more.'

'People have been talking about me?' I said, amazed. I'd only been doing my job, for heaven's sake.

'Like there's so much else happening around here that everyone isn't going to notice the impact you've had on Teddy.'

I blushed at the compliment.

'When Edward's in the office, Hugh and I have to stuff cotton wool in our ears otherwise we'd be sick of hearing about how perfect you are. It's Lucy this and Lucy that. Honestly!'

'Me? Perfect?' But inside I was glowing like a nuclear reactor at the thought that Edward valued me.

'So, come on, tell us the truth,' said Mandy, leaning forward and allowing her wine glass to tip at a perilous angle. 'You're not really called Lucy Carter. Your real name is Mary Poppins.'

I had a mouthful of wine and her comment made me almost choke on it. As it was, some of it ended up going up my nose and making my eyes water.

'God, she even went kite-flying,' shrieked Jenny and the pair of them launched into a tuneless chorus of 'Let's go fly a kite' from the musical.

When they had calmed down a bit I said, 'But Jo must have done all those things, surely?'

'No, Jo was frightened of getting her swanky uniform grubby. Poor little Teddy was never allowed to really muck about. His idea of getting down and dirty was to get away with not washing his hands before a meal.'

'You're joking.'

'We're not,' the pair chorused in unison.

A little bit of me felt I ought to be loyal to my professional colleague but a much bigger part wanted to know all about her. I fought my curiosity for about a second and then gave in.

'So what was she like?'

The two girls looked at each other and then Jenny started.

'Well . . .' And I got the complete low-down about how she liked doing handicrafts and was terrified of anything remotely creepy-crawly, how she thought pubs were common and that girls should never drink beer. She was paranoid about bacteria and swabbed everything with disinfectant and let Teddy do hardly anything in case he hurt himself. It was only after Edward had a blazing row with her that she agreed to take Teddy to the stables for riding lessons but she wouldn't help supervise him so she couldn't be sued. Jed was left to do it all himself.

'But didn't Becca want him to ride?' It didn't make sense to me.

'Becca was only interested in her own riding,' said Jenny with a dismissive snort.

'Besides, she took no interest in what Teddy was doing,' said Mandy. 'Jo had the poor little scrap completely wrapped in cotton wool but either Becca didn't know or she didn't care enough to demand a change. Until you got here Teddy spent most of his time on the nursery floor playing with his toys all by himself, while Jo got on with her knitting or sewing or whatever.'

Which explained a lot.

I remembered that was exactly what Teddy had been doing when I first walked into the nursery, but I didn't think there had been a lot of it since. Far too much other fun to be had. 'Didn't Edward say anything?'

'I imagine so, but I suspect Becca overruled him,' said Jenny. 'Becca was a great one for having things her way. And that included making sure that everyone knew she was a countess. She wanted a nanny she could be sure wouldn't let the side down so she got one from one of the top colleges, and the fact that the girl she hired wasn't much good wasn't half so important as the fact that she wore the right uniform.'

'Becca,' said Mandy, 'was always worried about her roots showing – and I don't mean her hair.' I must have looked bemused. 'Becca might have been loaded but her family weren't aristocracy. Jenny and I always thought that when she started this eventing lark, because she was mixing with people with "old money", she wanted the sort of respectability that a title would give her. And having nabbed one she was damned if she was going to give people an excuse to say she didn't fit in. I swear she paid more attention to etiquette and form than the royal family.'

'But Edward doesn't give a stuff about all that sort of thing,' I said.

'No, because he's been born into it. He isn't the least bit snobby, but Becca!' Jenny shook her head.

I was glad I hadn't had to work for her.

'Anyway,' continued Mandy, 'when Edward went out looking for a new nanny he obviously decided to hire someone who was the complete opposite of Jo.'

I remembered going to my interview thinking that my new prospective employer would want a girl with the right uniform and a double-barrelled name. It was lucky I had neither, I thought. For once it had worked in my favour – that and *Swallows and Amazons*.

For the following few days I kept thinking about Becca. She'd always seemed so fantastically perfect: beautiful, talented, rich, a sports star, a doting mother – and that was just the start of the list of things that the public loved about her. But first Annie and then Mandy and Jenny, who had all known her much better than the general public, had given me a glimpse of a different Becca, and having seen that recording of her training her horse I didn't have any reason to doubt them. But I couldn't square up what I'd found out with Edward's dedicating a whole room to her memory – unless he was absolutely devoted to her. Love, it's well known, is blind.

Of course, when I wasn't wondering about the Becca question I was walking on air because Edward liked what I was doing with Teddy. To be honest, I was so over the moon about that, the Becca conundrum wasn't really very important. I kept feeling as though I was being hugged by a pair of invisible arms. The feeling of being completely approved of was fantastic and one I hadn't experienced before. I was so happy I was almost beside myself.

I should have known it was too good to last. I should have known that a fly was about to land, splot, in the ointment. And I should have known that the fly would be called Dave.

My mum rang me up at the end of the week. I had just dropped Teddy off at playgroup and was walking back to my car when my mobile chirped in my bag.

'Hello, babes,' said Mum.

'Hiya.'

It was good to hear from her and we chatted about my cousins, the weather, what her neighbours had got up to – the usual stuff.

Then she said, 'Dave's been thinking.'

I refrained from answering that I didn't know he could. I confined myself to saying, 'Oh, yes?'

'He was looking at that postcard you sent.'

I'd forgotten all about it. I'd sent it weeks back.

'He said now the weather is better and the days are getting longer we ought to come and see you.'

Shit. 'Really?'

'Just for the day. Dave was impressed by the picture of

Arden Hall and thought we ought to take a trip to the country and see where you work.'

Why, oh why, had I sent her a picture of the house? Why hadn't I sent a postcard of the village, or kittens, or any damn thing but the bloody house? If I hadn't done that I wouldn't have put the idea in Dave's head, and Mum would never have thought of driving so far out of London just for the day.

And there was no reason I could come up with as to why they shouldn't. Still chatting, I got into the car and huddled my coat around me, feeling miserable. She finished the conversation with a breezy 'See you on Saturday'. I tried to sound pleased at seeing her again but inside I felt only despair.

There was no way I could pretend that she and Dave weren't anything to do with me. I didn't mind the idea of giving Mum a guided tour but Dave . . . He was such a loudmouth. He always had to voice his opinion and laugh too loudly and generally be a complete pain. Every time I met him I just wanted to curl up in embarrassment, although Mum always seemed to think he was so clever and funny. Ha!

I drove back to the Hall feeling down and made my way up to my flat to think about how to handle the forthcoming visit. By the time I had to go and collect Teddy I'd decided that the only thing I could do was to come clean and to meet them when they arrived. I could then ask the staff to call me when their tour finished, and take them off for lunch or tea in the village. The last thing I wanted was to take Dave up to my flat and give him an excuse to set foot in the private apartments. I certainly didn't want him running into Edward or Teddy – the bigger the distance I could keep between them and him the happier I'd be. I could just imagine the way he'd show off to his friends about meeting the Earl of Arden and pretending they were now bosom buddies. According to Mum he'd been full of it when I'd landed the job (although she hadn't put it quite like that) – the thought of what he'd be like if he actually got to press the aristocratic flesh made me shudder.

I rang my mum on her mobile and told her to buzz me when they arrived and I'd come down and meet them.

'I can't get you in for free,' I said. 'It's not in my gift.'

'That's all right, baby,' said Mum. 'Dave and I'll understand. Just because you live there doesn't make it your house, does it?'

On Saturday they pitched up around mid-morning. Teddy and Edward had gone off to get Toy Town and one of the other horses ready for a hack out into the grounds. The fact that they were safely out of the way made me feel quite light-headed with relief.

I met them in the huge entrance hall, where Dave was already sounding off about ormolu mountings, acanthus leaves and Hepplewhite furniture. I knew he was only doing it to show off; when he'd moved in with Mum all he'd brought with him were some IKEA bookcases, so what did he know about antiques?

Mum was standing by the ticket counter chatting to one of the guides. 'Lucy,' she called when she caught sight of me coming across the huge space. The other visitors turned to look at me and, as I was obviously arriving from the private wing, I suddenly felt hugely self-conscious. I could feel myself blushing but I plastered on a smile and tried to look pleased to see her. Which I was – it was just Dave who made me want to cringe.

I gave Mum a hug and managed to sidestep any contact with Dave before I entrusted them to one of the guides.

'I'll see you back here in about an hour,' I said. 'Then we can go and get some lunch. There's a nice pub in the village which does food.'

'That'll be lovely, won't it, Dave?'

'Isn't there a restaurant here?' he asked.

'There is, but it isn't licensed,' I lied swiftly, shooting a look at the guide and praying she didn't contradict me. No way did I want Dave hanging around the Hall for a moment longer than necessary. Luckily she either wasn't paying attention or had taken my hint, but whichever, she didn't say a word.

'Pub it is then,' he said predictably.

It was a great plan, apart from one flaw. I hadn't banked on Dave's battery going flat.

'No problems,' he said. 'I've got some jump leads in the boot. We'll go to the pub in your car and then start mine when we get back.'

'I'll go and fetch it. It'll only take me a minute or two. I'll be back in a mo.'

'No worries,' said Dave. 'We'll come with you.'

It was the last thing I wanted but I couldn't for the life of me think of an excuse as to why they shouldn't.

I hustled them through the ground floor of the private wing as quickly as I could to the garden room door. My mother dawdled, wanting to look round, but I wasn't having any of it. I held the door into the courtyard open and tapped my foot impatiently. I was determined to be out of the way before Teddy and Edward got back from their ride.

'This isn't very smart,' said my mother, gazing at the muddle of battered and broken belongings that cluttered up the garden room.

'Well, it's not something that they expect outsiders to see,' I said.

'Obviously.'

'So you're not allowed to use the front door,' said Dave.

I couldn't be bothered to explain that no one, not even the Earl, did, as it was easier to use this one. He wouldn't have believed me anyway.

I was just about to unlock my little Corsa when I heard another car pull up. I turned round expecting to see one of the staff and felt my heart sink as I recognised Zoë's red sports car. And there was me thinking we'd seen the back of her.

'Hello,' she said coldly as she climbed out.

I returned the greeting with a similar lack of enthusiasm. I saw her clock my mother and Dave and her forehead crease with a slight frown of disdain, but she didn't say anything or ask to be introduced before she waltzed over to the house as if she owned it, jangling her car keys as she went. She turned and gave them another look, though, before she went into the house.

Despite the fact that I really disliked Dave, Zoë's snooty reaction to my visitors made me livid. Who was she to judge my mum and her boyfriend? I felt prickly with resentment.

'Wasn't that . . .' my mum asked, awestruck, as she got into my car.

'Yes,' I answered shortly.

'What's she doing here?' she continued.

I shrugged. 'She and the Countess used to ride together.'

'She seemed very at home. Is she a regular visitor, then?' asked Dave.

'She's been here a couple of times before.'

He raised his eyebrows. 'She doesn't seem to like you. Because you're staff, I suppose.'

That was so typical of him – he always managed to say something to make me feel inferior and here he was, doing exactly that for the second time in as many minutes. First the snide comment about the front door and now this. I decided not to dignify his stupid remark with a reply.

'So are she and his lordship,' he continued, 'you know?'

'I neither know nor care,' I replied lightly. And it was true that I didn't know, but I realised with a jolt that I did care.

Very much.

The loss of the gold snuffbox from the Chinese salon wasn't noticed until the Monday, when one of the cleaning staff raised the alarm. There was a police car in the courtyard when I got back from taking Teddy to playgroup. Not unnaturally, I popped into the estate office to ask why.

'It was probably one of the visitors over the weekend,' said Jenny. 'Mind you, it'll be insured, so it isn't as if Edward'll be out of pocket.'

Which I supposed was true, but it didn't detract from the fact that someone had nicked it in the first place.

I returned to the nursery and got on with sorting out some of Teddy's toys and getting his lunch on the go so it would be nearly ready when I collected him from playgroup. The morning passed quietly. I saw a couple of police cars come and go but other than that everything was entirely routine. I assumed, once I'd collected Teddy and brought him home, that the afternoon would carry on in the same vein.

I thought nothing of it when Edward appeared in the nursery.

'Can I have a word?' he said as he made his way into my kitchen.

'Of course, if you don't mind me just finishing off Teddy's lunch.' I carried on mashing some potatoes.

'You know Zoë came back at the weekend?'

I said I'd run into her just as she was getting out of her car.

'She came to try to persuade me about Billy Boy again.'

'You can't say she isn't persistent.'

Edward nodded. 'She mentioned you had some visitors.'

'My mum and her boyfriend came to see me. They wanted to see where I live. Is there a problem?'

'No, nothing like that. This is your home too. Of course

you can have visitors. You should have told me. I would have made sure the guides knew to let them in for free.'

'Oh,' I said, slightly taken aback. 'That's kind of you. I didn't like to . . . I just assumed . . .' I was sounding foolish. 'I'll remember for next time.' Although I'd already made my mind up that there wasn't going to be a next time. Well, maybe it'd be nice to see my mum here again, but not Dave.

'Just one other thing . . .' His tone was unmistakably serious.

'Yes?' He'd moved round the kitchen so he was leaning against the counter beside me. I finished mashing the spuds and began to drain the peas. 'What's that?'

'Look . . . this is really awkward and please don't take it amiss.' I waited. 'It's just that Zoë said . . .' Another awkward pause. 'Well, she said if they hadn't been with you she would have wondered what they were up to. That they didn't look . . . Well, she said they looked a bit suspicious. And then . . . God, I really don't know how to say this . . .'

But I could see where he was leading. 'And then the snuffbox went.'

Edward went brick red. He nodded miserably.

'What? You think I'd let my relations waltz into your house and pinch stuff?'

'No, of course I don't. Obviously not. But . . .'

'But what?'

'But Zoë said as much to the police.'

I was so stunned I was literally lost for words. I opened and shut my mouth and all that emerged from it was some sort of incoherent splutter. That bloody woman. That bitch!

'I'm sorry,' said Edward.

'Sorry?'

Edward nodded miserably. 'They're sending someone along to your parents to take statements.'

'Dave's not a relation,' I said automatically before the bit about the statements registered. 'Oh, bloody hell. Just because Zoë saw them coming out of the private wing?' I was incandescent. 'I can't believe you trust me so little that you'd take Zoë's word and believe that I'd let my visitors raid your house.' I was shouting now. 'I mean, I was with them. Does she think I had something to do with it?' I didn't wait for Edward to reply. I was raging. 'Obviously I'm not as smart as Zoë, obviously my mum doesn't live in a posh house and obviously we're not rolling in it or I wouldn't be working as a nanny, but I'm not a thief, neither is my mum and nor is her boyfriend. If you want to think that we are then that's up to you, but as far as I am concerned you can go to hell.'

Edward looked horrified. His face was pale and he looked as if I'd physically struck him.

'Right,' he said quietly and then turned and strode out of the kitchen. 'Come on, Teddy,' I heard him say as he went through the nursery. 'I think we'd better leave Lucy alone for a bit. Let's see what Cook can find us for lunch.'

I heard the door shut quietly. Shit, what had I done? I felt sick and shaky and close to tears. I went into my little sitting room and sat on a chair, too shocked at what I'd said to him to even think.

After about half an hour I managed to rouse myself enough to write a letter of resignation; there was no way I could stay at Arden Hall after that and if I got in first I'd spare Edward the embarrassment of having to fire me. I owed him that at least.

I crept along to the estate office and checked to make sure that both Jenny and Hugh had gone to lunch before I nipped in and shoved my note on Edward's desk. I'd offered to stay until they found my replacement but in my heart I thought Edward would probably want me out of the way as soon as possible. People like me couldn't tell people like him to go to hell and not expect serious repercussions. I wondered about starting to pack. Maybe he'd want me on the next train, I thought dolefully. Maybe he wouldn't even want me to say goodbye to Teddy.

I felt tears start to well up. Sitting around feeling miserable wasn't going to get me anywhere so I decided to take myself out for a last walk in the grounds before I was railroaded off the estate.

I took some bread and went off to the lake to feed the ducks for one final time. I looked across at the boat house;

I never had learned to row, I thought. And now I probably never would. Morosely, I chucked scraps to the ducks and felt thoroughly sorry for myself.

I heard feet running towards me and turned to see who was approaching.

'Thank goodness I've found you,' said Edward, panting along the path towards me, Teddy scampering along beside him, trying to keep up. 'We've been looking high and low for you.'

'Did you think I'd done a bunk?' I said, biting back the words *with some more valuables*. Another bitter row with Edward wasn't appropriate with Teddy right beside us, although he must have had an earful of the previous one.

Edward ignored my cold tone and didn't seem angry with me for my previous inexcusable behaviour. 'I came to tell you the good news. It looks as though the snuffbox was nicked on Friday.'

'Friday? The day before . . .' I felt almost dizzy with relief.

Edward looked a bit sheepish. 'And I'm really sorry about . . .'

I nodded.

Teddy was looking up at each of us, not understanding a thing about the conversation going on over his head.

'So, have the police worked out who really did do it?' I asked.

'They're examining the tapes. They think there's every chance they'll be able to identify the culprit. They also think that, unless it was stolen to order, they'll get it back. If it was just an opportunist crime the thief will have a difficult time shifting it.' He smiled at me. 'And they hadn't got round to organising someone to see your par— your mother and Dave so there's no need to worry about them.' He met my eyes. 'I'm really sorry. I've caused you all sorts of worry and hideous embarrassment and I owe you an apology. I really need to make it up to you somehow.'

I shook my head. 'It wasn't your fault.' No, I thought angrily, it was bloody Zoë's, but I kept my thoughts to myself.

'I shouldn't have listened to what Zoë said and I was out of turn when I told you.'

I sighed. He was right, but just because Zoë was a bitch didn't give me licence to behave like one too. And at least I now knew for certain that Edward didn't share her assumptions. 'Well,' I said as lightly as I could, 'maybe I said a few things out of turn too.'

'I'm not surprised. When I saw your reaction I knew I was completely wrong and so was Zoë. Of course you wouldn't have been involved with anything like that and neither would anyone connected to you. You were perfectly right to get as angry as you did.'

'No I wasn't,' I protested. It was my turn to feel hideously embarrassed. 'I said some dreadful things.'

Edward shook his head. 'And I was way out of order.'

Teddy scuffed at some stones on the path. 'Come on, Lucy,' he said, tugging at my hand.

'I . . . um. I put a letter on your desk before I came out.'

'Yes, I know.'

'Oh.'

'I tore it up.'

'Oh.'

'You didn't seriously think I would accept your resignation?'

I stared at him and nodded.

Edward ruffled my hair. 'Don't be stupid,' he said quietly.

'Lu-u-uceee,' Teddy whined.

'Teddy's getting bored,' I said, thankful for the distraction.

'Then we must find something fun to do. Would you like that, Teddy?'

Teddy stared solemnly at his father as if weighing up the pros and cons of the offer. 'What?' he said after a pause.

Edward looked at the boat house. 'We could go for a row?'

Teddy jumped up and down. 'In a boat!'

'In a boat.'

'Can Lucy come?'

'If Lucy would like to.'

'Lucy would like to very much,' I said.

Edward led the way to the back of the boat house. He bent down by the door and pulled away a curtain of ivy growing up the wooden wall. 'Not secure,' he said, as he produced a large key from under the foliage, 'and the local bobby would have a fit if he knew, but there's nothing in here to pinch but the boat.'

The key grated in the lock and Edward swung the door open. The interior was cold, damp and dark, but I could see an oily gleam of still water.

'Just a minute, and I'll find the light.'

Edward disappeared into the building and a second later the darkness was replaced by the glow of electric light. Then I saw him move along to the far end of the shed and unbolt the big doors that led to the lake. He pushed them open and daylight flooded in. I killed the light and held on to Teddy's hand tightly as he began to jump up and down in excitement.

'A boat, a boat!'

And there it was, a wonderful old wooden rowing boat, lying perfectly still on the water.

'Well, what did you expect?' said Edward with a smile. 'An elephant?'

'Silly Daddy.'

Edward grabbed a couple of life jackets off a hook and stepped down into the little craft, which caused it to rock alarmingly. He held his hand out for Teddy, who stepped gingerly in to join his father. Edward instantly bundled him into the jacket and fastened the Velcro straps.

'Now you,' he said, and held his hand out.

I grasped it and stepped in. It seemed to me that Edward held on to my hand for longer than was strictly necessary. Gently I removed it and took the life jacket. I sat down next to Teddy and slipped the buoyancy aid over my head.

'Let me help you,' he said. Again, it wasn't necessary, but I allowed him to. In the musty old boat house and in the close confines of the little boat the feeling of intimacy was incredibly strong – even with Teddy watching us. Edward fastened the life jacket securely, our knees touching as he leaned forward to deal with the straps.

'There,' he said as he finished and sat back. I wanted the moment to carry on, but it was over. I smiled at him and he smiled back, but his was a smile of cheerful friendliness, nothing more.

'Come on,' said Teddy impatiently.

'You're right,' said Edward. 'What are we waiting for?'

I knew what I was waiting for, I thought, and I also knew how unlikely it was to happen.

I sat with Teddy on one of the planks that ran across the middle of the boat. I was sure there would be a nautical term for it but 'plank' seemed to do very nicely for now. Edward got busy with the mooring rope and then he sorted the oars out. With a few gentle strokes he had the little craft out of the boat house and into the sunshine. Teddy hung over the side trailing his hand in the water and I hung on to the waistband of his trousers while I revelled in the peace and quiet, which was broken only by the quiet plashing of the oars and the creak of the rowlocks. I was miles away when Edward's voice interrupted my thoughts.

'I remember I promised to teach you how to row. Do you fancy a go?'

'What, now?'

'Isn't now as good a time as any?' He patted the plank next to him. 'You take one oar, I'll take the other and let's see how you do. It isn't difficult.'

I hauled Teddy back into the boat and asked him to sit very still. Then, gingerly, I moved over to share the middle plank with Edward. The boat wasn't big and it seemed to rock dreadfully while I was moving the couple of feet to join him. Teddy hung on to the side and giggled at the movement. I had a feeling he thought that falling in might be a bit of a lark until I convinced him that the water was freezing, at which point he moved squarely to the middle of his seat.

Edward pulled my oar across my lap and told me to hold it with both hands. 'Then you move it like this.' He demonstrated slowly, and with just the one oar being used the boat turned in a little circle. 'Now you.'

The first stroke was fine. I dipped the blade into the water and felt the resistance as I pulled against it. The second time I didn't get it in deep enough and it skimmed across the surface. I nearly fell off the back of my seat.

'Try again,' said Edward encouragingly. He shipped his oar and put his hands over mine. He was sitting so close to me I could feel his leg pressing against mine. Now this other contact as well. I could feel my heart racing and it certainly wasn't from the effort of trying to row. I tried to concentrate on what I was doing but it was almost impossible. All I could think about was Edward and the feelings I had for him.

After a few more strokes I thought I understood the actions.

'I think I've got it now.'

'Really?'

I looked at him and his eyes were just inches from my own. I stared into their deep brown depths. I could feel his breath on my skin . . .

'Come on,' said Teddy.

I laughed and looked at him. He was adorable but his sense of timing was really off.

It was getting on for Teddy's teatime when we got back from the lake, laughing and joking about my shocking attempts at rowing as we walked into the house.

'You'll never be a threat to Steve Redgrave, that's for sure,' said Edward as we crossed the hall.

'I'm surprised you can be so light-hearted when you've lost some valuable property,' said Zoë from the den doorway.

The three of us stopped in our tracks.

'Hello,' said Edward.

'I came to see if there was anything more I could do to help solve the mystery.' I felt like saying she done quite enough. 'Give evidence, make a statement.' She stared at me.

'I dare say the police will get in touch with you if they need you,' said Edward lightly. 'They seem to have it all under control. They've worked out when it disappeared, on Friday.' Did I imagine it, or did he put extra emphasis on that word? 'I shouldn't think it'll be long before they get a result.'

'I see. Well . . .' Had she noticed that he was telling her Mum and Dave had nothing to do with the incident? If she had, she was doing a fine job of ignoring it. She moved towards Edward and stood next to him. 'I'm glad for you.' She smiled at him and then shot me a look of sheer triumph. She was staking her claim to him and reminding me that she was a friend whereas I was just an employee.

'I'll take Teddy upstairs,' I said, feeling superfluous. 'Thanks for the rowing lesson.'

Edward smiled at me. 'It was fun. We must do it again sometime.'

'Rowing? How droll,' tinkled Zoë as they walked off together towards the den.

I knew Edward was angry with Zoë and I knew he didn't particularly like her but his good manners stopped him from revealing it. And that was probably why he had been nice to me all afternoon – just good manners, to make up for the mistake earlier that day.

It was all it was.

I gave Teddy his supper, then we played some games, he had his bath and finally he got into his pyjamas, dressing gown and slippers.

'Shall we go and find Daddy and say goodnight? We could see if he wants to read you a story.'

'Yes please,' said Teddy.

I took his hand and led him down the stairs to the ground floor. Smith, with a tray of plates and serving dishes, was making his way across the hall.

'His lordship is in the dining room, miss,' he said, guessing my mission.

'Thank you.'

We crossed the tiled floor and I opened the door to the big dining room. I couldn't think of anywhere less cosy for dinner for two – it was fine for entertaining, but for a tête-à-tête? Acres of polished mahogany, all those pictures round the walls gazing stonily down on you? No thanks. Give me a tray and a TV set any day.

But I was wrong. There was Zoë almost snuggled up to Edward at the end of the table, a big candelabra spilling soft light into a pool, casting interesting shadows around them and enfolding them in a private space. And Teddy and I were gatecrashing.

'Teddy's just come to say goodnight,' I piped up breezily to cover my discomfiture at interrupting their intimacy.

Teddy ran into the room to give his father a hug while I hovered by the door. I saw Zoë shift her gaze to me. She regarded me coolly and leaned just a little closer towards Edward, her hand reaching out and touching his arm. I knew what she was indicating – that Edward had chosen to spend time with her and not me. She was there enjoying his company and I was about to be banished back to the nursery. She was silently underlining just where my place was in the great scheme of things. I was never going to be invited to an intimate dinner like this. My place wasn't here, being waited on by the staff. I was only going to be here when I was needed to look after Teddy. Without him I was completely surplus to requirements. And she was right.

Teddy finished saying goodnight.

'I'll be up in a minute to read to you. Choose a book – not too long though.' Edward dropped me a wink. 'Make sure he doesn't pick some huge great tome.'

I smiled back. Zoë looked daggers. 'Would you like me to read to you, Teddy?' she offered. I could tell the idea appalled her but she wanted to look as though she was taking some sort of interest in Edward's only child.

'No, thank you,' said Teddy, puzzled.

Keeping my face as straight as I could, I held out my hand. 'Come along, Teddy. Let's go and find a nice picture book.'

We went back upstairs. Teddy ran to his bookshelf and hauled out an old favourite, then trotted over to his bed and climbed in. I'd just tucked him up when Edward appeared. I left them to it while I pottered around the nursery, tidying Teddy's clothes, putting them in the laundry bin and clearing away the games we'd played with after supper.

Edward finished the story, Teddy snuggled down and I moved to switch off the main light.

'Would you like to join Zoë and me for a drink after supper?' Edward asked. 'You'd be very welcome.'

I contemplated the offer for a second. Was this another display of good manners? Did he feel sorry for me, stuck up here on the top floor? Did he really want my company? I couldn't work that one out, but I knew I'd make an enemy of Zoë if I accepted. Probably not a good idea.

'I don't think so.'

'Goodnight, then.' He shut the door behind him.

I wandered into my flat thinking I'd made the wrong decision, and feeling very lonely.

The week went on routinely: the police plodded on with their inquiries but assured Edward they would be recovering the snuffbox soon, and Zoë disappeared again. Teddy and I did our own thing and didn't see much of Edward. I knew he was about: I often heard him clattering around the private apartments, I recognised his voice coming from the offices near the nursery and I saw his beaten-up old Land Rover thundering around the estate. He popped in to see Teddy now and again but I found it easier to find things to do in my flat or in the nursery kitchen than to meet him. I wasn't sure why I didn't want to spend time in his company – after all, I knew I really liked him. It just seemed easier to keep some space between us. Anyway, I was staff and I should know my place.

The weather stayed sunny and bright and summer definitely seemed to be on its way. The trees in the park were vibrant in their new foliage, baby animals were everywhere and the days were longer and warmer. The end of the week was particularly glorious. After I'd dropped Teddy at playgroup I decided to treat myself to a few minutes on the roof. The sun was warm, the sky clear and the air still. I thought the view from the top of the house would be spectacular.

When I got back to the top floor I went along to the estate offices just to make sure that no one would have any objection if I took myself up the back stairs. There was no one in. Presumably Jenny was off in the main house sorting out staff or discussing a future event, and I imagined that Hugh and Edward were using the excuse of a lovely day to visit the farms or check out the gardens.

I took myself back along the corridor and found the hidden door. I flicked on the lights and climbed up the stairs. At the top I pushed open the skylight and climbed out. I wasn't disappointed. Around me stretched acres of park, the great trees now cloaked in shades of green that ran from vibrant acid to more subdued olive. The lake shone and glinted in the still air. No diamond sparkles today as the air was so still; today it was a pool of quicksilver. Over in the distance I could see the Home Farm sheep grazing peacefully on the hill and the bleats of the mothers and the higher-pitched ones of the lambs just reached me if I strained my ears. A blackbird, perched on one of the many chimney pots, was belting out his song. I knew how he felt. I felt like singing too.

I sat down on the warm lead that covered the expanse of roof and leaned against one of the huge chimney stacks. I was in full sun and completely sheltered. I basked like a cat and lapped up the warmth. Below me I saw the first of the days' punters start to arrive in the car park. A couple of coaches pulled up with a hiss and squeak of brakes. Several cars trundled up the long drive, their shiny paint gleaming in the sun. The voices of the disembarking tourists floated up to me, not distinctly enough for me to make out what was being said but clearly enough for me to recognise that the tone sounded happy; I could hear laughter in amongst the chat.

Reluctantly, after a while, I decided that I did actually have some work to be getting on with and this wasn't achieving it. I got up and made my way back down the steps. I was about to exit on to the landing when, in a fit of curiosity, I wondered where the stairs went if I continued on down. Edward had told me that they were so the maids could access various rooms of the house with supplies of coal and water without cluttering up the main stairs and getting in the way of the rich and titled occupants. I wondered which other rooms and areas were accessed from here. The stairs were precipitious and uncarpeted as I stole down them. I came to a tiny landing with a door. I tried it and it opened into one of the spare bedrooms on the floor below. I shut the door and continued down. The next door I came to was locked. I wondered if I would be able to get out on the ground floor.

My shoes clacked quietly on the stone steps as I crept down carefully, not wishing to miss my footing. The banister was a piece of rope attached to the wall by some antique-looking rings. If I needed it for active support I wasn't sure whether it would hold my weight. I didn't want to put it to the test. The stairs came to an end and I could see a rectangle of faint light gleaming round the edge of a door. Gently I pushed it and it swung open. I peered round the door and recognised the trophies and portraits: Edward's shrine to Becca. I stepped out, expecting to find the room empty.

'Lucy!' said Edward.

I nearly leapt out of my skin and I gave a yelp of shock. He was standing by the big desk.

'What are you doing here?' He didn't sound happy. Well, obviously. He'd come into the study to be alone with his memories of Becca, and then I barge in on him and destroy the moment. Of course he wouldn't be pleased.

I felt mortified. I could feel my face burning. 'I'm sorry,' I stammered. 'I went up on to the roof. I hope you don't mind, but it was such a lovely day.' I looked at him, wondering what he was thinking, but he was inscrutable. He was just staring at me and I still had to come up with an explanation as to why I was here. 'Anyway, on my way back down the stairs I thought I'd explore. I'm sorry,' I finished lamely. 'I didn't mean to intrude.'

His face softened a little. 'You haven't. Your sudden appearance was just a surprise.'

'I'll go. I'm interrupting.'

He looked puzzled. 'Interrupting what?'

'Well . . .' I stopped.

Edward stared at me. 'Yes,' he said after a pause.

I plucked up some courage from somewhere. 'You

must have loved her very much.' I gestured at the room and its contents again.

Edward gave me a smile accompanied by a shrug and a little shake of his head. I thought he looked immensely lonely and sad. 'Don't let me keep you,' he said.

I was being dismissed. He wanted to be alone and I was in the way. I edged to the door and scuttled out, feeling mortified for getting under his feet at such a private moment. I went back up to the nursery by the main stairs to while away an hour or so before I had to pitch up at the playgroup to collect my charge.

When I got to the village, just after twelve, Teddy rushed out of the hall to tell me about a story they'd had that morning involving kittens.

'Can we go and see Annie's kittens again? Please?'

It sounded like a good way of passing a pleasant sunny afternoon, providing we weren't going to get under Annie's feet or upset any plans she might have had. I promised I'd ring to ask if we could go over as soon as we got back to the nursery. Teddy's chatter, and later the business of cooking his lunch, drove all thoughts of my rather embarrassing encounter with his father earlier out of my mind.

Annie was thrilled at the idea of seeing Teddy so after lunch he and I piled into my little car and off we went to Home Farm. Annie was there to greet us and ushered us into the kitchen where Puss and her family had now taken up residence.

'I don't know why she never has them here in the first place. All nice and warm, not like the draughty old barn,' said Annie. 'But that's cats for you. They do their own thing.'

She found some old knitting wool for Teddy and some bits of paper he could scrumple up into balls, then made tea for us and poured a glass of creamy milk for him, although he was far too interested in hurtling around the kitchen table dragging a piece of wool in front of a posse of kittens to be the least bit interested in drinking it.

'They'll all be exhausted soon,' I said.

'Most young things only have "stop" and "go" buttons,' said Annie. 'And it's good to see how much he's livened up since you've been here.'

I felt warm with the praise. 'Was his dad like this as a kid – like Teddy is now?'

'Pretty much,' said Annie as she sipped her tea. 'He always liked animals and used to spend hours roaming round the estate as a child, watching the wildlife. And then, when I married Mike, he used to come over here in his holidays to help out.'

'Sounds idyllic.'

'I think he liked the company as well as the animals. There were always people here – you can't leave a farm to run itself.'

I thought of the big house and the staff that would have been there, all probably too busy with their duties to care much about one small boy. Even surrounded by dozens of people I could see that he might have been quite lonely.

Teddy had now given up running around and was lying on the rug in front of the Aga letting the kittens swarm over him. Their mother looked down on them from the arm of the sofa, her eyes closing drowsily; off duty. I knew the feeling.

Annie and I chatted on about life on the farm and the work her mother and her grandmother had done up at the big house; the entertaining, the dinner parties, the weekend shoots with a house full of people down from London.

Puss, her family and Teddy, I noticed, were all now asleep near the Aga, Teddy flat out on the floor with one kitten nestled in the crook of his arm, another curled up on his stomach and a third resting its head on his leg. I collected the trio and put them on the sofa near their mother. I didn't think the floor was an ideal place for Teddy to sleep so I asked Annie if there was a bed I could put him on, then picked him up and followed her upstairs. He didn't wake as I transferred him to a room he'd obviously used before, to judge by the toys and books on the shelves.

'Tell me about Edward when he was Teddy's age,' I said when we returned to the kitchen.

'There's not much to tell. He wasn't here very much. His sort get packed off to boarding school almost as soon as they're out of nappies. It might have been better for him if he'd had a load of brothers and sisters.'

'Shame Teddy hasn't any siblings,' I said.

Annie looked at me and raised an eyebrow. 'Yes, well.'

I'd put my foot in it again. Of course Teddy didn't have any siblings. Poor Becca had died so very young, she'd never had the chance to produce a little brother or sister for him.

'Becca wasn't maternal at all, you know,' said Annie.

Her directness surprised me but I didn't comment. I knew lots of people were of the opinion that a mother who employed a nanny did so because she couldn't be bothered to make the effort to raise her own kids. I also knew that, as a general rule, this absolutely wasn't the case, but I was equally well aware that you couldn't tell that to the 'earth mothers' of the world. And Annie had all the outward signs of being an earth mother. Don't get me wrong, I loved her to bits, but she was a nurturer by nature and she just couldn't understand that not all women were like her; that careers, driving ambition, the need to keep the family afloat financially or a dozen other reasons all made it impossible for some women to kick off their shoes and get up close to domesticity.

'And she wasn't no animal lover either,' said Annie.

That did shake me. 'What?' I shook my head in disbelief. 'But her horses. She must have had the most amazing rapport with them to be able to get them to do what they did.'

Annie shook her head vehemently. 'Huh!' She must have seen my expression of complete disbelief. 'Oh, that's what she wanted everyone to think. That's why they all voted for her as Sports Personality of the Year. Sports Personality of the Year, my giddy aunt. If the public had known how she treated her horses they'd have been ringing the RSPCA, not the BBC.'

'The RSPCA?'

'She killed one horse. Killed it by making it jump too high. It was entirely her fault that the poor beast broke its leg and had to be destroyed, and she didn't care at all. She and Jed were always having rows.' As Annie shook her head I remembered that video I'd watched, the one where Becca had lashed at a horse with her crop and then hit Jed. And I knew with cold certainty that Annie wasn't lying. 'She was a nasty piece of work. Not the saint the public thought she was. I tell you, she could be a hellcat, and that's why most of the old staff upped and left. They couldn't take working for her. One after another they gave in their notice. All Edward's old servants, or almost all, at any rate.' Annie sighed heavily. 'Of course, he blamed himself that some of his loyal old friends, because that's what they were, felt forced to go, but it was her or them.' Annie looked down at her lap. 'And it made him so lonely. But it was Hobson's Choice, so what could he do? Throwing her out was hardly an option.'

I thought back to all the pictures I'd seen in the glossy gossip mags, of him and Becca at all the balls and parties, and remembered that I'd thought what an exciting social life the two of them must have had with all those friends, all those invitations, and how I'd envied them and the glamour that surrounded them. I hadn't seen that she might be difficult – spoiled even – and very tricky to live with.

'So it wasn't a bed of roses,' I said slowly.

Annie shook her head. 'The trouble with roses is that they have nasty spiky little thorns.'

I'd never looked at it like that, but Annie was right. Roses, even beautiful long-stemmed ones, weren't something anyone would want to snuggle up with.

'Mind you,' continued Annie, 'I think Becca wasn't alone in the horsy world in being a nasty piece of work. That Zoë McMahon isn't any better than she ought to be.'

Well, I knew that. Look at what she'd said to the police about Mum and Dave.

'And now she wants Billy Boy,' continued Annie.

'So?'

'I think she'll play dirty to get him.'

'Oh, come off it. She can't be that bad.'

Annie gave me a steady look and raised her eyebrows. 'You don't think so?'

'Well . . .' I hardly knew the woman, although I knew I didn't like her. There had been that accusation, and she didn't like me – she'd made that perfectly clear. I had a suspicion that the two things were linked. However, I'd always got the impression that she was after Edward, and surely if she got him Billy Boy would be part of the package. 'But . . .' I started. I tried to articulate what had just gone through my mind, and made another effort. 'But I thought that Zoë and Edward . . .' I trailed off again. I was the new kid on the block here and I didn't want to look as if I had been prying into Edward's private affairs, but neither did I want to look completely dim. However, I suspected that right now I was managing to achieve both. Shut up, Lucy, I said to myself. Stop digging the hole.

'Edward isn't interested in Zoë; at least, I'll wager good money he isn't, if I know him. Which is why Zoë might do something underhand,' said Annie.

'But what on earth *could* she do?'

'There were rumours. When Becca was away there were stories about things she got up to.'

'I'm sorry, I'm not following.'

'There was a man. Well, men possibly, but one man in particular: Justin Naylor.'

I shuddered involuntarily. That drunken letch at the dinner party.

'He was on the international circuit with Becca and Zoë, and Zoë has hinted that she has evidence of what he and Becca got up to. Edward is desperate that it doesn't get made public. You know what the press are like, and he's terrified of a scandal that would haunt Teddy for the rest of his life. So if he doesn't let her have Billy Boy . . .'

'That *would* be playing dirty.' A thought struck me. 'So why doesn't he just let her have the horse? I mean, he doesn't ride it.'

'He's adamant she can't have it.'

'But why on earth not? I mean, if she might go to the press . . .' I shrugged. I didn't understand. Wasn't protecting Teddy more important than anything else?

'Because Zoë treats her animals no better than Becca did. Edward says Billy Boy doesn't need any more of that. He says he owes it to the horse.'

Now I was completely baffled. 'But Billy Boy killed Becca.' It didn't seem to add up to me. Teddy, Becca, Billy Boy . . . I just couldn't get a handle on Edward's priorities.

'It wasn't just the horse that died she treated badly. She beat all her horses something cruel. They jumped because they were frightened of her, not because they wanted to. And Billy Boy was no different,' said Annie. 'And Jed. If she didn't get results she blamed him. It was never her fault. It was never her riding that let her down. It was always his training. Or the horses. Some days he used to come home almost in tears. But he stuck with the job because he was afraid of the sort of trainer she might employ if he left. But he really hated her for what she did to those creatures. It was no wonder the police thought he might have had something to do with her death. Frankly,' she said grimly, 'the wonder was that he didn't.'

'He hated her that much?'

'He wasn't alone. You ask anyone who worked round the house. It was horrible while she was here. Horrible.'

'It must have been.'

'And I can't say that anyone on the estate was anything but glad when she died. Isn't that a dreadful thing to say?'

It must have been like something out of an Agatha Christie country house murder mystery. Except that it wasn't, and the butler hadn't done it, or the groom. It had been the horse who did it, not some shadowy figure lurking in the stables. It had been an accident. A very convenient accident, but that was all it had been.

'I suppose they blamed Jed because a horse was involved.'

'They thought he gave some signal which made Billy Boy lash out.'

'But he didn't.'

Annie snorted. 'Like Jed could do something like that.'

But I'd seen the way Becca had mistreated him and wondered if perhaps she hadn't pushed him too far. And I'd seen that spectacular move he'd taught Billy Boy – the one that involved leaping in the air and kicking out backwards. Of course Annie wouldn't want to think that her son might be capable of murder, but to be honest, if Becca had treated me like that I might have done it myself. But the police had concluded it had been an accident, so that was that.

Annie decided we needed more tea and bustled about the kitchen making it. I was left to think once again about Edward and Becca.

Had he turned a blind eye to Becca's faults because he loved her so much? Or had Annie exaggerated her faults because she was still harbouring a grudge about the way Becca had treated her only son – a son who obviously wasn't equipped to fight back?

And I could hardly go around asking awkward questions about my employer's dead wife of other people, no matter how curious I felt. Talk about food for thought.

Edward met me as I took Teddy upstairs for his tea. 'I'd like you to join me after Teddy is asleep.' It wasn't a request.

'Certainly,' I said, wondering what he wanted to talk to me about.

'Say, eight o'clock in the den.'

'I'll be there.' Teddy and I went on our way to the nursery. At eight o'clock, the radio alarm in my pocket and Teddy fast asleep in his bed, I presented myself in the den.

'Drink?' Edward offered.

'No thank you.'

'Sure? You're off duty.'

I shook my head. I had a feeling that this wasn't going to be a cosy chat.

'As you wish.' Edward poured himself a Scotch and added a splash of soda. 'Take a seat.' I perched on the big sofa. 'I want you to know that I think you've been doing a fantastic job with Teddy.'

I felt my face colouring, embarrassed by the praise. Why did this man always make me feel so mixed up? One moment he made me feel gauche or in the way and the next I wanted to burst with pleasure and pride at something he said. He seemed either to ignore me or to make me the centre of attention. Perhaps one day I would get used to such swings, but for the time being it did my head in.

'He's had more fun since you arrived than I can ever remember. He's really come out of himself. You've been wonderful.'

'Thank you.' I stared at my feet, feeling even more excruciatingly embarrassed by his praise.

'The thing is, Lucy, I'm worried you're not happy here. This place is in the middle of nowhere. I know you must have had much more of a social life when you lived in London and I wouldn't blame you if you'd had enough of us here.'

What? Was he trying to get rid of me? Surely not. I shook my head vehemently. 'No, I love it. Honest.'

'But that business with Zoë and the police. I mean, I handled that so badly. I wouldn't blame you if you decided you couldn't work for me any more.'

I stared at him. I couldn't work out what he was trying to do. Was he trying to make me feel I ought to leave for some reason? But why? He'd as good as told me I was doing my job perfectly. It didn't make sense. Unless . . . unless Zoë didn't want me around. My earlier conversation with Annie swirled around in my head but I wasn't Machiavellian enough to make use of it or clever enough to fish out the details I needed right now.

Maybe Edward took my silence for disapproval or something. 'I'm sorry, I shouldn't have mentioned anything,' he rushed on. 'You mustn't feel under any pressure. You must do what you feel is necessary.'

I shut my eyes and took a breath, even more confused. After what Annie had said about Zoë and fighting dirty . . . I wondered if I was adding two and two and making five, but on the other hand . . . But then I remembered Teddy. Suddenly I didn't care what Zoë's agenda was, but I did care about Teddy. 'No,' I said quietly and steadily. If Zoë wanted rid of me for her own ends she was going to have to really fight. There was no way I was going to give in if it meant Teddy's being left to her mercies. No way. 'You mustn't worry about me. I'm very happy here.' I was about to say more but something made me hold my tongue.

Edward stared at me very hard. 'I can't believe—' he started, but I interrupted.

'I really am very happy here. Honestly.'

He slowly put the glass down on the table. 'You mean it. Despite my monumental cock-up over that bloody snuffbox, and the fact that I was rather rude to you today in the study.'

I smiled and shook my head. Thank God I hadn't favoured him with my opinion of Zoë. Thank God for whatever twist of fate had made me shut up at a critical moment. I'd got it so wrong. This had nothing to do with the Zoë factor and a lot to do with Edward making a crap attempt at an apology, again. 'Hey, you made it up to me about the snuffbox when you took me rowing, and as for this morning – well, I gave you a helluva fright. Mind you, you gave me one too so I suppose we're quits. Anyway, I love Teddy to bits and I promised faithfully I'd stick around for at least three years – if you want me to, that is.'

'Actually, I do.' He was staring at me very intently.

He was messing with my head again and I felt flooded with confusion. To cover it up I said, 'Well, that's settled then.' I tried to say it lightly but instead it came out all brisk and prim.

A whimper issued from the radio alarm. 'That's Teddy,' I said, relieved. 'I'd better go.'

'Must you?'

'One of us must,' I said firmly, needing the excuse to be on my own to collect my thoughts.

I settled Teddy and sat by him while he dropped off to sleep again, then wandered into my own bedroom. I sat on my dressing-table stool and pulled open the top drawer. There, in the corner, was the scrumpled-up hanky – the one Edward had given me the night we'd first met, the night I'd brained him, the night I'd burst into tears. I took it out and pressed it to my nose. It didn't smell of anything much; cotton and a hint of fabric softener, but it had been his.

I sat there in the soft light of my bedside lamp and thought about Edward. I tried to tell myself I was just star-struck; besotted with a handsome celebrity who happened to toss me the odd kind word now and again. I was just overwhelmed with the closeness of a famous guy who was single and good looking and kind to me, who paid me compliments and gave me his attention. I thought about the visit to the roof, the trip in the boat on the lake, the book he'd put by my bed. Then I told myself that he had just been showing me round, trying to make me feel at home . . . But then there had been that look, and his relief that I wasn't going.

But who was I kidding, I asked myself angrily, making myself face reality. He might not want Zoë but she was much more his type. She, or someone like her, fitted seamlessly into his world and background, but me? Huh! I thought about how often I got the wrong end of the stick, how I hadn't been able to cope with the dinner party, how I didn't know how to deal with the awful Jason, how everyone else around him was completely surefooted in every conceivable social situation.

Of course he didn't fancy me. He was just being nice, trying to make me feel welcome, a valued member of his team and all that. I expect it was just the good manners of a proper education and good breeding. Being 'nice' again.

I stuffed the hanky back in the drawer and slammed it shut.

I heard a knock at the outer door of my sitting room – what was, in effect, my front door. I tramped through and opened it. It was Edward. My heart raced.

'I came this way in case Teddy was restless. I didn't want to disturb him if you'd been having trouble getting him back to sleep, and I thought going straight into the nursery might wake him again.'

'He's fine.' I had problems keeping my voice steady. 'Probably just a dream. He's out for the count now.' What did Edward want? There really wasn't anything else to say, was there? 'Did you want to see him?'

Edward lingered by the door. 'No. I don't want to risk disturbing him.'

There was more silence. I felt uncomfortable. 'I'm sorry,' I said. 'Did you want to talk to me about anything else?'

He gave me another long look, then said, 'No. That's fine. I'm sorry I disturbed you.'

But I was sure there was something else he wanted to say, to tell me, and hadn't.

I was awoken the next morning by scufflings and shufflings outside my bedroom door. It might have been Saturday, but kids Teddy's age don't do lie-ins.

'Come in if you want, Teddy,' I called. 'I'm awake.'

The door swung open and Teddy leapt in and bounced on my bed. He was followed by Edward bearing a tray.

Instinctively I pulled the covers up.

'What on earth is this?' I cried.

'I was awake early,' explained Edward, setting the tray down on my dressing table, 'and I came up here to see if Teddy was awake. He was and we both thought you might like some breakfast. So here it is.'

'But *you* don't make *me* breakfast.'

'Why not? Is there anything in the rules that says I can't? In fact,' said Edward, putting a mug of steaming tea on my bedside table, 'I think you'll find that this is my house, so my rules.'

'But what about the other staff? I mean, they'll think . . .' I blushed. What did I think they'd think?

'They won't think anything. I realised that I was going to be here on my own this weekend – well, apart from you and Teddy – so I gave them all the weekend off.'

'Your house, your rules,' I said, still a bit woozy with sleep.

'Exactly. There's no point making people hang about to look after me when I'm perfectly capable of taking care of myself.'

'I didn't say you couldn't.'

Edward handed me the tray, which boasted a plate of creamy scrambled eggs on toast plus some more slices of toast – brown and white – and a pot of home-made marmalade.

'I hope that's okay?' He sounded anxious.

'I told Daddy you always drink tea in the morning,' said Teddy.

'It's perfect,' I said. 'And quite right about the tea, Teddy. Well done.'

Teddy looked as pleased as Punch and climbed off the bed.

'Come on, Teds,' said Edward. 'Let's leave Lucy to eat her eggs in peace. We'll go and have ours.'

'Oh,' Teddy whined. 'Can't we have ours here with Lucy?'

'There isn't room. Come on, we need to have ours before it gets cold.'

Teddy dragged his feet out of my bedroom. Through the open nursery door I could hear him protesting that he didn't want to sit up at the table.

'Come on, Teddy, be a good boy for Daddy.'

Even from where I was I could tell that Teddy's silence was sulky. I listened for a couple of seconds to the sound of Edward trying to cajole him into eating his breakfast. I could see that this was likely to end unhappily so I shoved my tray to the end of the bed and swung my feet to the floor. Slinging my dressing gown on and then picking up my breakfast tray, I made my way back into the nursery.

'Do you know,' I said brightly, 'I felt really lonely in my room with you two having a nice cosy breakfast here. Would you mind if I joined you?'

'Lucy,' squealed Teddy, as if I'd been separated from him by at least a continent and several weeks, not merely a few feet and about thirty seconds.

I put my tray on the table and caught Edward looking at me with a warm smile. My insides flip-flopped.

'I'll just get my tea,' I said, lowering my eyes. Breakfast in bed and now that smile – he was having a very disconcerting effect on me and I needed a breather to get myself under control. I didn't think it would do either of us any good if he knew quite what he was doing to me. It could certainly compromise our employer–employee relationship.

Teddy was happily tucking into his eggs when I returned with my mug, having taken a few deep and steadying breaths in my room. Edward leapt to his feet and pulled my chair away from the table for me to sit down.

'Thank you,' I said, touched by the display of old-fashioned manners. Then I attacked my eggs. They were fantastic, just the right consistency and seasoned to perfection.

'These are delicious,' I said, forgetting my own manners and speaking with my mouth full.

'Don't sound so surprised.' Edward was laughing at me. 'Men can cook too, you know.'

'Sorry.'

'Don't you know any men who can cook?'

I shook my head and concentrated on my eggs, knowing I was blushing furiously.

'So what are we going to do today, Teddy?' he said. I felt relieved that he'd moved his attention elsewhere.

With a whole world of opportunities to choose from, Teddy was at a loss. He stared at his father. 'I don't know.'

'Well, if Lucy lets us borrow it, we could fly the kite. Or we could go for a ride together.'

'Could Lucy come with us?'

'But I don't ride,' I told Teddy.

'You don't ride!' Teddy was aghast. 'Why not?'

'There was nowhere to learn when I was growing up. I lived in a big city and it wasn't possible.'

Teddy looked at me. 'No horses?'

I shook my head. 'Sorry, sweetie.'

'So how about a riding lesson?' said Edward.

I gulped. I wasn't sure I wanted to get that close to a horse. Leading little Toy Town round the indoor school was one thing. Getting on board one of the brutes was something else entirely. It would have to be something a whole heap bigger than Toy Town if my feet weren't going to drag along the ground like stabilisers.

'Come on. I'm sure you'll like it if you give it a go.'

I wasn't nearly so confident. 'I'll hold you up and spoil your fun,' I said, hoping Teddy would agree.

'We'd only go for a hack around the estate. We're not going to do anything too energetic, are we, Teddy?'

I wasn't sure if Teddy knew the meaning of the word

energetic, but he got the gist. 'Come with us, Lucy,' he said, grinning irresistibly at me.

'What else have you got to do?' asked Edward.

He had a point. What was I going to do? I didn't have to clean, my washing was minimal thanks to the laundry maid, and Cook provided the nursery kitchen with whatever I needed so I didn't have to do any shopping.

'I could finish *Swallows and Amazons*.'

'You mean you haven't? But you've had ages. I'm disappointed.'

'It's probably because I'm overworked,' I said solemnly. Edward's eyebrows shot up. 'You have no idea how exhausting it is playing games all day. All that crawling around on the floor building Duplo forts, being a tiger, doing jigsaws. And as for the games of football, well! Then there're story books to read, board games to play, Snap, Happy Families. It's non-stop.'

Edward was laughing openly now. 'If this is a pitch for a pay rise, I don't think my heartstrings have been tugged nearly enough.'

I was embarrassed again. 'Oh, no. I wasn't suggesting . . .' Oh, God, he'd got the wrong end of the stick.

'Joke,' he said.

I blushed even more. *I'd* got the wrong end of the stick and I'd made a fool of myself – again.

'So what about it?' he said quietly. The mood shifted again. He was staring at me with his fathomless eyes. 'Will you let Teddy and me take you out?'

'Pleeeeease, Lucy,' said Teddy.

I smiled at Teddy. How could I resist? Besides, if a

three-year-old child could ride, surely I could. I mean, just how difficult was it?

An hour later I was in the stables regretting my decision. And I regretted it even more when Zoë waltzed through the huge doors looking immaculate in a summer dress and cardigan.

After slightly stilted greetings had been exchanged (or was that just me interpreting things to suit myself?) it transpired that Zoë had just dropped in on her way to somewhere else.

'Do come, Edward. It'll be such fun, and my invitation is for "Zoë and guest",' she purred, completely ignoring Teddy and me. She pulled a piece of stiff card out of her bag and waved it at Edward. 'Look.'

'Absolutely can't,' said Edward impassively, ignoring the invitation. 'I have promised Teddy faithfully that we're all going for a ride.' He gazed at her outfit and strappy sandals. 'Of course, if you've got a change of clothes you could join us. You'd just have time before you had to be at your party.'

But, sadly, it seemed she hadn't. 'Oh, dear,' said Edward.

I tried to keep the smile off my face, and when I found I couldn't I had to take a turn round the stables to admire the horses.

'Look, Edward, I really need to have a word,' I heard her say.

There was a pause. Then, 'Come with me while I get the tack for the horses.'

The pair of them disappeared into the tack room, and

Teddy came over to me and slipped his hand into mine.

'I'm glad Zoë isn't coming with us,' he confided. 'I'm glad it'll be just you and Daddy and me.'

I smiled at him but didn't trust myself to agree with his sentiment, afraid of the feelings it would reveal.

Teddy and I wandered up and down the central aisle admiring the horses in the stables and getting slightly impatient, waiting for Zoë and Edward to reappear. It was about five minutes before she did, looking extremely sour and lugging an armful of saddle and reins. I wondered what had passed between them, although I guessed it probably had something to do with Billy Boy – again. And I also guessed she hadn't got her way – again. Tough, I thought, but I smiled at her. My smile wasn't returned.

'Zoë's going to tack up Willow for you,' called Edward from the tack room door. He had a similar burden of leather. 'Willow's incredibly gentle,' he added reassuringly as he strode to Toy Town's loose box and dumped the saddle on the wrought-iron railings that divided the loose box from the central aisle. Toy Town, ears pricked, eyes alert, sniffed at the saddle, anticipating an outing.

I looked at the horse Zoë was approaching. Willow might be gentle but she still looked huge and I thought about how high I was going to be when I was sitting astride her. I felt a flutter of panic begin to turn my insides to mush as Zoë led the horse out and began to saddle her up.

Edward and Zoë were quick and efficient and it wasn't long before all three animals were tacked up. I felt my insides sink. I couldn't bottle out of this now, but I really didn't want to hoist myself up on to Willow's back.

Edward saw me looking at my mount and perhaps he mistook my fear for eagerness.

'We'll have you up there in a jiffy,' he said jovially. 'But before we do we need to get you a hard hat.' He dived through a door at the back of the stables and came back a minute later with a smart navy blue velvet one. 'Try this,' he said, dumping it on my head. He put his hand on top of it and gave it a jiggle. The hat seemed to stay put. 'That'll do nicely,' he said. Then he reached under my chin and began to do the strap up. I was acutely conscious of his hand brushing my neck, and his proximity. I could feel his breath, warm against my face in the cool, still air of the stable. I kept my eyes lowered, terrified he'd read my thoughts in them.

'Hurry up,' called Teddy from Toy Town's back.

'Just coming,' said Edward. 'Must make sure Lucy is sorted out properly.'

'Great,' I said, swallowing down my nerves. I risked a glance up at him.

He was smiling that lazy smile of his, staring right into my eyes. Hastily I lowered them again and headed towards Willow, trying to assume an air of confidence that I certainly didn't feel.

He handed me the reins and explained carefully exactly what to do next. 'Then you swing your right leg over Willow's back and sit down in the saddle. Don't worry about anything except hanging on to the reins and sitting up straight.'

All very well for him to say I wasn't to worry. I was going to be the one right up in the air, sitting on the back of a huge great animal, with not the first idea how to control it.

'Right,' said Edward. 'Give me your leg.'

I cocked my left leg as I'd been told, reached up, grasped the reins and the front of the saddle, and then Edward cupped his hands under my knee.

'One, two, three,' he counted and then, as I jumped, I felt myself being launched into the air. I lifted my right leg and took it over Willow's back and the next second I plumped down in the saddle.

'Okay?' asked Edward, grinning up at me. I tried to smile back but I couldn't force it. I hung on to the front of the saddle as tightly as I could. Willow shifted her weight slightly and I felt myself sway alarmingly.

'Right, Zoë, if you'd just like to finish everything off for Lucy, I'll hop on board Firefly and then we needn't hold you up any more. Don't want to make you late for your lunch date.'

I looked down at the top of Zoë's head as she dealt with the stirrups and then shoved my feet into them. She slapped Willow on the rump.

'You'll do,' she said. 'Enjoy your ride.'

Why did I think it seemed unlikely that I would? And did I detect a sneer in her voice? Very likely, as she could obviously see I didn't have a clue what I was doing.

Edward swung himself effortlessly on to his own horse. I looked across at him and with him now at the same height I didn't feel quite so lofty. Then I looked at the ground again and felt another lurch of fear.

'All fixed?' asked Edward.

I supposed so. I nodded.

'Right. Follow me.' He made a clicking noise and Firefly moved off smoothly. Willow followed. I stifled a little cry as the horse moved under me. I saw Zoë roll her eyes in disgust. I consoled myself with the thought that I was going out with Edward and Teddy and she wasn't. Ya boo, I silently crowed, childishly.

Edward looked back. 'Just let your hips move with Willow's back. Try to keep your head still, and let your body do the work from the waist down.'

I switched my attention from Zoë to what I was doing on Willow. I tried to obey his instructions. I knew the theory of it from running beside Teddy when Jed gave him a lesson. However, it was one thing watching Teddy do it; it was quite something else having to do it myself.

'You wouldn't be afraid of falling off a sofa, now would you?' said Edward.

I shook my head.

'Then just think of Willow as a slow-moving piece of furniture. Honestly, her back is almost as wide as a sofa. And we're not going to go any faster than we are at the moment.'

The promise of moving no faster than this sedate amble made me feel less tense and I began to allow my body to loosen up. We clattered out of the stable yard and along the path that led to the park. Little Toy Town and Teddy seemed to be dwarfed between Firefly and Willow and Teddy kept gazing up at the pair of us, a broad smile on his face as his eyes moved from Edward to me and back again.

Edward kept giving me little bits of advice about riding – toes up, heels down, head still, back straight, hands down, that sort of thing. It seemed to me that I could correct one fault at a time but as I did it everything else went to pot. If my heels went down my hands went up. If I got my hands right, my head was wobbling all over the place. I just couldn't get it all going right all at once. I felt like screaming in frustration. Edward and Teddy were having a great laugh at my expense. Well, I was so glad to be the court jester! At least someone was getting some enjoyment out of my riding, as I wasn't sure I was.

We had left the complex of buildings and cobbled paths that spread around the main house and were now out in the park itself. Teddy was itching to show off his trotting to his father but the idea of going any faster myself filled me with abject fear.

'Tell you what,' said Edward, 'Teddy and I will zoom off to that tree and back. Is that okay?'

The tree was about a hundred yards ahead, on the other side of a small clump of bushes. Edward and Teddy reined their mounts in and Willow stopped too.

'Willow won't try to follow you?' I asked anxiously.

'Lord no, she's far too lazy. You'd have to really spur her on to get her to move.'

'Well, I shan't be doing that.' I still felt desperately worried but I didn't want to be a killjoy. 'You go on. I'll be fine,' I added in what I hoped was a confident voice.

'Come on then, Teddy, last one to the tree is a sissy. But no faster than a trot, okay!'

But Teddy had gone, his little legs kicking Toy Town's

fat flanks. Edward threw me a grin over his shoulder and set off after his son. The distance between us grew, not quickly but steadily, until I was alone, astride Willow. I gazed after the receding pair and felt Willow shift under me, but it seemed normal and natural and I shifted with her. I relaxed. We'd stand here together until the boys came back, enjoying the peace and quiet, the birdsong, the still air and the view, content to savour the mild spring air and our beautiful surroundings.

The pair of them were side by side as they passed the clump of bushes. I could hear their voices floating back towards me. Suddenly a noise like a creaking gate erupted out of the bushes, heralding a startled pheasant. Making a krick-krick sound, the bird shot out of the undergrowth, wings whirring in a blur, skimming the ground and heading straight for me and Willow. Both of us jumped; me nearly out of the saddle and Willow out of her skin. I felt her tense underneath me before she shot forward at top speed.

I know I screamed but the next few seconds were a complete blur of utter, total, gut-wrenching fear. And although I knew that Willow was galloping, I seemed to be passing over the ground in slow motion. I saw Edward and Teddy turn and stare at me. I felt my bum bouncing all over the saddle, then one foot came out of a stirrup. I was being jounced around, my teeth jarring in my head, my backside smacking hard on the saddle with each stride the horse took. My hat bumped down half over my eyes and I knew I was going to fall. I grabbed the saddle, but I could feel the whole thing sliding under me. I could grip as much as I liked, but the saddle was moving slowly down Willow's side, taking me with it. I dug my hand into Willow's mane in a desperate attempt to stop the inevitable but it only seemed to make her go faster. Beneath me I could see her flailing hooves. All I could think about was one of them connecting with my body. I thanked God for my hard hat, but it wasn't going to protect the rest of me. I braced myself.

'Edward,' I screamed as I finally lost my grip.

It seemed an age that I spent in the air before I connected with the ground. As soon as I hit the earth time became real again. Willow raced off, and pain speared through me. And then I was rolling over and over, bouncing across the tussocky grass. Something connected with my cheek and more pain exploded, followed by the salty metallic taste of blood in my mouth. The rolling stopped. I suppose at that point I must have blacked out.

I came round to feel my hand being stroked.

'Lie still, Lucy,' said Edward.

I didn't want to move. I ached and throbbed all over, my head felt as if it was going to explode and I could feel something trickling down the side of my face.

'You're going to be okay. I've rung for an ambulance and Annie's on her way.'

I opened my mouth but I couldn't find any words. I began to cry; the pain was so bad I couldn't help it.

'Don't move,' Edward commanded again. He sounded fraught.

'Teddy?' I managed to whisper.

'He's here. Don't you worry about us.'

The tears continued to trickle out of my eyes but I managed to open them a fraction. Edward was hovering over me, white and shocked.

'You had a bad fall.' He stroked my hand. 'And it's my fault. I shouldn't have let Zoë tack up Willow.'

I didn't understand. It was just one of those things. It wasn't anyone's fault, but it was all too complicated. I felt sick and tired and my eyes weren't focusing as they should. I shut them again.

'Lucy, stay with me,' said Edward, patting my hand.

I wanted to, but the blackness and oblivion were pulling harder and I let myself slip into them.

I remember bits and pieces of the next few hours: being put on a stretcher, being carried to the ambulance, having a mask put over my face, being given an injection for the pain, strip lights flashing above me as I was wheeled along the hospital corridors . . . In between the memories were areas of complete oblivion. I think I must have been dipping in and out of consciousness, or maybe it was a subconscious way of coping with the awfulness of it all and I just blanked the worst of it. I felt too awful to be afraid, and once I got to the hospital I just felt relief that now the doctors would work their magic. They'd give me something for the pain; they'd heal me. Of course they would; that's what doctors do. I let my mind drift as others took control.

Maybe I was sedated too as my next memory was of dim lights, of feeling thirsty, of a cool cloth on my forehead and Edward's voice telling me I was going to be fine. I could feel him stroking my fingers and I think I felt him kiss them. Or maybe, with all the drugs and the pain, I imagined it. I sank back into sleep and dreamed about him.

The next time I came round I was conscious that I was much more lucid. From behind my closed eyelids I was aware of my surroundings: the clatter of a hospital ward, the clack of the nurses' shoes on the hard floor, the rattle of curtains being drawn round a bed and the smell of disinfectant and hospital food. I listened to the sounds and breathed in the smells and wondered what the time was, but my eyes were gummed together and opening them just seemed too much of an effort. I lay still, wondering how much it would hurt if I tried to move, and attempted to work out which bits of me had been damaged the most from the dull aches and throbs I could feel.

'Lucy? Lucy?'

It was Edward's voice. I made my sticky, heavy eyes open a fraction. It was daylight again and there he was, unshaven, drawn, pale, looking as if he'd been up all night. He was staring at me.

'Edward,' I croaked. I tried clearing my throat but my mouth was too dry. 'What are you doing here? Who's looking after Teddy?'

'Teddy's fine. He spent the night with Annie. You mustn't worry about him.'

I shut my eyes again, feeling exhausted. But inside I could feel a glow from knowing that Edward had cared enough to stay with me. The glow curled around my insides, warming and soothing me. I felt comforted, almost as if I was being physically held. And being comforted, I slept again for a while.

The rest of that day was a bit of a roller coaster. I felt unaccountably weepy when Edward left at lunchtime to go home, have a wash, get something to eat and see Teddy. The nurse noticed and doled out more painkillers, which made me doze again. As supper approached I felt so much better I was able to quiz her about my injuries: a cracked collarbone, several broken ribs and a fractured cheekbone. She said I would be able to go home the next day. In fact, if I hadn't been unconscious for so long I would have been patched up and sent packing that morning but they wanted me in for observation for a bit longer to make sure I wasn't suffering from concussion.

When the painkillers waned after my evening meal, so did my spirits, and since I had slept so much during the day sleep eluded me completely. I was bored and cranky and sleep was the only thing I wanted and I wasn't going to get it. All I could do was lie in my bed and brood about my injuries and my feelings for Edward. I knew I was falling in love with him. I knew it was more than just a case of being star-struck now. But why had I fallen for someone so patently unobtainable? Did I just love him because he was kind to me? Because he made the effort to include me in his family life? Because he made me laugh? I convinced myself that I'd got it all wrong, and he'd only stayed by my bed out of guilt over the accident. Of course he didn't care for me, except as an employer. I was deranged, deluded and mistaken to ever think otherwise. Guys like him didn't give girls like me, girls from the suburbs, a second thought. Just like *Swallows and Amazons*, what was allowed in books and what was allowed in real life were worlds apart.

Like Edward and me.

And to cap it all I was sore and aching, fed up with being bed-bound, wobbly from the realisation that I might have been killed and worried about how I was going to cope with my injuries and look after Teddy. And if I couldn't do that, how long would I be allowed sick leave and what would happen when everyone's patience ran out? Would I be sent packing? Would I be made to give up my flat at Arden Hall so a fitter, healthier nanny could take over? I felt lower and lower.

Unexpectedly Edward came to see me that evening. Why, I wondered. It was quite a journey to the hospital and surely he had more important things to do with his spare time. As he walked down the centre of the ward towards my bed I told myself that visiting me was his duty as my employer. Or maybe he'd come to find out how long he was going to have to make alternative arrangements for Teddy's care. The one thing I was sure about was that he wasn't here because he wanted to be. And part of me didn't want him to be here either. I was sure I looked like shit and I was in such a low mood I didn't think I was going to be very good company. I suppose my feelings must have shown on my face.

'You're not to worry about getting back to work,' were Edward's first words after he'd asked me how I felt and I'd lied and said I was fine.

'But . . .'

'No buts. Annie is going to help you until you're properly back on your feet. I'm also going to put you in one of the spare rooms on the first floor so you don't have to haul yourself up to the top of the house. You're not to worry about anything, least of all coping with Teddy, until you're completely better.' He'd also brought some toiletries and clothes for going home in. Inexplicably his kindness made me feel weepy again and I felt tears trickling down my cheeks.

Edward sighed and took his hanky out. 'Don't you ever have one?' he asked as he handed it over.

I snuffled into it, feeling foolish and overwhelmed in equal measures. 'I'll buy you some more for Christmas,' I said damply.

'I think it'd be of more use to everyone if *I* bought *you* the hankies.'

He sat by my bed and told me about Teddy tormenting Puss and her kittens by playing with them non-stop all afternoon. Everyone at the Hall had been asking after me, he said.

'Of course I've told them all that I'm entirely to blame for what happened.'

'I didn't have to agree to go riding, and anyway it was an accident.'

Edward raised an eyebrow. 'Really?'

'Of course it was. If that pheasant hadn't spooked Willow . . .'

'You might have stayed on if your girth had been tight enough,' Edward interrupted. 'It was my fault it wasn't.'

But Zoë had tacked up Willow. 'I don't understand.'

'Zoë failed to tighten the girth. I should have checked it myself and I blame myself for trusting her.'

'Well, maybe it just slipped her mind.'

Edward raised both eyebrows. 'Zoë is a professional equestrienne. She wouldn't forget. It'd be like you forgetting to strap Teddy into his car seat when you set off on a journey.'

Well, put like that . . . 'Have you mentioned it to Zoë?' I asked.

Edward snorted. 'I did this morning. She says I'm mistaken. She even suggested you might have loosened it to get attention.'

'What!'

'Yes, that was my reaction too. You could sue her, you know,' he added.

I considered what he'd said. 'But supposing it just came loose by accident?'

'Trust me, girths don't, not if they're tightened properly.'

I didn't want to believe Edward's implication. It was deeply uncomfortable to think that Zoë hated me *that* much. And if I did something about it I would have to face that fact. On balance I thought I'd rather not. 'Look, what happened happened. And I'm okay. A bit bashed and battered, but okay. You can't beat yourself up about it. Maybe it was just one of those things.' Edward opened his mouth to disagree but I held a hand up to silence him. That was a mistake as it hurt like hell and I winced.

'Are you very sore?' asked Edward.

'Only when I do that.'

'Don't do it then,' he said with a wicked grin.

I laughed and that hurt too. 'Best I don't laugh either,' I said as a spasm of pain shot through my chest.

Edward stared at me. 'That's a shame,' he said quietly. 'Your face lights up when you laugh.'

'Anyway,' I said quickly, 'I didn't have to go riding with you and Teddy. I don't want to believe Zoë would have done such a thing deliberately and I don't think that making a big song and dance over it is going to help anyone. So let's forget it.'

'If that's what you want,' said Edward.

'It is.' But I wasn't sure how I'd cope if I ran into her again. Best I stayed out of her way, I resolved.

I was pronounced fit enough to go back to Arden Hall after the doctor had done his rounds the next morning. However, it was one thing being told I could get myself dressed ready to go, another thing entirely getting into my clothes with one arm strapped up and my ribs sending pain shooting through me every time I moved. I managed to struggle into my knickers and trousers but putting on a bra was out of the question. I was feeling sore, crotchety and exhausted when I finally managed to get my sweater on over my head and my one good arm down a sleeve, with the other one tucked in under. I struggled to the bathroom to drag a comb through my hair and was shocked by my bruised and battered face. Shit, no wonder it hurt when I smiled.

I leaned in to the mirror to examine the damage more closely. A nurse bustled in behind me and saw me staring.

'Don't worry,' she said cheerfully. 'The bruising will go down in a few days. In a week or two no one will be able to tell.'

'A week or two?' I was horrified. I looked like a freak. Things weren't helped by the state of my hair, but, frankly, tidying that up wasn't going to make a significant difference. I looked as if I'd come off worst in a brawl. I wondered what people would think when they saw me.

'By the way,' said the cheery nurse, 'your sweater is on back to front.'

I looked down and saw she was right. Did I have the energy to try to turn it round? I sighed. Bollocks to it. It could stay like that. It went with my lank hair and bruised face. I looked like an advert against domestic violence.

'You didn't tell me about the bruising,' I said to Edward when he appeared.

'You didn't ask,' he said with a hint of a grin.

'Funnily enough, when I meet people I might sometimes worry about having lipstick on my teeth or a smut on my nose, but I don't usually feel inclined to ask if I've got some hideous bruises.'

'They're not hideous,' said Edward.

I stared at him. 'Are you off your rocker? They're shockers.'

'I'll grant that they're impressive.'

'I could get a job in a circus looking like this,' I said.

'Only if you learn to ride a horse properly.'

His comment was so outrageous, given recent events, that I found myself giggling in spite of everything.

'That's better,' he said. 'You looked really miserable when I got here. Only to be expected, I suppose, but I'm going to make sure that you get spoiled rotten once we get you home. Your every wish will be my command.'

'Every wish?'

'Why, what do you have in mind?'

His eyes were locked on mine and I had a feeling this conversation was getting out of control. Time to change the subject. 'Come on,' I said, handing him my carrier bag with my odds and ends in it. 'I've had enough of this place.'

We made our way through the maze of shiny corridors with ugly strip lighting and worse linoleum on the floors until we got to the sliding doors at the front of the building.

'Where's the car?' I asked. I tried to sound bright but the walk from the ward through the hospital had taken more out of me than I had anticipated. If it was going to be another schlep to the car park I thought I might just ask if I could wait while he brought it round.

'It'll be here shortly,' said Edward. 'There are some advantages to being filthy rich and having staff.'

'You don't say.'

A large and very old-fashioned Rolls-Royce purred round the corner as he spoke. I could see Smith at the wheel.

'Blimey,' I said. So what had he done with the crappy old Land Rover?

'I got Smith to get this out of the garage. I thought you'd find it more comfortable than anything else.'

Smith pulled up beside us and Edward opened the back door for me to step in.

The seats were huge and soft and I sank into one gratefully, taking in the smell of polish and leather. Passers-by stared at the pair of us with curiosity. I could tell from the nudges that several of them recognised

Edward before they transferred their attention to me and then tried to work out what on earth he was doing with a woman who looked as if she'd just got out of A & E after a night of binge-drinking and fighting.

Edward reached behind me and pulled my safety belt across me. He arranged it as gently as he could and then plugged it into its socket.

'Don't want you getting hurt again,' he said. 'Okay, Smith, as smoothly as you can.'

'Yes, sir.'

I didn't even feel the car start to move as Smith pulled away. I relaxed back into my seat and enjoyed the luxury. This was a lifestyle I could get used to, I thought, not that it was ever likely to happen. It was bizarre enough that I was in a Roller this once in the company of one of the most famous men in the country. What were the chances of its ever happening again?

Not great.

Smith pulled up at the front of the private wing of Arden Hall, invoking more curious stares, this time from punters making their way from the car parks to the grand entrance. Obviously a Roller could only mean that someone of note was arriving, and was therefore worth a few seconds of rubber-necking.

'How do you feel?' asked Edward as the car drew to a halt.

'Okay. Sore, but I'll live.'

'Pleased to hear it.'

'What? That I'm sore?'

'No. That you're going to live.'

He pushed open the door and got out. I followed him gingerly. As I straightened up my ribs decided to protest and a shaft of pain shot though my side. I gasped and leaned against the car until it subsided. Edward thrust my carrier bag of bits at Smith and stepped up close to me.

'Put your arm round my shoulder,' he commanded. I did so, thinking he was going to support me into the house. Instead he bent down and in one fluid movement swept me up into his arms. I gasped again, but this time in surprise. 'I didn't hurt you?' he asked worriedly, turning his face towards mine. Our noses were inches apart.

I shook my head, too overwhelmed by his proximity to trust myself to speak. I was aware of my heart thundering in my chest and I could smell the warm clean scent of his clothes. I resisted the urge to rest my head on his shoulder and tried to look nonchalant, as if being carried by a member of the nobility was something that happened to me every day.

Edward smiled at me and my thumping heart did flip-flops. 'This is giving the punters something to gawp at,' he said lightly. 'I wonder what they're making of it.'

I glanced over at the visitors, thankful for an excuse to break the spell Edward was casting over me. And what *were* they making of it? I didn't dare think. One or two seemed to be trying to take photos, which was bizarre. I hadn't been on the receiving end of this much attention ever before, but then I realised it was Edward they were snapping, not the girl in his arms, although I had to assume they must be wondering who the hell I was, and why I was in such a state.

What would it be like to be the sort of person who got stared at and papped all the time? I suppose it was commonplace for Edward – or it would have been when he'd been married to Becca. She had never missed an opportunity to get their pics in the press. But the only photos I'd ever had taken of me were the ones my mum and aunt took for the family album. Now I was the focus of strangers and I looked as if I'd just lost a prize fight. I consoled myself with the thought that they weren't interested in me and only wanted a souvenir of seeing Edward.

When we got to the door it was thrown open by Mrs Porter. She must have been looking out for us. I thought I detected a look of disapproval on her face, but maybe I was mistaken as she asked after my health.

'I'm glad to see that you're much recovered,' she said, but she didn't look it. The way she looked at me and then Edward left me in no doubt that she utterly deplored what Edward was doing. I suppose she thought he ought to have got a minion to lug me into the house. I wanted to tell her that it wasn't my idea, but before I had the chance Edward spoke.

'I'm taking Lucy up to the blue bedroom,' he said blithely. 'It is ready, isn't it?'

A flicker of annoyance crossed Mrs Porter's face. 'Of course. You left instructions.' Seeing how efficient she was I suppose she would be a bit cross that Edward would dream of thinking that she might have failed.

'Look, this isn't necessary,' I cut in, rather hoping that I might be able to smooth her ruffled sensibilities, since it seemed to be entirely my fault that she felt put out. 'There's no need for anyone to go to any trouble on my behalf. Put me down and I'll go up to my room.'

'I'll do no such thing. You need looking after, and Mrs Porter and I are going to make sure you get the best care we can provide. Isn't that right, Mrs P? Your room is fine but a long way away; it'll be a whole lot easier for all concerned to have you on the first floor. Besides, Mrs P won't have to climb so many stairs.'

Mrs P looked a little mollified. 'Whatever you say, my lord.'

Edward smiled at me. 'That's settled. No more arguing.' He carried me upstairs to the first floor and pushed open a door. The room was sumptuous: big, light and airy, with wonderful soft furnishings in a delicate pale blue and a huge bed that dominated the space. He laid me gently on it and straightened up, grimacing slightly.

'Sorry. I hope carrying me hasn't put your back out.'

'Not a bit of it. You're a featherweight.'

I raised an eyebrow. I knew what the bathroom scales said.

'Now get into bed. The doctor told me that you need to rest for several days.'

I stared up at him. 'Right.'

'Can you manage?'

I thought about my struggle to get into my sweater and wasn't entirely sure I was going to be able to get out of it again. I shrugged. I wouldn't know till I tried, but I didn't fancy another struggle – not with the state my ribs were in.

'Want a hand?'

I thought about my bralessness and felt my face flushing. When Edward had held me in his arms had he been aware that I hadn't been fully dressed? Besides, Edward undressing me? What a thought that was.

'Perhaps Jenny could come down,' I mumbled.

Edward nodded his head vigorously. Had he had similar thoughts? 'Yes. Jenny. Of course. I'll get her.' He picked up the house phone by the bed, dialled the office number and had a quick chat with Jenny. 'She'll be down in a sec.'

I nodded. Silence fell while we waited for her.

'Hmm, you'll need a TV,' he said. 'And what about a radio?'

'Thank you,' I said. 'That's very kind of you.'

'Can't have you getting bored.'

'No.' I wished Jenny would hurry up. The effect Edward was having on me was doing me no good at all. I could feel my heart racing and God alone knew what had happened to my blood pressure. I was desperately worried he'd guess how he was making me feel.

Finally Jenny appeared and Edward slipped away, muttering about finding a TV set for me.

'Wow,' said Jenny, staring at my face. 'That must have been some fall.'

'It was.'

She began to pull the sleeve of my jersey down my arm. 'Tell me if I hurt you.'

'Don't worry, I will.'

She managed to slip my good arm out of the sleeve

without causing me to wince too much; then she bundled up the garment ready to pull it over my head. She whistled when she saw the bruises on my shoulder and back. 'I bet that's sore.'

'It's not a load of laughs, that's for sure.'

'No wonder Edward was in such a state about you,' she said. 'He got me to come in on Sunday to get some clothes and washing stuff sorted out for you. Racked with guilt is the expression I'd use to describe the state he was in. And livid. In fact livid doesn't even come close to describing how angry he was.' I was so riveted by Jenny's revelations that I barely felt her whip my jersey over my head. 'He kept banging on about bloody Zoë not tightening your girth. I was around when he came back from taking in your washing kit and clothes and I accidentally overheard his phone call to her.' She grinned. 'Well, maybe *accidentally* is a bit of an exaggeration; I did have to push his office door open a bit to make sure I didn't miss anything. Anyway, he had this monumental row with her down the phone. I could tell she was protesting her innocence but Edward didn't seem to want to believe her. Anyway, I don't think she'll be visiting here again any time soon. It was quite a set-to they had.' My jaw must have slackened visibly. 'So has Edward told you what she did?'

'Well . . . he said she couldn't have tightened the girth, but, I mean,' I hesitated, 'it could have been an accident, couldn't it?'

Jenny looked at me as if I'd suddenly grown another head. 'Not tightening the girth is just *not* something she'd forget to do.'

I nodded glumly. 'That's what Edward said.'

'Well, there you are. Case proved.'

But I still didn't want to believe it. It was too horrid. And why me? What threat was I to her?

'Anyway, he blames himself for not tacking up Willow himself.'

'Well, he shouldn't. I don't blame him and I've told him so. He can't hold himself responsible for what happened. Besides, I still think it was an accident. Just one of those things.'

Jenny sniffed in disbelief. 'If that's what you want. Anyway, he's still beating himself up about it. He thinks you'll hate him for ever. I told him you wouldn't bear a grudge but he didn't believe me. Maybe he will if he hears it from you often enough.'

Jenny helped me slip my nightie over my head and gave me a hand off with my trousers. Then she pulled back the covers and tucked me in.

'Anything you need?'

'You couldn't pass me my pills, could you?' My shoulder was giving me grief again and I was about due for another shot of painkillers.

Jenny passed them over and poured me a glass of water from the carafe by the bed.

'Teddy's desperate to see you. Up to it?'

I swallowed my pills and nodded. 'I hope the poor little mite wasn't too upset by my fall. I mean, what with the fact that his mum was killed by a horse it couldn't have done him any favours to witness another riding accident.'

'Annie said that he did ask if you might die "like

Mummy did", which was a bit awful,' admitted Jenny.

'But thank God you didn't,' said Edward from the door, making me jump. 'Can I come in again?' he asked as an afterthought, although as he was already halfway into the room it struck me as a bit late.

'Good job she's decent again,' said Jenny drily. 'An impressive set of bruises, though.'

Edward looked stricken. 'I am so incredibly sorry, Lucy. I really am. I should never have made you get on a horse. You said you didn't like them that much and yet I really pushed you into coming with us. And then letting Zoë . . .'

'Shush,' I said. I really didn't want to face the Zoë issue. I just wanted to bury the whole thing and not think about it ever again. 'I've already said it was almost certainly an accident. I'm not blaming anyone or anything except that blooming pheasant,' I said firmly, ignoring the look exchanged by Edward and Jenny. 'If that hadn't shot out of the bushes like that it would never have happened.'

The house phone by the bed rang and Edward picked it up. He exchanged a few words with the caller.

'Jenny, there's a rep from some firm to see you. Something to do with place mats for the gift shop, Hugh said.'

Jenny glanced at her watch. 'Shit, I'd forgotten. Got to dash.' And she legged it out of the room.

For about the fourth time since Saturday morning I was very conscious of being in bed in the presence of my boss. Not a situation many employees would ever find themselves in, and certainly not several times in as many days.

'Penny for them,' said Edward.

Knowing that I must have looked a bit embarrassed, I thought it was best to be upfront so I told him what I'd been thinking.

'I don't suppose it's happened to you before,' I added, trying to lighten the situation. 'Visiting the maids' bedrooms is all rather Edwardian, I suppose, not how the modern gentry carry on.'

'Well, seeing as they all live out these days it's not as convenient as it used to be. Nope, I have to say you are the first. But there are extenuating circumstances, aren't there?' There may have been now, but on Saturday, when he'd brought me breakfast in bed, I hadn't been able to think of any. 'Anyway,' he continued, sitting down on the edge of the bed, 'it's jolly pleasant. Or at least I think so.' My heart, which had calmed down, battered around under my bruised ribs once more. Then Edward reached out and took my hand. 'Besides, I don't think I particularly want to see most of my staff in their beds.' I laughed nervously, not knowing where on earth this conversation was going. 'But I'm quite prepared to make an exception for you.'

There was a quiet knock at the door. Edward removed his hand.

'Come in,' I called, absurdly grateful for the interruption.

'Sorry to interrupt, sir, but I've got the television you wanted for Miss Lucy. I took the liberty of taking the one from the study. I hope that is in order.'

'Fine, Smith. I think the only person who's watched

that one recently is Lucy while she was waiting for the aerial in her room to be fixed.'

'Yes, sir.'

Smith disappeared and came back a few seconds later accompanied by Jed, lugging the big set. Jed put the TV gently down on the big dressing table under the window and set about plugging in the lead and the aerial socket.

'Would you like me to switch it on to make sure it is working properly?' said Smith, as Jed finished.

'Please,' I said. Jed nodded at me and gave me a lopsided smile as he sidled out of the room.

Smith pressed the button and the television clunked as the power surged into it, and then the screen lightened to reveal a daytime chat show.

'That's all fine,' said Edward. Smith switched the TV off with the remote, handed the gadget to me and then withdrew. We were alone again. And Edward was still sitting on my bed.

Silence fell. I felt, maybe incorrectly, that he was plucking up the courage to say something to me. Eventually he said, 'I'll bring Teddy in to see you this afternoon.'

Not what I was expecting, so I'd obviously, yet again, read him wrong. 'I'd like that. And I'm really grateful to Annie for stepping in like this. Still,' I added, 'it shouldn't be long before I'm on my feet.'

'You're to take as long as you need. We can cope here. It isn't as if we're short-handed, now is it?' He took my hand again and patted it. 'You just concentrate on getting better. Teddy loves Annie deeply, but she's not as good at football as you and he says she's rubbish at hide and seek.'

'She doesn't have the advantage of having a house the size of this to play in.'

'Or your imagination.'

I blushed at the compliment.

'It's true,' said Edward. 'Teddy's had a ball since you've been here. You have wonderful ideas for keeping him happy.'

'I'm sure I've done no more than anyone else.'

'But you have. The last nanny was okay on the childcare side but hopeless at playing. Well, she didn't do boisterous and she didn't much like the outdoors.'

'So all this must have been wasted on her.'

'I suppose so. But Becca liked her and Jo could cope with Becca's moods. I wasn't going to rock that boat. I wonder what you would have made of Becca,' he mused.

'I would have thought her very beautiful and talented,' I replied carefully, not wishing to reveal that I'd been listening to gossip.

Edward put his head on one side. 'No you wouldn't. You wouldn't have been taken in by her at all.'

I sighed. 'Look, whatever else she was, and I can't possibly judge as I never met her, she *was* talented and she *was* beautiful.'

'And manipulative and dangerous.' Edward turned my hand over in his and examined my palm.

'But you loved her very much despite all that,' I said.

'Loved her? If you only knew.' He gave a hollow laugh. 'Well, I suppose that's what we wanted people to believe.'

'Wanted people to believe?' I shook my head, baffled, and I knew I was gaping like a stranded goldfish. 'But . . .'

Edward looked at me and sighed. 'It was sham,' he said quietly. 'From start to finish.'

I still didn't get it; the whirlwind romance, the fairytale wedding, it had all been so perfect. The press, everyone, had held them up as the perfect couple.

'But . . .' I thought about all the pictures and memorabilia in the study. Her shrine. 'But the study,' I stammered eventually.

'I put everything in there so I didn't have to look at it. People would have talked if I'd chucked everything out, so I shoved it all in one room and closed the door.'

'So it's not . . .' I didn't quite know how to phrase the question I was burning to ask. 'It's not so you can, sort of, be with her.'

Now it was Edward's turn to look baffled. 'Be with her?' He shook his head slowly. 'Oh, my God. You think . . . I suppose it does look as if I'm besotted still. Unable to move on. Christ, if people knew the truth they'd think differently, that's for sure.' He sighed and let go of my hand. 'But I'll say one thing for her, she kept her part of the bargain. I got an heir and the whole world thought we were the perfect couple.'

I could feel my brow wrinkling as I tried to get my head round what he was saying. 'But you were.'

Edward snorted. 'She was a self-obsessed bitch, but she was also as good an actress as she was an eventer. We had a pact: I gave her the name, the title, the stately home and the background she wanted; I got an heir, a trophy wife, the perfect hostess and her money.'

I couldn't believe what I was hearing. What he was

saying was shocking. I couldn't believe it was only about the money. I was lost for words.

He must have seen the disgust on my face. 'No, it's not a fairy tale, is it? Of course we made it look like one, outwardly it was hunky-dory, but once she was the Countess of Arden and had produced Teddy she and I had almost nothing more to do with each other.' Edward turned away from me and stared out of the window. I stared at him. This was unbelievable. Except that it wasn't. Annie had said as much.

'You know, I can't think why I'm telling you all this,' he said, still not looking at me.

I couldn't think why either and I rather wished he wasn't. He continued to stare out of the window and I tried to come to terms with the reality of what he'd just told me. The silence went on.

'But why?' I asked eventually, after it began to get uncomfortable.

'Why did we agree to such a Faustian pact?' He laughed again. 'You may well ask. I suppose because we each had something the other needed. Becca never quite fitted into the social scene she wanted. Her father made his millions in business; she wanted to be one of the elite, as she saw it, but could never be fully accepted as she was. She always felt they looked down their noses at her, and she hated that. But as the Countess of Arden, well, that was a whole other ball game. One of the oldest titles in the land. And what could she offer me in return? Arden Hall needed money – millions. She had them, I wanted them and she knew I loved this place more than anything in the world. Well, until Teddy came along.

'You know, it isn't that hard to sell your soul to the devil. Not if the devil has something you want badly enough. And when I actually came to live with her I discovered that was what she actually was.'

I was so utterly shocked by his confession I was completely stunned. 'So, you *never* loved her?'

Edward snorted. 'I could have done at the start. But not after she moved in. I tolerated her, but I think she actively loathed me. And the reason I couldn't renege on the deal was that she gave me the one thing that means even more to me than the house.'

'Teddy?'

Edward nodded. 'Not that she gave the poor little chap a second look after she'd had him. She'd lost a season's eventing while she was pregnant and she had to claw her way back up to the top of the heap. Of course it was handy for her when Zoë's horse got killed. If it hadn't so obviously been a complete accident I might even have thought that Becca had arranged it.'

'No!'

'No? She would have been capable of it. She didn't have a nerve in her body. I've never come across anyone so completely cold and heartless. Still,' he added on a lighter note, 'one oughtn't to speak ill of the dead.'

I couldn't help thinking about those scenes I'd witnessed on the video tapes, the hints Annie had dropped, the conversation I'd had with Jenny and Mandy, and I knew that Edward wasn't lying.

'But I still don't know why you're telling me all this,' I

said quietly. 'It's none of my business and maybe it would be better if people didn't know the truth.'

'Maybe. But I want *you* to know the truth.'

I shook my head, not understanding. Why should I know?

'I was terrified when you had that fall,' he said.

'It must have brought back some dreadful memories.'

'I didn't mean it like that. I mean, yes I was scared about how badly hurt you were, but I was frightened you might decide you'd had enough of this place, what with one thing and another.'

'Had enough? Why on earth?'

'Because of everything – the snuffbox, Zoë, the misunderstanding and now this accident.' The way he emphasised the word 'accident' left me in no doubt he still didn't think it was any such thing.

I shook my head. 'But I don't want to leave. Honest.'

'Really?'

'Really,' I said with feeling. 'But as for horses, I don't mind leading Toy Town around but I don't think I want to get any closer to one than that again.' I smiled at Edward. 'No offence but I really, *really* don't like riding.'

He grinned ruefully. 'Point taken. I think you're missing out on a great experience but I can see you've made up your mind. Just as long as you stay.'

'I've no intention of going anywhere. The disruption wouldn't be fair on Teddy.'

'It wouldn't be just Teddy who got disrupted. It would upset me too.'

'Yeah, well, you won't have all the hassle of advertising

for a replacement and organising interviews, because I'm going to stick around for a bit longer.'

'That wasn't the sort of upset I meant. I don't want you to leave here ever, Lucy. I don't think I could cope if you did. And I don't mean that as a parent, but as a person.'

It was like that moment when I'd come off Willow, when time had assumed a whole new quality. I knew, in the real world, it was passing at ordinary speed because I could hear the clock on the mantelpiece ticking away steadily, but in this weird place that I now found myself in, it had stopped. I wasn't entirely sure if my heart was still beating. I certainly wasn't breathing. What Edward said, what he'd implied about how he felt, just didn't make sense, although his actual words had been quite simple ones.

Dumbstruck, I stared back at him.

'I would mind very much if you left.' Edward was staring at me intently. I still didn't know what to say. I hadn't expected this and I was dumbfounded. It was quite mad. I shook my head to try to clear it, to try to make sense of everything.

'I'm sorry,' said Edward. He stood up and walked over to the window. 'I don't know why I thought that you might have any feelings for me. I mean, I'm years older than you, I have a failed marriage behind me and I almost kill you by making you go riding. The whole idea is preposterous.'

He turned and looked out of the window, leaving me to stare at his back.

My vision seemed to clear, as did my head. It was one thing my falling for him – and I had – it was quite another to have him falling for me. He was right, it *was* preposterous. 'Yes, it is,' I said slowly, 'but not for those reasons. I mean, I'm the nanny, for God's sake.'

'What's that got to do with it?' He spun round, looking almost angry.

'Everything.' Couldn't he see how wrong it all was? This was just ridiculous and one of us needed to spell it out as Edward had clearly lost his reason. 'I'm Lucy Carter, you are the Earl of Arden. You live this rich, glamorous life, you hobnob with the titled and famous because that's what you are too and I'm just ordinary, plain old me. The whole country knows who you are and no one has ever heard of me. You throw swanky dinner parties and I don't even know what a fish fork is. We're worlds apart and I don't think I would ever fit into yours, just as you wouldn't fit into mine.' I paused for breath. 'How many ways do I have to put it before you get it?'

'We're not living in the nineteenth century any more, Lucy. None of that matters now. Not to me, not to anyone.'

I shrugged. Mistake – it hurt. 'People like you don't go out with girls like me.'

'Yes they do, it's just that no one makes a song and dance about it these days. Like I said, none of that matters now.'

'But I'm so ordinary.'

Then he leaned forward and kissed me very gently on

the lips. 'That's where you're wrong. I think you're the most remarkable person I've met,' he said. 'Everyone who has met you completely adores you, you've transformed Teddy's life and you've transformed mine.'

'I think that's an exaggeration.'

'Definitely not.'

'And I don't think your friends would like it.' I didn't want to mention Zoë but she was a perfect example: one of his set who obviously resented me.

'Who?'

I sighed. 'Well . . . Zoë.' Obviously.

Edward snorted. 'Like that matters to me.'

'But it matters to me. And supposing she isn't the only one? Supposing your other friends take against me? I really don't fancy being a social pariah. I know from kids I've worked with that it's not funny being on the outside looking in.' I'd had lots of experience of just how miserable children could make life for the one they marked out as different, and I knew that adults were capable of doing the same – just more subtly.

'But I wouldn't let that happen.' Maybe not when he was around, but he couldn't be with me all the time.

'But . . .' I sighed. It would be so much more suitable for Edward to find happiness with someone like Zoë; someone from his world. Besides, I couldn't forget what Zoë had said to me that day in the nursery bathroom – that Edward only fancied me because I was on the premises and available. A handy shag – wasn't that how she'd put it? Wasn't that the likely reason why he found me so attractive?

Edward shook his head. 'Look, I don't care about any of them or what they think. It's just you I care about. Very much.'

But I was still filled with self-doubt. I wanted to be sure that he wanted me because loved me, not just because I was handy. He'd told me he cared but he hadn't mentioned the word love. Maybe that was because he didn't, not really. And I couldn't let myself fall for him completely and utterly until I was sure. 'You may not care about the views of your friends, but Zoë cares about you.'

Edward looked exasperated. 'Does she? Only because of Billy Boy. It's not me she wants, is it?'

Did I detect some bitterness there? Oh, my God, I wished I had the confidence to say, okay, cards on the table; tell me exactly where I stand. Or ask him outright if his apparent dislike of Zoë was because she wanted Billy Boy more than him. But I didn't. I fluffed asking the direct question because I was terrified that if I asked him outright if he loved me not her, I wouldn't get the answer I wanted to hear.

I tried to lighten the mood. 'You don't seem to have much luck with women.'

'Not until now.' He smiled at me. My breathing seemed to stop again. 'Anyway, Becca wasn't bad luck but a crap miscalculation. I knew my title was the thing that attracted her to me, and I won't pretend that her money wasn't important to me, but I really believed that there might be affection there too. Well, she might have loved the idea of being a countess but she never loved me. That became obvious almost immediately.'

I didn't know what to say.

'Anyway,' he sighed, 'I resolved to make the best of it. Becca said she'd honour her promise to give me a child – which she did. And whatever else I feel about her, she gave me Teddy.'

'I should think almost anything would be worth having him.'

Edward nodded. 'You're right. The trouble is, his arrival brought with it a whole new set of problems. Becca decided she didn't have to alter anything once he was born – that she could carry on as before.'

'But surely you didn't expect her to give up eventing.'

'Oh, no, it wasn't that. I could have coped with that. No, that wasn't what caused the final showdown between us.' Edward got up and paced across the room. He leaned with his back to the window sill and stared back at me. 'She threatened to take Teddy away from me.'

'But why? You said she never really cared for him.'

'Oh no, *she* didn't. But she knew *I* did.' He sighed again. 'I got worried about the way she was behaving: the parties, the rumours . . .' He paused. 'The lovers; Justin Naylor was just one in a string. Oh, there was never any proof, but people talked so I asked her to stop or at least be more discreet, if only for Teddy's sake. I couldn't bear the idea of him growing up reading scandalous stories about his mother in the press.'

'I see.' I was shocked. 'How did she react?'

'She laughed. She said, "Make me." '

'Didn't she deny it?' I was horrified.

'She didn't care. She was rich, she had her title, she'd

fulfilled her side of the bargain. So she just laughed and asked what I planned to do about it. I said that divorce seemed to be the only option. She said I wouldn't dare, that I wouldn't want the scandal. But I think she knew that I'd have called her bluff.'

'And would you?'

Edward nodded emphatically. 'Yes. I knew she didn't want her fairytale image – perfect Countess, eventing champion, wonderful mother – damaged by a divorce. And she was afraid all her swanky new friends only liked her because she had a tangible connection to me and Arden Hall. We both knew what sort of shallow types a lot of them were and she wasn't prepared to risk having the doors that she now found opening to her slammed shut again. So she said that if I divorced her she'd not only take away every penny that she'd brought with her, but she'd take Teddy as well. I knew she meant it. Actually, I didn't give a stuff about the money, we'd have coped here somehow, sold another picture or two, but Teddy?'

'But she couldn't have known she'd get custody.'

Edward looked at me levelly. 'And how often do judges give custody to fathers?'

I shook my head. I had no idea.

'Far less frequently than mothers get it. I couldn't risk it.'

'Couldn't you have told the judge what you knew about her behaviour?'

'And have the whole sordid mess broadcast to the world? That was exactly what I was trying to protect Teddy from.'

'But he's too young to know or understand. Surely by the time he was old enough no one would remember.'

'Do you really think so? Because I don't think it works like that. If enough mud gets thrown around quite a lot of it will stick. And it isn't as if Becca hadn't made sure that we were never out of the glossy mags. People would have remembered, I'm sure of it.'

'It must have been terrible,' I said, not knowing what else to say.

'It was,' he said grimly. 'But the problem is solved now – thank God.'

Without warning, I yawned. 'I'm so sorry,' I said. I couldn't believe I'd just been so rude.

'I shouldn't have unburdened my problems with Becca on to you. Forgive me.'

'No, I don't mind,' I protested hurriedly. 'I wasn't bored. It's the painkillers. They make me drowsy when they kick in.'

'Then you need to sleep.'

'Maybe.'

'I'll leave you in peace. I'll get Mrs Porter to organise some supper in an hour or two. What would you fancy?'

'Nothing very much. I'm not doing much to work up an appetite.'

'But you must keep your strength up,' said Edward. He kissed me again, pulled the covers up under my chin and left the room quietly, closing the door behind him.

As I drifted off to sleep troubling thoughts began to gather. I was still completely confused by Edward's feelings for me. I couldn't believe the emotion he seemed to profess was real, not with Zoë's catty observation echoing constantly at the back of my mind. And furthermore, although there was nothing to suggest that Becca's death had been anything but a terrible accident, a feeling of dreadful uneasiness persisted. It had been awfully convenient and because of it Edward had kept his son and her money.

I was woken by Edward, switching on the lights. Outside there had been a complete change in the weather. A gale had blown up, and rain was now lashing against the old sash windows. Edward crossed the room and drew the curtains.

'I've asked for someone to bring you up some supper,' he said as I came to.

I looked at my watch. Seven o'clock! I'd been asleep for ages.

'Thank you.' I yawned widely.

'Boring you again?' asked Edward, grinning.

'Just waking up properly.' I momentarily forgot about my injuries and moved too suddenly. The pain made me hiss.

Edward shot me a worried glance. 'Are you all right?'

'Stiff and sore.'

'Let me help you.' He came over to the bed and gently eased me upright and forward, plumping my pillows so they supported me in a comfortable sitting position. I sagged against them gratefully.

'Thank you.' I suddenly noticed the temperature in the bedroom. It was perishing. 'Could you pass me my dressing gown?'

Edward brought it to me and draped it over my shoulders. 'I'm really sorry that it's a bit cool,' he said. Cool? Arctic, more like. 'But the heating's bust. I'll get Mrs Porter to organise a fire in here.'

'That's okay. I'm all right here in bed. Is it the whole house that has no heating or just this bit?'

Edward nodded. 'All of it. That's the trouble with an old place like this. Things are always breaking down. I expect the entire system needs replacing, but it's not something that we can embark on lightly. For a start, we don't know where half the pipes go, as when it was put in the plumbers just shoved them where they thought best. I imagine Hugh will get someone to come out and patch up the boiler and fix the bits that are really desperate, and then we'll hope that it keeps going for a few more months, maybe even a year or so.'

'I'm glad it isn't my problem,' I said, thinking how horrendous the bills must be. There was a tentative knock at the door. 'Come in,' I called.

Teddy, with his hand clasped firmly in Annie's, appeared. 'Hello, Lucy,' he whispered. 'Annie says you're not so poorly now.'

'No, Teddy. I'm a lot better.'

Annie let go of his hand and he ran across the room to the bed.

'No jumping on it,' said Annie. 'Remember what I said.'

'That Lucy's very sore,' said Teddy gravely. He turned back to me. 'Are you?'

'A bit. But climb on the chair and lean over so I can give you a kiss.'

Teddy scrambled on to the chair beside me and gave me a wet smacker on my unfractured cheek. I rumpled his hair. He really was an adorable kid.

'Tell me what you've been doing.'

'Jed played football with me and I played with the kittens. Then Daddy took me out on Toy Town.'

'That must've nice,' I said, trying, but probably failing, to sound enthusiastic. Horses were off the menu for me from now on. 'And how has playschool been?'

'Okay. Miss Wilson said I ought to draw a picture for you to make you feel better.'

'That would be wonderful. Just the thing to perk me up.'

Teddy looked about the room. 'Are you going to be sleeping here for ever?'

'Only till I get a bit better. Then I'll come back up to the nursery with you.' I could see the look of relief on his face.

'I'm glad. I'm going to sleep at Annie's tonight. Daddy says it's too cold in my room.'

'That's right,' Annie said. 'And if we're going to get you bathed before bedtime we must make tracks, young man.'

'Ohhh,' Teddy whined.

'Jed and Mike are going to want their supper. Just because you've been fed doesn't mean there aren't other folk who are hungry. And remember what I said about not making Lucy too tired.'

Teddy climbed reluctantly off the chair. 'I'll bring you your picture tomorrow.'

He and Annie said goodnight and left. Without Teddy providing a distraction I became more aware of how cold the room was. I was okay from the waist down – that was all tucked up under layers of blankets and an eiderdown – but my hands were frozen and even my shoulders, wrapped in my dressing gown, were cold. Perhaps I looked cold too as Edward suddenly mentioned a fire again.

'And I'll chase your supper.'

After he'd gone I lay against my pillows and thought about him and wished I understood him better. My troubled thoughts returned. Who did I believe – him or Zoë? He'd made a declaration but Zoë's poisonous words made me wonder just what sort of relationship he might be after. I mean, it just wasn't going to happen – a bloke like him ending up with a girl like me – so was I really just a stopgap until someone more suitable caught his eye?

I was just starting to feel sorry for myself again when Maria clattered into the room lugging a scuttle full of coal in one hand and firelighters and an old paper in the other.

'No wonder his lordship said you needed a fire. It's perishing up here,' said Maria as she got busy at the grate. Deftly she crumpled up the paper and then began arranging small bits of coal over and around a firelighter. When she'd got it all arranged to her satisfaction she lit a match and carefully applied it to several different places. The paper flared and then the lighter and the coal began to catch. Maria sat back on her heels as she watched to make sure that her fire-laying was completely successful. A faint, acrid, sulphurous smell of coal-smoke wafted across the room.

'So how are you?' she asked over her shoulder.

'Much better, thanks.'

'His lordship was that worried about you.'

'Well, it's understandable,' I said. 'Another accident involving a horse – he must have had a nasty flashback.'

Maria snorted, then glanced guiltily at the door. 'Well,' she said in a low voice, 'he might have minded that Becca got killed but there's plenty around here that didn't.'

I didn't answer. After all, it wasn't the first time I'd heard that, so the shock factor had gone completely. Maria dusted her hands on her apron as if to cover up my lack of response. 'Well, I'll tidy up and get your supper.' She bustled out, taking the coal scuttle with her.

I lay in bed and watched the flames licking higher and higher as the fire began to blaze properly. The warmth hadn't yet managed to reach me across the large expanse of the room but it gave the illusion of cosiness.

A few minutes later Maria reappeared carrying a big tray laden with a bowl of soup, a couple of buttered brown rolls, a decanter of wine and a glass.

'His lordship said to tell you he'll be up in a minute to make sure you finish it all up,' said Maria as she dumped the tray across my knees and put the decanter on the bedside table. 'We don't want that going everywhere.'

'Thank you,' I said. The soup smelled delicious and despite the fact that I'd done nothing but lie in bed all day just sleeping and eating now and again, I felt ravenously hungry. I tore into one of the rolls. It was warm and moist and the butter had partly melted into it. I couldn't resist dipping it into my soup as I had when I was a little girl and sucking the broth out of it. It was wonderful. I picked up my spoon and began tucking in with gusto.

Feeling warmer, better and more comfortable I laid my spoon down after a few mouthfuls and reached for the TV remote. If I was going to loaf I might as well do it properly and watch some early-evening action on the box while I ate. I flicked through the channels and finally settled on the tail end of *Emmerdale*. I hadn't watched the soap for ages and had no idea what was going on in the characters' lives, but the Woolpack and the sets were all comfortingly familiar, as was the scenery, and I was happy to watch what my mum used to call 'moving wallpaper' while I slurped my soup.

The theme tune was fading away as I scraped the last drops from the bowl and polished it clean with a final morsel of bread.

'May I join you?' said Edward. I looked round and saw he was carrying another wine glass.

'I was a bit concerned about your message,' I said, greeting him with a grin. I hoped it disguised both my feelings of relief that he wasn't ignoring me and the sheer elation that I felt just because he was near. As casually as I could I added, 'Maria said you had given orders that I was to polish off everything. This carafe of wine is a bit of a challenge, so if you can see your way to helping me out I'd be very grateful.'

'I'll see what I can do,' said Edward, picking it up. He

sloshed out two glasses and put the decanter back on the tray. Unfortunately he put it down awkwardly and must have caught it either on the edge of the tray or on the rim of my soup bowl, as the next instant the decanter was on its side on the bed with red wine flooding everywhere. It didn't help matters that the shock of the accident made me jump and more wine slopped on to the bedding out of my glass.

'Damn, blast and buggeration,' exclaimed Edward, grabbing the neck of the decanter and righting it again. There was still some wine left in it but I could feel the remainder seeping wetly through the bedding and over my legs. It was cold and clammy. Edward took my glass and dumped everything on the dressing table, and then returned to me. The puddle of wine was sinking into the eiderdown like water into sand. Edward stared at the mess.

'You can't stay there, that's for sure,' he said.

Even I knew that I couldn't spend the night in a sodden bed. 'I can go back to my own room,' I offered.

'You can't. The nursery is freezing. You'd catch your death up there.'

'Couldn't Maria make me a fire?'

'I've sent the staff home for the night. It seemed ridiculous to keep them on in this perishing house when they could be tucked up warmly in their own places.'

'Well, isn't there an electric heater I could borrow?'

Edward shrugged. 'I imagine there is, but I haven't the first idea where Mrs Porter would keep it. That's the trouble with having staff.'

I looked at Edward gravely. 'You know, it's the only reason I've never bothered with my own household. I just can't imagine the sheer irritation of not being able to lay one's hands on one's kit in an emergency.'

'Are you taking the piss?'

'Might be.'

Edward shook his head. 'You just can't get the staff these days, can you? Anyway, this doesn't solve the problem of where you are going to sleep. I think there's nothing else for it – as there's a fire going in my room, you'll have to spend the night in my bed.'

I stared at Edward, the tension palpable between us.

'Well, where else are you going to sleep?' he said in exasperation.

I could think of dozens of places. Just how many bedrooms were there? So why was he suggesting this? My God, sleeping in Edward's bed! And exactly where was he planning to sleep? My heart raced as I considered the implications and the possibilities and I could feel my colour rising.

'Well, let's get you out of there and then we can think about what to do next. I don't want you catching a chill from lying on a damp mattress.'

He began to pull back the bedding. I hoped to God that my nightie wasn't all scrunched up round my waist. With relief I realised it wasn't.

By this time the wine had soaked through all the old-fashioned layers of eiderdown, blankets and sheets, through the lower half of my nightie and into the bottom sheet and mattress. The bed was awash.

'What a waste of wine,' I said.

'Never mind that.' He dabbed at the wine on my

nightie with a clean and dry bit of the top sheet. It went from soaked to damp, although it was still uncomfortably wet next to my bare leg. 'Go and stand by the fire and keep warm,' ordered Edward, helping me off the mattress and supporting me across to the fire. 'At least your dressing gown was spared the flood.'

For which I was grateful, given the fact that the fire had hardly made any difference to the air temperature in the room. Despite Edward's ministrations, I was conscious that my nightie still managed to drip wine on the pale blue carpet as I tottered over to the fireplace.

'Mrs Porter is going to kill me in the morning,' he said.

'Why? It's your house.'

'She doesn't see things quite like that,' said Edward. 'She runs it. She feels responsible – even if it's me cocking things up for her.'

Standing made my ribs ache badly and my discomfort must have been reflected in my face.

'You ought to be sitting down,' he said. But when we looked round the room the only seat that could be easily moved nearer to the fire was a rather uncomfortable-looking dressing-table stool. 'Come on. Can you manage to walk a step or two?'

'I should think so. It's my collarbone that's broken, not my ankle.'

He grinned at me. 'No one likes a smartarse.' Then he tweaked my nose.

He gave me his arm for support as we made our way out of the blue bedroom and across the corridor to an open door. Through it I could see a vast bed and a roaring fire and mounds of books, papers and clothes on various surfaces including the floor – it looked incredibly welcoming and cosy; much nicer than the beautifully appointed and practically perfect spare room I was vacating.

'Sorry about the mess,' said Edward.

It didn't bother me and I said so.

'You can sit here and keep warm while we think about what to do next. And perhaps your nightie will dry off a bit.'

That would be good, I thought. I didn't want to have to face the necessity of stripping it off – something I wasn't going to be able to do without help. And Jenny had gone home.

Maybe Edward was thinking the same thing, as there was a pause before he added, 'I'll be back in a minute.'

He disappeared, leaving me with the dressing gown wrapped round me and a fire roaring away just a few feet from me. I felt toasty warm as I snuggled into the armchair in front of the grate and waited for Edward's return. I wondered if he had suddenly thought how inappropriate it would be for me to spend the night in his room and hoped that he'd gone off to sort out some alternative arrangements for me. He might have been waited on hand and foot all his life, but surely even he was capable of making up another bed and lighting a fire?

I looked about me; the room was full of soft flickering shadows which danced over the dark, heavy furniture. Along one wall was a large bookcase which seemed to be filled with battered and well-read books. The blanket box at the end of bed was strewn with the previous Sunday's papers and more books. There was a pile of clothes heaped up on a tatty old sofa under the big bay window and a threadbare teddy lolled against the mirror on his dressing table. This room seemed to be a reflection of his character – without any sorts of airs and graces and focusing on comfort and contentment rather than style and show.

I stared at the flames and wondered about Becca. I couldn't see her sleeping in a room like this. Somehow the blue bedroom seemed to be much more the sort of place she would have wanted to call hers – cool, stylish and expensive.

Becca, I thought, appeared to have had it all and yet I hadn't found anyone at Arden Hall who seemed to be able to find a good word to say about her; Annie, Jed, Maria and even Jenny had all found reasons to dislike her. She'd done nothing to bond with her son and she'd alienated a husband who had tried to love her, and as for the way she'd treated her horses . . . I felt her memory's power to intimidate me fading. In a perverse way I felt sorry for her. I couldn't imagine how life would be with everyone you came into contact with disliking you. The nation might have viewed her as some sort of paragon, a beautiful successful sportswoman, a wonderful mother, a veritable goddess, and collectively sobbed itself silly over her death, but the eyes of all those who had really known her had probably remained resolutely dry.

Which made me wonder once again about her death. Edward had been adamant that Jed had had nothing to do with it – a fact I could easily believe. But there was still something not right. Maybe it *was* an accident, but all the same . . .

Instead I began to think about the present. I wondered what Edward was doing. Perhaps he was having problems finding bedding and another room. For some reason I suddenly realised that I wanted him to fail in his search. So maybe Zoë was right – he fancied me because I was around and available. So what? Would it be so bad? I told myself to stop having such idea. As if he'd want to. As if I'd be able to in this state. But a girl could fantasise.

'Here we are,' said Edward. 'How's the invalid?'

I jumped as I crashed back into reality. 'Fine,' I said, to cover up my awkwardness at being interrupted while thinking about sharing a bed with my boss. Edward looked at me curiously. I knew I was blushing.

Edward brandished a bottle of wine and held out two glasses. 'As you didn't get a drink earlier and if I promise not to throw this lot over you, will you join me while you dry off and warm up?'

I smiled. 'Sounds good to me.'

Edward poured the wine and sat in the armchair on the other side of the fire. I tried not to stare at him although I could feel a magnetic tug between us. Here was I, Lucy Carter, in the Earl of Arden's bedroom, sharing a bottle of wine with one of the most desirable and eligible men in the country. Was I really falling for him or was I in love with the attention he was giving me? And was it love or infatuation? I didn't know but I did know I cared for him very much and that my insides felt juddery with excitement just because he was sitting close to me.

I contemplated my wine and thought about the kiss he'd given me earlier. 'Brotherly' just about described it. It hadn't been a kiss of passion or desire. He'd said he couldn't cope without me, he'd said he had feelings for me, but he hadn't said he loved me. And when I'd remonstrated with him about the ridiculousness of the idea he hadn't really disagreed with me. Maybe he wanted me for a casual relationship as he had nothing better on offer at the moment. Or maybe he was feeling guilty about my accident and hoped that if he was nice to me I might forgive him. I wished I was more sophisticated and knew how the hell to handle this situation, or how to talk to him in order to find out what was really going on.

'Penny for them,' said Edward.

I glanced up. In the firelight, with soft, flickering shadows caressing his face like fingers, he looked even more handsome. My heart lurched.

'Not worth that much,' I said glibly, trying to disguise my feelings.

Edward cocked his head on one side as if he was considering my answer. 'I think you're fibbing. You were deep in thought. Miles away, even.'

At least I could refute that last bit. 'I wasn't miles away.'

'So where were you?'

I lowered my eyes. Not a question I wanted to answer. Edward slid off his chair and came and sat on the floor by my feet.

'Where were you?' he repeated softly.

'It's not important.'

'If the look on your face is anything to go by that's another fib.' He rested his hand on my knee.

I took a deep breath. My doubts weren't going to be sorted out if I didn't answer his questions. 'I was thinking about you.' I could feel my face burning at my directness.

'What about me?'

'About what you said earlier. About not being able to cope without me.'

'And it's true. This has nothing to do with your job, and everything to do with you.'

I didn't know what to say. I put my wine down on a table by my chair. My hands were shaking so badly I was afraid of spilling it.

'Do you,' said Edward softly, 'think that, despite our differences, you might ever feel anything for me?'

'But . . .'

'No buts. And don't tell me about all the things that might come between us – all those dreary reasons you listed earlier. This is the classless society now. It's official; the PM decreed it years ago.'

'But it's not how it works in reality. I'm poles apart from your friends – the ones I met at that dinner party. Jason Naylor reckoned I was fair game. He felt he could make a pass at me because I was *just the nanny*. You see, things haven't changed so very much.'

'If you recall,' said Edward, 'that dinner wasn't my idea and the people who turned up weren't really my friends either. Zoë organised it all, remember?'

'But they're still people you know.'

'That doesn't make them friends, or people whose

opinion I value. I've got far more time for Annie and you than I have for any of them.'

'But you'll still see them, move in their circle. And I won't fit in.'

'You will when they get to know you.'

I heard what Edward was saying but I knew he was wrong. I was a poor kid from the suburbs. They would never accept me. They might be polite to my face, I might even get invited to functions providing I went with Edward, but I was never going to be part of their set. I think that's why the idea of being divorced from Edward had terrified Becca – without his support and presence his circle would have cast her aside because she wasn't 'one of them'. They'd have closed ranks once more and shut her out. I wasn't sure they would ever open their ranks wide enough to let me in in the first place. And, frankly, thinking about the people Zoë had been so keen to hobnob with, their attitude to their kids and their awful braying comments, did I really want to be friends with them? A firm no. And that was another point: if he didn't like my mates and I didn't like his, would our feelings for each other be enough to carry us forward?

Edward was still sitting at my feet, staring up at me, expecting an answer, and what could I say?

'I can see you have too many doubts still,' he said eventually. 'I'm rushing you. I'm not being fair.'

I nodded. 'I need time,' I admitted. 'I need to think.'

Edward moved back to his chair. 'How's your nightie doing?'

I was grateful for the change of subject, and bent

forward to feel the fabric. Damp but not very. 'Getting there.'

'Good. That's good news. The bad news is I can't find where Mrs Porter keeps the spare bedding. I'm sorry, but you're stuck with me tonight.'

I froze. Oh, my God.

'Don't look so horrified,' said Edward. 'I promise I won't make a move on you. Look at the bed – it's huge. If you lie on one side and I lie on the other we'll be miles apart.' He was smiling at me as he said this, trying to reassure me that it was okay.

'But the staff?'

Edward shook his head. 'I'll be up and out of the way long before anyone will come into the bedroom, and if you're concerned about your reputation I'll say I spent the night on the sofa. I'm not going to because I have in the past and it is truly the most uncomfortable piece of furniture in the universe. I'm sorry, but I'm not prepared to do that again. Nor, I'm afraid, am I prepared to freeze in some other bedroom because I can't find the blankets.'

'Okay,' I said slowly. I took a slurp of my wine. I needed Dutch courage before I went to bed with my boss.

My nightie had pretty much dried so Edward helped me into his bed. I snuggled down under the covers, which smelled very faintly of his aftershave, and watched him bank up the fire and set the guard in front of it.

'It will no doubt go out before morning but I'll light it again when I get up. We won't freeze tonight, that's the main thing.'

I nodded from my position on the very edge of the mattress, where I lay feeling hugely self-conscious and nervous. Supposing I snored and kept him awake. I thought of other noises I might make in my sleep and cringed. I shut the thought from my mind.

Edward disappeared out of the room for a few minutes and came back in his pyjamas and dressing gown. He walked round to the other side of the bed and climbed in. He was right, there was a huge space between us, but there was no denying we were sharing a bed. He leaned over and dropped a kiss on my forehead. 'Sleep tight then,' he said quietly as he switched off the bedside lamp and snuggled down.

The flicker of the fire in the otherwise dark room was

quite hypnotic. I lay in the near darkness and watched the shadows pulse and move until the wine and my painkillers combined to make my eyelids close.

When I awoke the room was pitch dark and cold. It took me a second or two to remember quite what my situation was. When I did, I realised I could hear Edward's quiet, slow breathing. A frisson thrilled through me. In bed with the Earl of Arden, I thought. Who would believe that Lucy Carter was lying next to one of the most desirable men in the country? I almost giggled at the incongruity of it. With a struggle and very careful movements I managed to push myself semi-upright using my good arm. With a similar effort and a lot of silent cursing I then managed to swivel round enough to take a look at the luminous dial of the bedside clock; it was just after three in the morning – and I felt wide awake. That would teach me to go to bed so early.

Having got myself into this position with a lot of effort, I wasn't inclined to move again, despite the fact that the top bit of my body was exposed to the chill air. I lay slumped against my pillows, aware that my shoulders were perishing, my dressing gown was out of reach and my painkillers were in the other room.

Tough, I thought. Worse things happen at sea.

I shut my eyes and tried to make my mind a blank, but all I could think about was the incessant dull ache in my shoulder and ribs. The trouble is, in the cold dark hours before dawn, every least niggle, worry or discomfort assumes proportions that are completely unreal and exaggerated. It wasn't long before the dull throb had almost reduced me to tears, my inability to go back to sleep transformed into a totally obsessive frustration. All I could think about was the bottle of painkillers by the bed in the blue bedroom.

I suppose the pain made me restless, because I slowly became aware of a change in Edward's breathing. Then I heard an almost inaudible whisper.

'Lucy? You all right?'

'It's all right. I'm awake,' I said.

'What's the matter?'

'I've left my painkillers in the blue bedroom.'

Silence. Then, 'Do you really need them?'

'I'm sorry . . .'

'Of course you do. I shouldn't have asked.' There was some shuffling, then he switched the bedside light on. 'I'll go and get them.' He slung on his dressing gown, stuffed his feet into a pair of slippers and crossed to the door.

'I'm just going outside. I may be some time,' he said.

'It's not that cold.'

'All right for you to say. You're tucked up in bed.' Edward opened the door and disappeared. The draught of chill air that sliced across the bedroom made me take my words back. He was going to get frozen, even just fetching my pills.

I was beginning to get concerned when he hadn't returned after a couple of minutes. The blue bedroom was only across the corridor; what was taking him so long? Five minutes passed. Ten. I was really beginning to worry now. Then the door swung open again and there was Edward with not only my pills but two steaming mugs.

'I thought we could both do with some cocoa to help us get to sleep again.' He put a mug and the pill bottle down beside me before trekking round to his side and clambering in.

'Are you very cold?' I asked.

'Been warmer,' he said cheerfully, clasping his hands round his mug. 'Never mind. I'll soon warm up.'

'You'll warm up quicker if we share body heat,' I said.

Edward turned his head and looked deep into my eyes. I lowered them. I'd gone too far. Overstepped the mark. What was I thinking of?

He took my cocoa out of my hand and put my mug next to his. Then he shuffled across the bed. I leaned towards him and he kissed me gently on the lips. 'A cuddle would be lovely and I promise not to hurt your poor shoulder.'

I searched his face and saw only kindness and I trusted him absolutely. I smiled up at him and snuggled deep against him. I felt safe, secure and completely loved. Even my arm had stopped aching.

The next time I woke up it was the sound of fire irons rattling in the grate that roused me. I started guiltily when I remembered that my last thoughts had been about trusting Edward. I bolted upright, gasped with pain as I jarred my collarbone and then sighed with relief when I saw that Edward, empty cocoa mugs and wine glasses had all disappeared.

'Morning, Lucy,' said Maria, seeing me awake. 'Sleep all right?'

'Yes, thank you,' I said, hoping I didn't sound guilty.

'I don't think his lordship did. By the looks of things he ended up on the floor of the blue bedroom. He says the wrecked mattress was entirely his fault, so he gave up his bed for you.'

'He did spill the wine, when he brought me my supper,' I conceded.

'Well then.' She tutted expressively. 'It was the least he could do, wasn't it?' She turned her attention back to the cold grate and riddled the ashes out of the fire basket. 'You stay in bed now till I get this sorted out and a nice blaze going. You don't want pneumonia on top of everything else. Soon have it done, then I'll bring you your breakfast.'

I lay back against the pillows as Maria clattered around by the hearth, and remembered the wonderful feeling of falling asleep in Edward's arms. In my mind I recreated that happy, secure feeling of being cherished. I found myself smiling at the thought of that old-fashioned word, but it was the right one. I *had* been cherished and it had felt fantastic. The sound of a match striking brought me back to reality.

I opened my eyes and watched the flame beginning to grow and lick around the lumps of coal that Maria had piled carefully over the kindling and a firelighter.

'I'll just make sure it gets a proper hold before I fetch your breakfast.'

'No need,' said Edward from the doorway. 'May I come in?' He was carrying a large wooden tray on which several dishes were steaming enticingly

'It's your bedroom,' I answered. The waft of bacon reached my nostrils. My mouth watered.

'Not at the moment.' Edward put the tray down on the table by the sofa. He filled the cup on the tray from the big teapot and brought that over to me first. Then he returned to the tray and removed the pot and put it on the hearth.

'Don't want another accident,' he said.

'And whose fault was the first one?' asked Maria, getting to her feet. 'Mrs Porter is going to go mad when she sees that mattress.'

'I know, I know.' Edward sighed. 'But I'm sure it's not ruined. Once it dries out I expect we can put a cover on it and no one will know.'

'Mrs Porter will,' said Maria darkly.

'Let's get you sorted out,' said Edward, ignoring Maria's comment. Very gently he eased me forward and plumped up the pillows, then pulled the eiderdown up to my armpits to keep me as warm as possible. Then he fetched the tray and placed it on my knees.

'Voilà.' He removed the dish cover with a flourish. 'And Cook says she doesn't want any excuses, you're to eat it all up.'

On the plate was bacon, scrambled eggs, toast, mushrooms, tomatoes, beans and sausage. I stared at it aghast.

'I can't eat all that. I'll burst. I had a huge bowl of soup and rolls for my supper, remember, and I've done nothing but lie about in bed since.'

'Do your best, then,' said Edward. 'I've been up since six and Cook was so determined to spoil you she only had time to throw me a crust.'

'A likely story,' I retorted. Like Cook would allow him to start the day with just some bread.

Edward looked aggrieved. 'Anyway, if you can't manage it all I might be able to help out.'

I began to tuck in. Maria left, saying she had several other fires to lay and light and couldn't afford to hang about and gossip all day. She shut the door 'to keep the heat in' and Edward and I were alone again.

'Don't worry,' he said as I chewed on a mouthful of bacon, 'I was long gone before Maria made an appearance. By the way, do you know you snore?'

'No!' I felt my face flaring. How embarrassing.

'Don't worry, they're pretty little whiffly ones, not thundering great wall-shakers. They're quite endearing, really.'

Like that made me feel better. I had a bet with myself that Becca hadn't snored. I changed the subject as I forked up some creamy scrambled eggs. 'How's Teddy?' I asked.

'When I phoned Annie this morning he was fine. He's busy doing that drawing he promised you before he goes to nursery this morning. They're going to bring it over at lunchtime.'

I felt a glow that little Teddy cared enough to spend the time on me. I realised just how much I cared about him. He'd become a big part of my life. 'I shall really look forward to that.'

Edward smiled at me. 'You really mean that, don't you?'

'Of course. He's such a lovely kid.'

'Thanks.'

'Well, look at his dad. Why shouldn't he be wonderful?'

'Hmm. He might have taken after other relatives of mine. I have a couple of seriously dodgy cousins.'

'We've all got a dodgy relative or two.'

'He should have had a mother like you,' said Edward.

I decided to make light of his comment. 'What, one who can't stay on a horse?'

'Apart from that, obviously.'

I pushed my plate away. I was feeling stuffed and, when I considered the damage I'd done the mound of food I'd been presented with, it wasn't surprising.

Edward wrapped a piece of toast round an unwanted sausage and bit into it. 'So,' he said not entirely distinctly, 'what are your plans for today?'

'Oh, I thought I'd go for a row on the lake, possibly followed by a workout and a jog round the park, and finish off by giving the nursery a thorough spring clean.'

'And in the afternoon?'

I grinned. 'I'm sure Teddy will have plans to keep me busy if I ask him.'

'So how about sacking those ideas and doing a bit of light loafing, read a book or two and listen to the radio this morning, and maybe get thrashed by Teds and me at spillikins after lunch?'

'Oh, that sounds a bit strenuous. Not sure I can manage to pick up those big heavy sticks.'

'Well, if you rest this morning, maybe you'll have conserved your energy enough to manage it.' Edward noticed my teacup was empty and refilled it. Then he picked up the tray. 'If milady requires nothing else . . . Sorry, but I've got to earn my keep and make an effort to run this place, to say nothing of 'fessing up to Mrs Porter about the mattress in the blue bedroom. I'll pop up later to check you're okay. And I'll make sure Maria comes up in about an hour to see to your fire. Hopefully the heating will get fixed today. Hugh's on the case and is giving it his full attention. The fact that his office is as cold as charity must spur him on a bit.'

Edward disappeared and I lay against my pillows sipping my tea and watching the flames leap and dance. Outside, the sky was grimly gloomy. The promise of summer had been put on hold, swept away by this last gasp of winter. It seemed a really pleasant option to be snuggled up in bed given the dreary weather and the temperature of the house. Trouble was, boredom set in with astonishing rapidity. With nothing to occupy myself I began to focus on my aches and pains, on imagined lumps in the mattress and a draught that played over my shoulders and the back of my neck, and I became more and more dissatisfied and fed up.

There had to be something to do that would occupy me, surely. I stared at the big bookcase with its shelves of reading material. There must be something there that would keep me entertained for a couple of hours, mustn't there? Well, only one way to find out.

I pushed the bedcovers back and gingerly swung my feet to the floor. I was definitely better than the day before although still not completely pain-free. The room wasn't warm but it was certainly a great deal warmer than it had been when Edward had gone for my pills. I draped my dressing gown over my shoulders and wished I had my slippers. Maybe I'd ask Edward to get them for me when he next came to see me. I padded over to the shelves and began examining the spines of the books there. I worked my way along titles trying to convince myself that I would find *Martin Chuzzlewit* a ripping yarn or that *Heart of Darkness* was something I ought to read before another day passed. However, these weren't books for show, judging from the state of their covers; these were old favourites of Edward's.

Didn't he read anything other than classics, I wondered. What was wrong with Colin Dexter, Jill Mansell or Dan Brown? I'd even settle for the *Beano* annual. Frankly, compared to the dry-as-dust selection on offer, the back of a cornflake packet had a certain appeal. At the end of the second shelf I noticed a couple of orange paperbacks – old Penguin editions – and pulled them off the shelf to get a better look at the titles. As I did so something rolled off the bookcase from behind them and clattered lightly on to the floor. I bent down to pick it up. At first I thought it was a small wooden door knob. I looked at it more closely and my second thought was that it was a toy, a toy bird. A wooden wren. Then I realised what it was. It was Jed's whistle.

I stared at it for several moments. Jed's whistle. The whistle he'd lost before Becca's accident. The whistle he'd used to train Billy Boy to perform those fantastic manoeuvres.

I knew Edward couldn't whistle. But with this . . .

The cherrywood wren in my hand began to blur as all sorts of implications and connotations raced around in my brain, all of them frankly unpleasant. I tried to deny the reality which was elbowing its way to the front. I told myself that it was just coincidence. There could be any number of ways the whistle had found its way on to that shelf. Teddy could have picked it up and hidden it here. Or Edward had found it and put it on the shelf for safe-keeping. Of course he meant to give it back to Jed, but he'd just forgotten . . .

That was it, of course, that was what happened, although in my heart I knew I was deluding myself. I tried to back up my thought process with further logic; in all the hullabaloo of Becca's death a little thing like returning Jed's whistle wouldn't signify. I moved to put it back on the shelf and hide it with the books once again.

'Lucy. What are you doing out of bed?'

I leapt. Literally. My feet actually left the ground. And the whistle spun out of my hand. I watched it arc through the air and clatter to the floor at Edward's feet.

There was silence after that small insignificant noise. I watched Edward's face and saw him looking at the whistle. I willed him to make some exclamation – *You've found it! Jed will be pleased. How did that get into my bedroom?* Or *Good heavens, I'd forgotten I had that.* But nothing. Instead I saw the colour drain from his face and he raised his stricken eyes to meet mine.

'I can explain, Lucy,' he said.

And I felt a nauseating feeling of dread seep through me. Shocked, I stumbled back to his bed and lowered myself on to the edge.

Edward bent down and picked up the whistle. 'I should have got rid of this.'

Too right, I thought. He must be regretting hanging on to it. No whistle, no evidence, no awkward questions.

'It's not what you think,' he said lamely.

I found my voice. 'And what am I thinking?' I said shakily.

'You think I had something to do with Becca's accident.'

I nodded, afraid, sickened. I knew it had been too bloody convenient.

Edward turned the whistle over in his hands, then looked at me. 'I did. But it wasn't intentional.'

I wasn't sure I believed him. Part of me felt he would say that, wouldn't he? Now he'd been caught out. I stared at him. 'Go on then,' I said.

'I wouldn't blame you if you don't believe me.'

'How do you know I won't? I haven't heard what you've got to say yet.' But he was right; I wasn't sure I was going to. I might not know much about the psyche of a grown-up found out but I knew a lot about kids when they got caught lying, and generally they tried to shift the blame or find a plausible excuse.

He pulled a chair up and sat down opposite me. 'I found the whistle a couple of weeks before the accident. Jed must have dropped it in the yard between the stable and the indoor school. I was busy at the time so I shoved it in the pocket of my old jacket, meaning to give it to him next time I saw him. Anyway, there was a problem with staffing, Hugh went sick, the day became hectic and the whistle just dropped off my radar. Then a couple of days later Becca went off to some trials on the other side of the country and Jed drove the horse box for her. He was away for the best part of a week and what with one thing and another I forgot about it completely.'

'That's handy,' I said.

Edward looked at me. 'Yes. But the whistle has only assumed importance because of the accident. Then it was just a piece of kit. Anyway, when Becca got back I could see she was in a vile mood. She'd not done as well as she'd hoped and as usual she blamed everyone else for her shortcomings: Jed, Billy Boy, the other competitors, the judges. She was never one to wonder where she might have gone wrong; whether maybe she was at fault. The next day she was in the indoor school making Jed put extra hours in with Billy Boy. It had been the dressage that had let her down, apparently, and she thought that extra training would sort out the problem. Of course, it was Jed she expected to solve whatever the matter was. Becca would observe, Becca would criticise but Becca wasn't one to do the hard graft herself – that's what she had staff and servants for. Anyway, I had work to do on the estate and was away from the Hall for several hours. When I returned and parked up I could hear shouting coming from the indoor school. I could hear her laying into Jed.'

I remembered those training videos I'd seen when she'd been caught on camera screaming and yelling at him like a banshee. Those ugly, hateful moments when I'd seen a different side of the nation's favourite horsewoman, the side the nation hadn't known about.

'She had a filthy temper and Jed was getting the full force of it,' continued Edward. 'Whatever was going wrong, it wasn't fair of her to take it out on him. She wanted to compete, she wanted the glory, but she couldn't see that it wasn't Jed's job to deliver it on a plate. I felt that just once in a while she ought to get her own hands dirty. Besides, I wasn't having her treat anyone – and certainly not a member of my staff – like that. I went into the school just as she was going to hit Jed with her riding crop. She stopped when she saw me and pretended that it was an idle threat, told Jed to get along and get some lunch. She thanked him very prettily for the work he'd done on Billy Boy that morning. But I knew it was all an act. I could see Jed was scared stiff and from the way Billy Boy was acting up, she'd had a go at him too.

'I told her what I thought about her training techniques and that Jed might be happier if he worked somewhere else on the estate. I told her it was about time she took responsibility for her failures and stopped blaming the staff. She went ballistic. I mean, I knew she had a temper but I'd never witnessed anything like it. It was almost as if she was possessed.' Edward's face was expressionless as he recounted Becca's outburst. He stared at me and there was something in his eyes, a flicker of pain, that convinced me he wasn't lying about this. He rubbed his hand over his mouth and chin as if he were wiping away some sort of bad taste. 'I couldn't stop her. Obscenities, profanities, curses, just poured out of her. She railed about everything and anything. She was yelling and screaming. I thought she'd gone mad. I pleaded with her to stop but she just carried on and on. Then she picked up a whip and began to lay about her. She went for me and Billy Boy. It was awful. I had to stop her. I tried reasoning. I tried to hold her, but she was beyond control. I thought about hitting her but I've never hit a woman in my life. I pushed my hands into my pockets to stop myself and I found Jed's whistle. I don't know why but I blew it. Maybe I thought the noise might bring her to her senses, I don't know, but I put it in my mouth and blew as hard as I could.' Edward looked at me, imploring me with his eyes to believe him. 'I never thought about what might happen, that Billy Boy might react. And he did. Maybe it was the way she was treating him, maybe it was the whistle, I don't know, but one minute he was standing stock still while Becca went mad, lashing out, hitting him, then I blew the whistle and he lashed out at her.' Edward's face was ashen at the memory of the moment. 'His hoof caught her on the side of her head. I think she must have been dead before she hit the ground. I don't know what was worse, the noise of Billy Boy's hoof hitting her or the silence that followed. I didn't mean to kill her. I just wanted her to shut up. I wanted her to stop hitting Billy Boy. I wanted her to calm down. It was an accident.'

I stared at him. I felt sick. His revelation was appalling, dreadful. What he'd done might not have been premeditated murder but the result had been the same. He'd been responsible. He'd killed her. And the ugly fact was that the man I'd fallen for had committed a truly dreadful act. But as I stared at him I realised that he was still the same person I'd spent the night with, the same man who would do anything for his son and the same man whose staff adored him. But did I believe him? I weighed up what he'd told me. No question. I wasn't blinded by love, I was sure, but I knew he hadn't made this up. This was the truth. I nodded.

'I shouldn't have panicked. I should've called an ambulance there and then but I was so shocked I didn't think straight. I could see she was dead. There was no question that anyone would have done anything for her. So I just left her there with Billy Boy and came back to the Hall.' He sighed. 'I regret that moment of utter cowardice more than anything I've ever done.'

'And then Jed found her.'

Edward nodded. 'And the police thought . . . Well, it never crossed my mind that they would come to the wrong conclusion until it was too late. I should've thought, but I was in such a state.'

'Poor Jed.'

Edward nodded. 'Do you know, I can justify what happened to Becca, but Jed? No. I torture myself about that every time I see him.'

I shook my head. 'You should have owned up when they began investigating.'

Edward sighed. 'I know. I can't believe I was such a coward. I suppose I didn't think they'd believe it was an accident. I was afraid they'd arrest me for it. I was terrified of what might happen to Teddy if I was taken away. He'd just lost his mother . . . If I told you I did it for Teddy, would you believe me?'

Loving father or total coward. What did I think? Maybe, I reasoned, the answer was somewhere between the two. What would I have done in the circumstances? How would I react if I saw someone mistreating an animal or a lovely gentle person like Jed? Would I have flipped? Maybe. And besides, was it such a crime to blow a whistle? Or to panic and run away from the consequences? How many people could put their hands on their hearts and swear they had always done the right thing? Not many, I reckoned. Certainly not me.

'So that was why you were so adamant that Jed had nothing to do with it.'

'I could hardly say anything else, could I? I knew he was innocent.'

'If you hadn't convinced them, would you have come clean?'

'I like to think I would have done. In fact I know so. I might be a coward but I couldn't have lived with myself if I'd thought that Jed would end up taking the blame.'

I wanted to think that too.

31

Edward sat on the edge of his chair and searched my face.

'Do you believe me?' he asked eventually.

I nodded. I did; this man wasn't lying. Whatever happened to Becca had been an accident, a terrible incident which hadn't been foreseen. He hadn't planned it, he hadn't even wished for it, it had just been one of those things.

The trouble was, even with my shaky grasp of the law I could see that he might be guilty of manslaughter, but would it benefit anyone if he was charged? I couldn't see that it would. Apart from anything else, what would happen to Teddy? Maybe, in law, I ought to go to the authorities, but I decided there and then that I wasn't going to.

I leaned forward and took the whistle out of Edward's hand.

'I expect this'll come to light in the stables one day soon,' I said, examining the craftsmanship of the object.

Edward frowned. 'I don't understand.'

'You know what men are like,' I said lightly. 'They're

hopeless at looking for things. Jed will think he just didn't search in the right places. And I think he ought to get it back, don't you? Besides, I don't think you ought to keep it. Someone else might come across it and jump to some absurd conclusion about you having something to do with the accident, like I did. You wouldn't want that to happen again, would you?'

Edward shook his head slowly.

'In the meantime, I suggest you put it back where it was.' I handed him the whistle.

Edward went across the room and shoved it back on the shelf behind the books. He returned to me and sat beside me on the bed.

'I can't get over the fact that you believed me. I was sure that if you found out you would be so shocked you'd leave.'

I smiled wryly. 'You thought my fall off Willow would get rid of me. That didn't work, so now you try shock tactics.'

'And that hasn't worked either.' Edward took my hand. 'But the important thing is that you believe me and that's all I care about.'

'I can't think my opinion matters that much,' I said.

'It does to me. More than anything.'

'But I'm only the nan—'

Edward put his finger on my lips. 'You are *not* "only the nanny",' he said firmly. 'You're far, far more than that. You've brought real light into Teddy's life, and you mean more to me than I can say.'

I stared at him in puzzlement.

'Lucy, don't you understand that I love you? I fell under your spell at that first encounter. Your bravery, your spirit – everything – just blew me away. But you've always been so wary of me. I thought I'd done something to upset you. Every time I tried to get close to you, you backed off. I never thought I had a chance. And then I thought I'd made you hate me.'

'I never hated you. But I didn't dare show you how I felt because you're . . . well, you're you.'

'I know I'm me. I'm a bloke like any other bloke except I just happen to live in a big house. And I'm a bloke with a little boy who deserves – who needs – someone like you until he's big enough to fend for himself. And I'm a bloke who is in love with a remarkable, beautiful girl.'

I didn't know what to say.

'So does this bloke have a chance?'

'But—'

'The answer to whether or not I have a chance doesn't need to use the word but.'

I clasped my hands in my lap and stared down at them. This was too surreal to be true. Guys like Edward didn't want girls like me. But *he* did. How much clearer could he make it? My heart was thudding out of control, battering against my sore ribs like a bird trying to get free. I felt shaky and apprehensive and scared and elated and . . .

'Lucy?'

I raised my eyes. He was looking at me with such tenderness that I knew he had meant every word.

'Lucy, you won't move back up to the nursery, will you?'

'I . . . But what about Teddy?'

'He can cope with you sleeping on a different floor. I don't think I can, though.'

'And the other staff . . .' It worried me that they would mind. That they would think me some fast piece on the make.

'The other staff won't mind a bit. Honest.'

I wasn't convinced. 'You're fibbing.'

'Even Mrs Porter likes you.'

I giggled. 'Now I know you're fibbing.'

'She likes you as much as she likes anyone, honest.' Edward leaned towards me and kissed me very gently on the lips. 'I really want to take you in my arms and give you the most enormous hug, but I daren't in case I hurt you more.'

'We could risk a little hug,' I said.

And he folded his arms around me incredibly sweetly and I laid my head on his shoulder and I felt utterly loved and wanted. It was as if this was the moment I'd been waiting for all my life. I relaxed against him knowing more happiness than I'd ever experienced before – and knowing that it was going to last for the rest of my life.